# SEASON OF SEDITION

## LILY

### THE HAWTHORNE SISTERS
### BOOK TWO

## ISABELLA THORNE

MIKITA ASSOCIATES

# SEASON OF SEDITION

## OF

*THE HAWTHORNE SISTERS*

# PART I

# A MEETING OF MINDS

*L*ady Lillian Hawthorne, eldest daughter of the Earl of Thornwood, shivered with delight as she listened to the conversation around her. These brave men and women fired her heart. Of course, they might not be so congenial if they knew who her grandfather was, so she was, for the moment, silent, bearing the name among her compatriots as Miss Lily Hawkins rather than Lady Lillian Hawthorne.

The gathering, ostensibly, was nothing more than a dinner party, unusually well attended, perhaps, by a strange collection of both men and women. Ever proper, the ladies and gentlemen occupied both sides of the long, meticulously set dining table, each dressed in fine outfits befitting an evening of wine and socialization, but many were not ladies and gentlemen at all. They were a collection of shopkeepers and merchants, farmers and prostitutes, and although there was the occasional gentleman, to Lily's surmise, she was the only lady. It looked like a lovely, slightly crowded private party, the likes of which were often held in homes of the aristocracy throughout London each evening, but this dinner party was anything but proper, and most of the attendees were not aristocracy. Lily knew that those who attended could be called treasonous, and be locked in a dungeon without a key, transported to some wild untamed land, or even summarily hanged without so much as a by your leave. No, the Crown would squash any such individuals without allowing them any recourse, but together, they were strong and brash. Together, they could accomplish anything, even freeing their dear Napoleon Bonaparte who was at this very moment captured and imprisoned.

What was also not so mannerly was the topic of conversation at this particular table, less sparkling and more incendiary. "It is a crime," one young man opined, his eyes burning with passion, "that our own government should keep General Bonaparte imprisoned on St. Helena. Free the man. Send him back to France. Let him do his work! Can they not see the vision he had for France?"

A rumble of assent swept around the table. Some glasses were lifted in agreement. Lily sipped her glass, simply listening. She would let them get their grievances out before she attempted to speak. The thought sent a spark of excitement through her. She had only spoken a handful of times, but with each utterance, she felt bolder and more alive. What was life without a purpose? She was certain she had found hers here with these people and their quest for freedom.

"What happens in France is not our business," said another. "Are they not a sovereign nation?"

"What happens in France has always been our business," muttered another. "Since the Hundred Years War and Henry VI."

"Humph," said another. "Do you think the trouble started in the 1400s? I beg to differ."

One after the other, the members spoke their minds, words which if spoken in aristocratic company would get them killed, but here among like-thinking neighbors, they felt safe and bold.

Finally, when the turmoil quieted, Lady Lillian Hawthorne stood, and here, under the pseudonym of Miss Lily Hawkins, she began to speak with all the passion she could never show to her own family. Her eyes, too, were alight with fire and intelligence.

"The aristocracy fears Napoleon," she remarked boldly. Never mind that her own family were aristocrats. She was here among the people she could call her surrogate family. "They fear the people rising. The British monarchy fears the power of Napoleon's ideals, the power to the people. While Prinny parties, and tables are laden with delicacies, the masses starve here in our beloved England. This should not happen. We have a madman and a spendthrift at the helm. This is the legacy of the aristocracy. The bluebloods. They are no better than any other man or woman. Their blood is no different. As proven in France, they still bleed red. Why should they rule? Simply because they are *men*." She paused briefly, but she gauged her audience. As much as she loved Mary Wollstonecraft's ideals, this was not the place to speak of the plight of women. She could not alienate half of the audience or more. There would be time enough. Baby steps, she thought.

"Simply because they are men," she repeated,

5

"whose blood and birth allowed them to rule? God, they claim. Divine right. But is that right? Moreso, what gives them the ability? Is the mad king smarter than you? Or you?" She pointed out several in the audience. "Is Prinny more versed in economics than you?" She gestured to one of the prominent businessmen. "I think not. It is no different than it was in France a decade ago under the Austrian queen." Lily shook her head, dark curls swaying with the motion as she thought of the swift retribution of the guillotine, and she paused.

Finally, Lily, along with many others in the hall, nodded agreement. "They do not care about the people. They care only for their own coffers. It is not about what is right. They do not care what is right. They only care about power. It is about power and control," said Lily. "And coin. That is all those people think about…" She trailed off, thinking of her own grandfather who seemed to want to even control how his family breathed. He certainly made her feel as though she were suffocating.

"How so?" asked another, and Lily was forced to answer. "It has been so throughout history," Lily said. "The powerful gain more power and subvert the weak. Greed is the problem. Not the aristocracy per se, but greedy men."

A few of the merchants muttered their disagreement, but Lily continued. "Power and greed are what keeps men and women from being equal. Is this what the golden rule has taught us?"

"He who has the gold, makes the rules," added a tipsy woman from the corner with a giggle and an upraised glass.

"You are right," Lily said raising a finger and

6

holding her audience at bay. "But it doesn't need to be that way. The aristocrats are few; a tiny oligarchy which has risen up under our ineffectual king." A few of the company shrugged and looked confused. Perhaps they did not understand her words. She explained. "They are but a small group of weak men grabbing power," she expounded. "We have the numbers, and in numbers there is the real power." This is what Wollencraft had said about the French Revolution, but in the end, even she lost her nerve. Lily would not.

Lily Hawthorne's comments were well received, punctuated by a smattering of applause from her peers at the table. As always, after speaking out during one of these clandestine meetings, she was thrilled by a rush of adrenaline. Here, she was appreciated. No one in her home ever listened to her. No one gave any credence to her ideas. They did not know or care that she could recite verbatim practically every book in her grandfather's library, and they did not value her intelligence.

Certainly, her father and grandfather did not. Her mother was a milksop who was not worthy of Lily's respect, and even her sisters, who she knew loved her, did not understand her need to make a difference in the world. They saw her as a dreamer, silent and weak, because she bided her time. They did not expect her dreams to come to fruition. Never did Lily feel more alive than when she was putting her thoughts out into the world. Someday, her audience would be bigger than the dining room of a London manor. She just knew it. Someday, she would change the world.

Some differences of opinion arose. Even in this small room, they could not agree. But Lily hoped that as they listened to one another they could come to a consensus. If they could, they could change the world.

"Are you saying the aristocracy is not wicked?" asked another.

"Of course not," Lily countered. "There is wickedness in all men, and greed releases it. But what control can the aristocracy have if the press is truly free to print the truth?"

"The press prints what the aristocracy allows," commented another.

"Exactly," Lily said, raising a finger and nodding. "But if the people are represented as the colonies demanded…" She paused, thinking of some of the French and Colonial newspapers of years past that she had read like contraband. "If the press were truly free to print the truth, imagine the changes that would occur in such a world, with the common man as the watch dog of the aristocracy. I tell you; the world is changing. We stand together with our demands, rather than accepting the crumbs as a privileged few see fit. After all, there are many more in the masses than there are of the aristocracy," she added to the gentleman. "If we stand together, we cannot fail."

"I intend to stand in the back," said one man. "The frontline will be shot."

Some of the crowd chuckled nervously. No one wanted to be reminded of the price of their gathering.

"The promise of freedom is too great a sword to allow the people to wield," called an audience member. "It cannot be done. We are all risking getting our necks stretched, and for what? It will all come to naught."

"Did it come to naught in France?" observed an individual in her audience. "Heads rolled. Aristocratic heads."

Several audience members nodded, but others were already into their drink. Still, it did not take the entirety of the populous to make a difference. A small but committed group was all that France had, and look how the world changed.

"For freedom," Lily said, raising a glass. "Freedom for each man and woman. If the people rise up and demand equality for every man and woman as they did in the colonies, what a world it would be! The people will lead themselves!"

"The people will riot," said another merchant said grumpily. "Yes, the decadent aristocracy must be curbed, but that must be done by people of merit, those who have proven that they can run a business and therefore a country, not the rabble."

By old men, thought Lily. No. She was not risking her neck to see the monarchy pass from one old man to another, both of which had the same delusions of grandeur and lust for power. She truly believed that if a woman were in charge, the world would be different. But how would that come to pass?

As much as she wished it, that moment had not yet come. However, over the last few months, Lily had seen the size of their little troop of radicals double and then triple. The magnetic influence of their leader, a brash but broadly charismatic man named Roger Montgomery, had begun to seep out beyond the walls of their secret meeting spaces. Some of the bravest members of the group were passing leaflets out to the public and whispering into curious ears. Ah, the power of print, she thought. It was truly glorious.

Lily had yet to do any of the recruiting herself, though there was certainly no lack of desire on her part. She just had no time to do so. It was hard enough to escape her family home to come to these meetings. She could not do more and steer under her grandfather's watchful eye. How her heart pounded at the thought of that tiny, folded square of paper transferring from her palm into someone else's! Like her sister, Eleanor, had poetry, Lily had her iron-clad ideals, and she was just as determined to have them heard.

It was only a matter of creating the right time and place. Unfortunately, for the eldest daughter of the esteemed Hawthorne household, such circumstances were hard to come by. Lily's comfortable singleness had already placed her upon the thinnest of ice as far as her family was concerned. The first warning had come by way of her father, and then her grandfather. Lily was sure there would not be many more warnings. No, they would be planning her wedding. Gads! She could only hope that they found a free-spirited sort of man for her, but that was unlikely given her grandfather's iron rule and conservative politics. She would simply trade one jailer for another, but her personal life must give way to her loftier goals at the moment.

The pursuit of liberty was fast becoming Lily's greatest love, both the country's liberty and her own. Lily could contemplate no greater horror than being pinned under the thumb, and quite literally the body, of a man she would never love. No part of her desired to be the submissive, faithful wife her mother modeled every day. What Lily wanted was to change the face of England for the better and forever. If she could not rule her own life, how could she do that? There would be a way, she promised herself. There was always a way; hadn't her own younger sister Eleanor proved that? Who would have thought that meek little, poetry-loving Eleanor would have balked both Father and Grandfather? And yet she did. How could she, Lillian Hawthorne, do less?

Of course, Eleanor did not come through unscathed. Still, if she could do it, so could Lily, and moreso. After all, even Grandfather, much to his chagrin, had to admit that Lily was the most intelligent of his progeny, although Lily's eldest brother, Robert, would beg to differ. There was a tyrant in the making.

She brought her mind back to the matter at hand. The meeting was nearly at a close, and like always, Montgomery stepped forward to say a few galvanizing words. The man was brilliant. A first glance at the fellow with his stocky physique but relatively average stature might not have conveyed the impression of leadership, but the energy, the strength, the inspiration, flowed from him each time he opened his mouth. He was not handsome; he did not need to be. Every syllable reverberated through the air when he spoke. His voice was like a beacon in the meeting room calling all to heed him.

"Our movement grows, my brothers and sisters. Keep your ears open in the city streets, and you will hear our message spreading on the breeze. Be committed. Be courageous." His voice dropped to hold a sincere edge. "Be careful. Look toward the bright future we seek to build, for it will be here before we know it."

Lily took those words and tucked them close to her heart. Like many others from days past, she would hold them in perpetuity as she returned to her own isolated island within the Hawthorne estate. There were no friends of General Bonaparte there. Indeed, she had no doubt that if her father and the old earl knew of the sorts of things she was getting up to, they would have beat her and then disowned her long ago. Likely, they would have had her committed to bedlam.

"Miss Hawkins?" The voice arrested her as Lily made ready to depart discreetly from the house. No one knew she was the granddaughter of an earl and rightly called a lady, and she wanted to keep it that way. Thus, here, she was only Miss Hawkins, not Lady Lillian Hawthorne. The attendees made their way to the street in carefully orchestrated waves, designed to maintain the illusion of couples and friends dispersing from a fulfilling social engagement. Waiting her turn inside the front hall of the manor, Lily turned to see Mr. Roger Montgomery approaching.

Immediately, she smiled. Although she could not call Montgomery a friend, he was dear to her in the way that an idol is dear to his devotees. Never before had they exchanged more than a passing glance and a few perfunctory words, but they were bound together by a common cause. Now he held out a gracious hand, which she took politely, shaking his hand instead of waiting for a perfunctory kiss against her gloved digits.

"It is an honor to speak with you, Mr. Montgomery." Lily inclined her head. "To what do I owe the pleasure?"

He laughed. "To the wisdom of your own words, I suppose. You have quite a way with them, you know."

The compliment both surprised and delighted her. Montgomery had something of a pugnacious reputation, and she had assumed he was there to take issue with one of her points, or to start in on a spirited discussion. He had been known to debate his favorite issues far into the depths of the night. Such an opportunity for discourse lay far beyond Lily's reach. She had to be home within a certain time frame, or she would be caught out, but she yearned for the freedom of discourse, nonetheless.

"Thank you, sir. I am pleased to hear you say so." Lily's smile widened. "I must say, it is refreshing to be present in a space where all opinions are equally encouraged, even if those opinions come from one of the weaker sex."

Montgomery nodded eagerly. "Yes, well, we are all risking life and limb. We must be allowed to express our divergent opinions." His eyes brightened, attaining their habitual gleam. "But what you say is true! And your presence here has only served to illuminate the greater need for female voices within the radical realm." His animated face grew serious, though no less intense. "I want to amplify your voice, Miss Hawkins. The women of England must hear your speech. I have no doubt many would be moved to join our side, and of course, there is the added benefit that women can go where some men would be banned."

Lily blinked. Of all the things Montgomery could have said, that was not what she had expected. So surprised was she that she very nearly asked him to repeat himself. "Again, I thank you, Mr. Montgomery. I could not receive any higher praise."

"Come now, don't be modest!" He grinned expansively. "I'm quite serious, Miss Hawkins. And to prove it, I'd like to invite you to speak again in a more formal venue, to the larger group, when we gather on Tuesday next. What do you say?"

"Well, I—" Lily paused, buying time to quiet the sudden buzz of thoughts inside her head. Of course, she had no shortage of material to speak upon, and she knew exactly the sort of rhetoric upon which her fellow Bonapartists thrived. Had she not spent countless afternoons ensconced in her father's library, dreaming of this very scenario? The moment had arrived, as she sensed it would. Rather more abruptly than she had anticipated, perhaps, but Lily knew she could not back away from her calling.

"Yes?" Roger Montgomery regarded her with the air of a man who knew what she was going to say. On most of his peers, that attitude would have rankled Lily to no end. Montgomery managed to wear his self-assured confidence with a pride that made it palatable.

Finally, she nodded, her heart a flutter with anticipation. "Yes. I am glad to accept." There. The words were out. A nervous, euphoric jolt rushed through her veins. Although Lily had been attending Montgomery's gatherings for some time and speaking in small groups, she had not imagined he would take notice of her specifically. Yet here she was, being offered the chance that she had always wanted. A real chance to affect change in a larger way.

"And I'm glad to hear it!" he declared. "Be proud, Miss Hawkins. You are about to become a genuine pioneer. When your daughters' daughters look back, generations from now, they will see you standing here at the beginning of it all."

With that, he let go of her hand and was gone, off to work his peculiar bardic magic on another rapt follower. Lily stood in silence for a moment, stunned. The conversation played back in her mind as she resumed her place by the door. Roger Montgomery, leader at the heart of London's growing Bonapartist movement, wanted her to speak! No longer would she be a face in the approving, anonymous crowd, speaking only to small groups, but now, she would speak to the Bonapartists at large.

Lily bit her lip. The revelation of losing her anonymity brought reality crashing back full force. If she were to step out as a voice in the radical underground, word might reach the family estate and the earl. The absolute last thing she needed was her father or grandfather discovering these illicit, rebellious activities, her only source of personal freedom. Nor did she relish the idea that enemies of the movement could target her family. It was one thing to risk her own life, but quite another to risk those of her sisters.

But political ideals never came without risk. Perhaps the American, Patrick Henry, said it best. *Is life so dear, or peace so sweet, as to be purchased at the price of chains and slavery? Forbid it, Almighty God! I know not what course others may take; but as for me, give me liberty or give me death!* The thought sent a shiver through her, but Lily knew that England needed to find a way forward, to break the chains that the elite had upon the common people. They were all people under God, both men and women, and regardless of her misgivings, she could not turn back.

Wherever she looked from her vantage point high among the peerage, she saw others below her struggling to gain equal footing, fighting injustices she could not stand.

Stepping out onto the bustling London street, Lily took a deep breath of city air and vowed not to let apprehension dim her morals. She was in the progressive fight, and nothing was going to stop her. With a deep breath, she hurried towards home.

THE LOOMING FAÇADE of the Hawthorne estate looked to its eldest daughter like an elaborate mausoleum. Lily felt her face settle into the habitual flat mask she wore in the presence of her family elders, just in case she should be so unlucky as to encounter any of them on the way in. She hoped that at least the men would be gone, off to another session of Parliament about which she was not permitted to ask, because of course, as a woman, she would be too stupid to understand politics anyway. Each day, her own family bound the common man in a tighter vise, and she could do only this. She would not stop. She would not be silenced.

The hallways appeared blessedly quiet. Lily crept toward her chambers, praying under her breath that she wouldn't be seen. She had almost made it to the foot of the stairs when a familiar figure exited the drawing room. The two girls narrowly avoided a collision.

"Lily!" She stood face to face with her sister, Grace, who was always quiet and gentle. She was everything Lily was not, but still, Lily loved her younger sister with a passion. Grace's eyes flicked over her, and a light of resigned understanding came into them. She sighed softly. "Father and Grandfather are at Westminster. Robert is at his club. No one knows you were gone."

It was Lily's turn to let out her breath, relieved. Her youngest brother, Matthew, who may have given her some support, was away at school. "Thank goodness for that," she murmured. Grace hesitated. Her gaze had not left Lily's face. It was evident that something lingered on the tip of her tongue, and that she was unsure whether to release it. The older girl crossed her arms, barely resisting the urge to roll her eyes as well. "Come on, then. Let it out." She knew what was coming.

"I worry about you, Lily," Grace allowed at last. "About what you are doing, associating with such riffraff."

"They are not—" Lily began hotly, and Grace waved away her protest.

"What if Father should find out? Or worse Grandfather?" Grace frowned, her forehead furrowed with consternation. "Even if Robert catches wind of what you are doing, he will certainly bring it to Grandfather's attention."

"They will not find out." Lily spoke firmly, with all the implicit authority of an eldest sibling. "Unless you would tell them."

"You know I would not do so."

"And even if they did, it would hardly matter, Grace."

"Worse, what if you should run afoul of some blackguard?"

"I have Patton with me," she said. The old footman was hardly protection. He was nearly deaf, but he was large, and therefore some deterrent to anyone who would mean Lily ill.

Grace chewed on her lip, and for an instant, Lily wondered if her sister would rat her out. No. Never. The sisters were always there for one another, although it was a good thing that Grace did not know the extent of Lily's involvement in the movement. "Evelyn did her share of sneaking about," Lily said, although she knew that attending poetry salons was hardly part and parcel with attending, or speaking at, radical political meetings. A thrill ran through her at the thought. "I cannot renounce my beliefs just to please Grandfather, Grace. I will not," she said.

This was a duel that Grace had attempted before and never won. She made the judicious choice to end the current bout in surrender. "Be careful, Lily. Please." She paused. "For our sake, and for Mother's. If not your own. After the debacle with Eleanor, I think knowing you were associating with such people would kill her. You know her health is frail."

Lily chose not to answer. She would not be made to feel guilty for her passion. She sighed and climbed the stairs in silence, her jaw tight. With every step, she reminded herself that it did not matter if things inside this old house could not change. For now, she was becoming poised to change the world outside of it.

## A CONFLICT OF MINDS

*L*ily studied the pilfered news sheets from France and the colonies as well as the older historical tomes until late into the night, formulating her speech for the meeting on the following Tuesday, but when Tuesday dawned, she was summoned to the library to pay court to her grandfather, the Earl of Thornwood. She knew it could not bode well.

For one awful moment, she wondered if her grandfather had found out about her clandestine meetings with the Bonapartists. Surely not. He could not even fathom that a woman would have the wherewithal to conceive of such a bold plan. No, she assured herself, her secret was safe. Nonetheless, her hands were sweating within her gloves as she paused at the library door.

Angley, the footman who stood at that door, smiled at her. "Do you know what he wants?" Lily asked in a whisper.

The footman answered in the negative. He said only

that the earl wanted to speak with her, but Grandfather did not have discussions. He gave orders.

"Thank you, Angley," she said with a nod as he opened the door to the library and announced her. Both her father and her grandfather were in the room. That did not bode well.

The earl gave her no preamble. Instead, he got right to the point as was his wont. "Lillian, you will marry before the beginning of next season," he said.

"Before?" Lily gasped. "I am not to have a Season?"

She threw a glance at her father, who stood at her grandfather's side, but she knew there would be no help there. Her father capitulated to the earl on every issue. On more than one occasion, she had hoped that her father would grow a spine. It was doubtful that would ever happen.

"You have had one," the earl said.

"That was two years ago," Lily protested. Two years ago, before the kerfuffle that ended in her younger sister Eleanor's marriage to the most unsuitable Lord Firthley. No doubt, her grandfather was holding her personally responsible for her sister's sins, since she was the eldest, and well, in truth, she had known about the secret meetings of the poetry society, and she had kept her younger sister's secret.

However, Lily did not want to marry two years ago, and she did not want to marry now, but that was hardly the point. Surely, she would be given another chance to choose her own husband. "But Grandfather," she began, hoping to appeal to his humanity instead of the earl. She was, after all, his blood. She made an effort to speak in a reasonable tone although the anger bubbling within her was murderous.

"You squandered your time, and now you will pay the price, young lady," the earl interrupted, not allowing her to even defend herself. "You are a spinster already, and I do not see the point in wasting money on a Season when you will not take it seriously. I shall not have it. You are a Hawthorne, and the Hawthornes are not left on the shelf. I will not see your spinsterhood paraded before the Ton, nor will I see your sisters shortchanged."

"But surely," she sputtered. Normally, she could go toe to toe with her recalcitrant grandfather, but this meeting had so blindsided her that she was out of her depth. She had been busy preparing for tonight's meeting, and she had not expected her Season to be taken from her. It was not like the earldom was poor. There was plenty of money for a Season for both her and her sisters, Grace and Betty. Grandfather was simply being cruel and punishing her for being a bluestocking.

"Lily, you were raised to be a lady," her grandfather said, leaning heavily on his cane, although the old man was spry as the devil. He did not need the cane at all. She thought he used it only to lull people into thinking that he was old and infirm. He was not. He was more likely to hit someone over the head with the cane than use it as a crutch, at least figuratively.

She narrowed her eyes as he spoke. "You were not raised to become an old maid. I will not have it. Do you understand me?"

"I am hardly an old maid," Lily protested. True, she was six and twenty; she was certainly past the first bloom of youth, but surely there was a man out there who wanted a woman for a wife rather than a child bride, not that she wanted this fictitious man for a husband.

"It is Grace's turn and then Betty's. You will not deprive your sisters of their chance to shine in the sun."

"Of course not," Lily said. "I never intended it to be so." She loved her sisters. She did not want to steal their light. She only wanted her own freedom, and she would have it, she thought as she narrowed her eyes. She vowed it so in her heart. Her grandfather would not clip her wings.

Her father's frown deepened, but Lord Hanway said nothing. There was no help there. Only her grandfather, Lord Thornwood spoke. Grandfather was king here. Yes, he was the earl, but he might well have been the king. He ruled with such absolute authority. No one crossed him.

"Your younger sister, Eleanor is already married," he said.

Oh, well, except for Eleanor. Perhaps that was the issue here.

Lily did not point out that Eleanor had married David Firthley against all of the family's wishes. She did not want to antagonize her grandfather by reminding him of how Eleanor had undermined his authority with that marriage. Likely, if she did, he would lock her in her room, and tonight of all nights, she could not be so confined.

"All of your cousins have married—"

"Not all," she muttered.

"Attend me!" he snapped, and she grew sullenly silent. "Your father and I are worried about you."

She sincerely doubted that.

"We've watched your social circle shrink over the last few years. Your father and I have been talking…"

More than likely Grandfather spoke and Father listened, she thought, kowtowing to Grandfather like he always did. She gritted her teeth against the protests that sprung to her lips. She had to be silent. She could not be censured. Not tonight.

"… and we have decided that if you can't find a suitable husband within the month, then we will pick a match for you."

"A month!" Lily gasped and sat down, defeated.

"Likely, within the month, the Corsican problem will be dispatched, Parliament will close by then, and we can get out of this sweltering city. I doubt it will be longer than a month." As Lily stared at her father in disbelief, she felt a wave of anger rising up in her chest. How could he do this to her? Why couldn't her father have some gumption? And her grandfather… How dare he try to control her life like that! With her hands balled up at her sides, she said through gritted teeth, "And who would you have me marry? Lord Rumford?" The man had been sniffing around like a dog.

"Lord Rumford might be a good match," her father said, gazing off into the distance as if he were thinking about that possibility. Lily's stomach did a flip flop.

"Father! He's practically your age!" Lily exclaimed. Besides, she knew that Lord Rumford had no liking for bluestockings. He had his eye on Lily's sister Eleanor, but now that she was out of his reach, perhaps he would settle for Lily. The thought was appalling.

"If Lord Rumford is who your father and I choose,

23

then that is who you will marry," Grandfather said. The earl paused, as if giving her a chance to rebut the possibility, but he knew she could not. She had no direct recourse if the earl pushed the issue. Her nimble mind was searching frantically for an escape. Surely, there must be something she could do to stop this travesty.

"I doubt you are going to find someone in the next month, but your father wanted me to give you the option, so consider this your chance. If there is someone you favor, speak now," the earl said.

A chance! she thought belligerently. This was an outrage. The retort was on the tip of her tongue. She wanted to yell at them, *I won't do it. I won't marry!* But of course, that would only bring Grandfather's wrath down upon her head. She could not scream with all the force she felt. She could only bide her time. She inhaled slowly. "Is that all?" she asked with quiet dignity.

"Yes," Grandfather said. "See that you do not embarrass the family any more than you already have with your bookishness."

WITH THAT, Lily turned on heel, grabbed her lace shawl from the back of the chair where she had flung it earlier, and walked out of the room with her head held high. Tears were brimming in her eyes, but she was not sure if they were tears of anger or frustration. Her mind was running like a panicked filly, but she held herself aloof. She would win this. She would find a way out of this if it was the last thing, she would ever do... and it quite possibly might be.

As she bolted from the room, she passed Angley,

who waited on the earl's pleasure. "Have my supper sent to my room," she ordered. "I have megrim coming on."

AN HOUR LATER, Lily was dressed for travel. Her black hair was braided into a tight plait which hung down her back, and her clothing was nondescript. She had borrowed it from one of the maids so that she would not be recognized as gentry. The supper tray sat mostly untouched. She was too nervous to eat.

"Lily," said her sister Grace who sat on her bed. "I wish you wouldn't go. This is folly on any night, but moreso tonight. Tonight, of all nights, remain at home."

"I must go," said Lily as she donned her black cloak. She did not tell her sisters she was to speak at tonight's meeting. She did not need to add more worry to their minds. It was enough that they would cover for her absence.

"Who knows," she said, "perhaps I will find a husband." With a wink, she pulled the hood up to shield her face and went out into the night. A hired cab was waiting for her at the end of the lane.

When she arrived at her destination, a crowd had gathered. There was some altercation brewing. She had a moment of hesitation as she realized some of them were unsavory characters.

"Bonaparte scum!" cried one, flinging offal in the direction of Lily's destination. It hit a man she knew, who threw a punch, and suddenly the crowd was moving with intent. She took one step back and another. She glanced towards the hired cab which had already moved down the street. That option was out of reach. The angry mob was between her and her destination, and she had nowhere else to go.

∼

LORD REGINALD BARTON hoped that his work for the Crown would see a lull. The past few months were busy, but with the war in the peninsula now all but over, he could rest and take a holiday. He, like most of Europe, was glad that at last the Corsican business was at an end. Napoleon Bonaparte had been captured—*again*—and this time, he expected that the man would stay imprisoned on whichever island the Crown decided to inter him, alive or dead. Lord Reginald did not really care which. The man was a menace. Some had touted that his bid to take over the world was centered in evil and that the man himself was the antichrist. Lord Reginald was not so inclined. He was just glad to be home in England. London, in fact, even though it was long past time to retire to the country. The city was sweltering, and the stench was overwhelming in the heat. He brought his perfumed handkerchief to his nose.

The carriage in which Lord Reginald Barton was traveling slowed, and his driver called out. "I'm sorry, my lord. The road ahead is blocked. Some rabble. Shall we go around?"

"What is it, Helms?" Reginald wondered, sticking his head out of the carriage to see.

"Bonapartists," his driver spat. "Next, they'll be calling for blood. Best just avoid them. I can turn around at the next juncture."

"No," Reginald said, squinting into the night. There was a woman ahead. Something in the way she moved seemed familiar. Like a dance. She was dressed in a black cloak... in this heat. Still, nothing to set her off, but there was something different about her. She moved with grace. She took one step back and another trying to avoid the rabble, but he could see she would not succeed. The fight had broken out, and there were shouts and insults. The anger was growing. Mobs did that. They had a life of their own, and like a wild animal, they attacked without reason. The woman stumbled and took another two steps back, but she had nowhere to go to escape.

"Pull closer," Reginald demanded.

"Sir?"

"You heard me, Helms." Reginald flung the door open and jumped out of his conveyance, just as the woman went down. The crowd swarmed over her like ants on honey bread, but he kept his eye on her in the fray. With two steps forward and a shove and a punch, he reached her. A fist connected with his eye, but he ducked the worst of it.

"I've got you," he said, pulling her free of the rabble, but she had been hit and was knocked senseless. She stared at him with wide dark eyes. Those eyes...

He lifted her bodily from the fracas, and she roused herself, putting her hands on his chest and pushing.

"Let me go!"

He assumed that she could not tell her rescuer from the rabble, and he ignored her protests, pulling her away from them, wrapping his arms around her waist and lifting her, putting her into his carriage out of danger.

"Unhand me!" she cried, and he realized from her words and her speech, that he was right. She was no commoner. Somehow, a lady was amidst the riot. He did not know who she was or how she had arrived at this state, but he knew she did not belong in the street at night, especially not this street.

"Now, Helms. Away," Reginald said, and the carriage lurched forward, making haste away from the riot.

The woman made a dive for the door, and Reginald realized that she must think she was being kidnapped. Perhaps she had been separated from her protector.

"Peace, Miss," he said laying a hand on her arm. "Where can I see you to safety?"

"You can bloody well take me right back where you found me," she snapped. "I wasn't lost."

Had he misjudged her? From her movement, he had thought she was a lady in distress, but her language belied that. Her dark eyes were flashing fire now, and her black hair was coming loose from its plait. She was utterly marvelous, like a dark avenging angel.

No self-respecting whore would wear hair like that in a severe braid, and yet, she was exactly to his taste, dark and fiery. He was not in the habit of finding a doxy on the street, but he was intrigued. He caught her chin and turned her to look at him.

Her face was angular and perfect, with dark brows and dark eyes. Her nose was long and straight and her lips… oh, her lips. They were full and absolutely kissable. Her nostrils flared a little as she raised her chin while attempting to pull out of his grasp, but he held her fast. He leaned close, his lips almost touching hers. She smelled of lavender water. Definitely not one of the unwashed masses. What was she doing here? "If you do not have a protector," he said in a low voice, "I might be persuaded…"

Her right hook caught him on the jaw and rocked him. He caught her hand before she could hit him again.

"I am no doxy," she spat.

"Then, I was right. You needed assistance," Reginald said reasonably. He was correct in his first assumption. She was a lady in distress, but she was no shrinking violet this one. Violet. He thought. Why did she remind him of a flower when she was so utterly not flower-like?

"I did not," she argued. "Why do men always think women need or want their assistance?"

"What is wrong with you, woman?" Reginald asked, getting angry now. He had just risked life and limb to rescue her, and she was not the slightest bit grateful. Moreover, she had clocked him nearly as hard as the rioters had. He wanted to rub his jaw. He realized he was going to have a bruise on his face, perhaps two. "Those Bonapartists would have ripped you limb from limb."

"They…" she began, and then she seemed to think better of her words. "Thank you," she said, suddenly subdued.

He looked at her, trying to fathom what had caused this sudden change in tack. They sat quietly for a moment while she thought, and Reginald caught his breath. Who was this woman? He wanted to know.

"Let me assist you," Reginald said at last. "Lord Reginald Barton, at your service," he said. He gave her a slight bow in the confines of the carriage.

Her eyes opened wide. She knew him then, or at

29

least knew of him. She did not offer her own name, but of course, this was the most uncouth introduction he had ever known. He could not blame her for being uncertain.

"No doubt someone is worried for your safety," he said softly. "Let me take you home to your family." At least if he took her home, he would find out who she was, and he realized he wanted to know this dark siren's name. There was something so familiar about her, he wondered if they had actually been introduced at some event. Surely, she could not be a member of the Beau monte ton? He couldn't imagine her as one of the simpering ninnies at Almacks. Not this firebrand. Maybe she was a widow… or a married woman? In which case, who was the negligent husband who allowed her out with such rabble in the dark of the night? The man should be horse whipped.

"You are not going to ask how I arrived at this particular corner?" she asked warily.

"Not unless you would like to tell me," Reginald said, leaning back and crossing his arms over his chest. He waited. His clandestine work these past months had made him remarkably patient.

She stared at him tight-lipped, frowning. He could almost feel the anger coming off of her in simmering waves.

"I DID NOT NEED your help. I am perfectly capable of taking care of myself," she said in a snit.

.  .  .

"Forgive me, Lady," he said, his voice softening. "My instinct was to protect someone in danger. I did not mean to imply that you were incapable."

"Your chivalry is misplaced, Sir," she continued icily. "Women are just as strong and resilient as men. We do not need saving. *I did not need saving.* I was perfectly fine exactly where I was."

"I beg to differ," he said.

"I do not care what you think! Let me out of this carriage at once."

Now that they were clear of the rabble, she reached for the door as if she meant to leap from the moving conveyance.

He acted on instinct, catching her, and she leveled a cuff at his head.

"Enough," he said, lifting her bodily onto his lap and catching the hand that reached out to slap him again.

He was used to subduing grown men in his work, so this slight woman was no challenge. Putting both of her wrists in one strong hand, he held them together above her head against the side of the carriage. The other he wrapped around her waist and pulled her close, pinning her between the door of the carriage and his own body. She was still spitting with anger as she struggled. He tightened his grip, holding her effortlessly immobile until she realized the futility of her rebelliousness and quieted.

FEAR FLASHED THROUGH HER EYES, and he almost relented. He never wanted a woman to fear him, but hard on the heels of that thought came another.

Good. Maybe she should be afraid. Perhaps she realized how foolhardy she was traipsing about the street at night without protection.

"YOU ARE NO GENTLEMAN," she snapped.

"YOU WERE NOT in the company of gentlemen," he reminded her, his lips quirking up in a sardonic smile. She smelled so good, a mixture of lavender and her own sweetness. Her bosom heaved as she again attempted to twist out of his hold. Then, she stilled, and there was a sudden heat in the moment.

THIS HAD GONE FAR ENOUGH. Perhaps too far, he thought. He released her abruptly, and she scuttled to the other side of the carriage.

. . .

LET ME OUT, IMMEDIATELY," she said pulling the thin summer shawl around her person as if it were a cloak of some protection. She crossed her arms over her chest.

"I WILL TAKE YOU HOME," he said with a decorum he did not feel. "And I trust you will remember that sometimes, even the strongest among us could use a helping hand."

SHE STUDIED HIS FACE. He could practically hear the grinding of her teeth. She did not like to be bested, and there was such an intelligence in her gaze that he thought she was not often foiled in her desires. What she lacked in strength of body, she made up for in wit, he was sure.

HER GAZE WAS CALCULATING.

SHE WAS TRYING to gauge his sincerity or perhaps his honor. Her dark eyes were filled with wariness and a passion he wanted to explore, but not here. Not now. He rubbed a hand over his face. What on God's good earth was he doing? Regardless of her circumstance, the woman was a lady, and he had never in his life taken a woman against her will, lady or not. He relied upon his honor. "I could not, in good conscience, leave you on the street after such an ordeal," he said.

. . .

"Your concern is noted," she said tersely. "I can find my own way back now. Truly. Please, let me out."

"Where do you live?" he asked again.

"You are not going to let this go, are you?"

"I am not," he said. "Knowing how easy it is for a man to subdue a woman, I cannot in my role as a gentleman let you go unescorted into the night. You should know that too now."

Lily hesitated, rubbing her wrist. He winced, hoping she did not bruise. Perhaps his demonstration was a bit too harsh, but if it kept her safe… He realized, suddenly, he wanted to keep her safe.

"Mayfair," she said at last.

He smiled. There were many of the gentry who lived in Mayfair. He knew them all. "Helms, take us to Mayfair," he said to his driver. "Are you going to give my driver more specific instructions?" he inquired.

She gnawed on her lip. He found the gesture endearing. It reddened her lips, making them seem irresistibly kissable in the shadows. After a few moments, she said. "Stop the carriage. I can find my way from here. Truly. We are only steps away from my destination."

Reginald ordered the driver to stop, but instead of allowing her to disembark alone, he got out of the carriage too. "I will walk you to your door," he said and began to do just that. The carriage followed.

"You will not!"

He considered the neighborhood and narrowed the families down to a dozen possibilities. Even fewer had girls her age in the family. Girl? No, she was a woman. She was old enough to have had a Season. She had a certain poise about her. She had to be out. Besides, there was a niggling familiarity about her. Who was she?

"I thought I made it clear that I have no intention of leaving you on a street corner," he said. "Even if that is where I did find you." He grinned at her, suddenly finding humor in the situation.

She folded her arms protectively about her person and glared at him.

He paused. "Might I assume that you do not want your family to know of your whereabouts?" he inquired.

She gnawed harder on her lip. "You cannot walk me to my door," she said. "We are not introduced."

He gave a sharp bark of a laugh. "That is the excuse you are going to use?"

"Yes," she said solidly.

He looked at her, his grin widening. Eventually, she began to chuckle too. It was ludicrous to speak of introductions.

She had inadvertently slowed as they approached one of the townhomes. He glanced up at it and suddenly had the neighborhood narrowed to one.

"Well, I suppose I should thank you for being my knight in shining armor," she said harpishly.

He shook his head, clarity coming in that moment. "Not a knight," he said. "A dragon, and you are a lily...

35

Lady Lillian Hawthorne." He gave her a courtly bow and smiled. "Until we meet again," he said with a tip of his hat as he climbed back into the carriage. He had a satisfied smile on his face.

He watched the amazement fill her face as she tried to puzzle out where they had met. The realization that she would spend the rest of the evening thinking about him brought a rush of pleasure through his veins as he watched her round the corner of the walk and head for the servants' entrance, but he knew she was no servant. He knew exactly who she was, and although they were not introduced by name, they were introduced… by none other than Rudolph Keening, the Earl of Keegain, during his holiday masquerade. Reginald had even danced with the firebrand, and then she had disappeared from society, but he had found her now. He did not intend to lose her again. He had dressed as a dragon that night, but it was she who breathed fire. He had always liked dragons.

Whistling softly, he leapt up to his carriage and ordered Helms to drive on. London had just become much more interesting, and perhaps hotter than was warranted by the summer weather.

～

"UNTIL WE MEET AGAIN, LADY LILLIAN," he had said, his hawk-like hazel eyes fixed upon her, branding her as his. She shivered in the summer heat. She was just being fanciful.

"Until we meet again, Lord Barton," Lily whispered to herself, her heart pounding as she made her way to the servant's entrance. She glanced back as she reached the door, and only now did his carriage begin to move forward. As much as she loathed to admit it, she couldn't shake the feeling that their paths were destined to cross again. And when that day came, she would be ready to face him, armed with the same determination that had fueled her fight for equality thus far. She would not be bowed by his arrogant attitude. He was just another haughty aristocrat filled with hot air.

Hot, she thought as her body remembered the effortless way he had lifted her into the carriage, and then the moment when he pinned her hands and held her close... protecting her. No. Enslaving her. She would not give the moment another thought, and yet the thoughts did creep in—the feel of his hard body against hers, the scent of him in the closed carriage, tobacco and wood smoke, and perhaps cloves. Beneath it all was something entirely alien, something entirely male, and she did not hate it as much as she wanted to...

Once inside the dimly lit servant's corridor, Lily leaned against a cool stone wall, her breathing labored. She closed her eyes and allowed herself a moment to absorb the safety that enveloped her like a familiar embrace. Her heart still pounded in her chest, but with each steadying breath, she felt the adrenaline of the night's events begin to recede.

"I'M HOME," she whispered to herself, her voice shaky. A glance at the mirror in the corridor told her she was monumentally disheveled. No wonder the man took her for a doxy. Her hair had come loose from the braid, and her cap had been lost in the fray. She brought a hand to her bosom where sweat pooled between her breasts and stained her garments. The summer heat caused ringlets of hair to cling damply to her forehead. Overall, her black hair was in a tangle that made her look wild, to say nothing of her soiled and torn clothing.

Her maid would wash and mend the dress if it was possible to mend, but tonight was too close. The weight of her rebellious actions threatened to crush her spirit when she remembered the cost of discovery, but she reminded herself that many of the nation's poor had survived worse challenges than this. She was resourceful. She was brave. That was what was required of those who stood with Bonaparte to bring a new world into being. She straightened her spine, squared her shoulders, and took one last deep breath before venturing further into the house. She needed to send a footman to find Patton, who would be worried when he could not find her and bring her home.

She was home. The moment of security faded into the normal feeling of suffocation that filled her in her family's grand estate. She was home, back under the misanthropic thumb of her grandfather, the Earl of Thornwood. Would she ever escape?

# SISTERLY LOVE

rue peace was a rare commodity in the Hawthorne household, at least as far as Lily was concerned. She had escaped for a brief respite to the drawing room, intending to read in the coveted quiet, but her mind could not quite let go of last night's proceedings. She had been denied her chance to speak at the event, but no doubt the rally broke up early anyway due to the riot.

She wondered what had happened to cause it, and then her mind went to why a gentleman like Lord Reginald Barton was in that section of town to begin with. He did not belong there any more than she did. She couldn't help but be glad that he was there, but if he hadn't been, she was sure Montgomery would have come looking for her. He was expecting her, after all.

She didn't need a man like Lord Barton in her life. He was everything she was fighting against—the entitled rich. The man had the audacity to proposition her in his very carriage only moments after he had set eyes on her.

That was only because he thought she was one of the lower classes. Upper class men tended to regard lower class women as mere sport, and she could not forget that Lord Barton showed his true colors when he thought she was one of that class, available at the whim of the Quality. It was a bitter truth—a truth Lily longed to change. A shiver went through her at the thought of how effortlessly he had immobilized her. The man was a beast, but he had showed himself a gentleman. He had delivered her safely home. Just like a man to ignore her wishes entirely though. She had not wanted to come home. Her thoughts were in a tangle.

She sat with the book open on her lap, grateful for the moment of privacy, but her mind was racing. As was their wont, her family inevitably found her and intruded upon her thoughts. She often wondered how it could be that they managed to find her in every nook and cranny, no matter where she tried to hide. And the remarks were constantly the same.

"You are always *reading*, Lily!" Her youngest sister, Betty, sat down on the cushions beside her and peeked over her shoulder. She was the youngest of all of them— four girls and two brothers. Betty was perhaps the most vivacious. She hung in the tenuous balance between girlhood and womanhood, her debut on the horizon. Lily often found her profoundly irritating. Now, Betty smiled slyly. "What if I were to take your book away?" Playfully, she put her hands on the top edge of the spine and tugged.

Lily's grip tightened in response. She pulled the volume firmly into her lap. "You had better not," she warned, eyes narrowing. After checking for their mother's presence, she added, "Don't you have anything better to do?"

Betty pouted. "Not until Cousin Catherine is done with her lessons."

Lily had forgotten her aunt and young cousin had come to visit. They were just another set of individuals in her way. Oh, bother.

"I thought you would be happy to see me," Betty said. She craned her head to read the lettering on the book's front cover. "You've been sneaking into the library again! Is it a naughty book?"

"Hush!" Lily snapped the tome shut and shoved it under a pillow on the chase in case anyone might have heard Betty's outburst. "Must you always shout so? You will raise the whole house with your carrying on. Anyway, it is nothing Father or anyone else will miss." The book was a history text, dry but informative, definitely not as enlightening as Thomas Paine's pamphlet, *Common Sense*. Lily was surprised her grandfather even had such a periodical. Perhaps it was a gift, or her brother brought it home from school and accidentally left it at home. In any case, Lily had been soaking up all the information she could find that might be relevant to her cause. She was a firm believer that knowing others' mistakes in history would keep her from repeating them in her own life.

Betty laughed. She never seemed to have a care in the world, always floating with her head in the clouds. Lily was, by turns, amused, exasperated, and sometimes just a little envious of the girl's peculiar ability to fly above the earthly concerns of others. She did not expect her younger sister to grasp the weight of the issues with which she currently grappled. None of them did, of course, but Betty least of all.

"I wish you would have more fun," she said to Lily now, all but proving Lily's inner thoughts. She grasped her sister's hand. "Come to the shops with me and Catherine today. It would be good for you to get out. Do you not think so?"

Lily opened her mouth to reply but was abruptly cut off by the austere clearing of a throat. Both girls looked toward the drawing room doorway, caught off guard by the sudden intrusion. Lily's heart sank when she saw their father standing at the threshold. He stared at his children, stern and mildly disapproving.

"*I* do not think so, Betty," he declared. "The last thing Lily needs is yet more frivolous distraction. She is no longer a child."

"Neither am I," Betty protested.

Lily straightened her spine and inched subtly over to shield the pillow that concealed her pilfered book. "Hello, Father." She made her best attempt at a smile, which was not very convincing. Even Betty's permanently cheery demeanor had slipped. They were all a little chastened in their father's commanding vicinity, but at least it was not Grandfather who interrupted them. Father, on the other hand, could not best Grandfather, and so he continually held his fist over his wife and daughters.

His eyes fell on his oldest daughter, their gaze as tangible as a physical weight. "I trust you remember what we have discussed?" he inquired.

Lily nodded. "I have, Father." How could she forget the quest to find her a husband, to marry her off to someone deemed worthy by martial means alone? Lord Hanway had offered the illusion that Lily had any say in her choice of a husband at all, but she knew he was chafing at the bit to choose one for her, and Grandfather's choice of Lord Rumford was appalling. It was no secret that the earl's son did not trust the judgement of his progeny; no wonder after Eleanor. Truthfully, he didn't trust his own judgement either and would bow to whatever Grandfather said. He always did. They were the same. All men were.

Lily's aversion was to the very idea of wifehood. She felt no man suitable for her needs, at least not any she knew. The thought had crossed her mind of late that perhaps she could marry a fellow Bonapartist, but that would require leaving her family completely behind. In no reality would her father and grandfather ever agree to giving his daughter away to a politically minded radical. Grandfather would probably have an apoplexy, especially after Eleanor's previous engagement. Even though she felt the old man would live forever, she had to be cognizant of the fact that her grandfather was old. Such strain could not be good for him, and yet, he seemed to thrive on adversity.

"Dare I ask, have you made progress?" The question was barbed, as Father's tended to be. It was clear that he wanted her to know his patience was waning, which meant of course, that Grandfather was impatient. Father was only the messenger. She would not be granted an infinite well of time to make her selection. And she had been well informed of what would happen were she too sluggish.

Lily tried not to purse her lips. She kept her face

smooth and calm. "Regrettably, Father, I have not." She had no interest in men who did not share her ideals. There was no future for her unless she and her would-be husband could build the future together, side by side.

Father's eyes darkened the way they did whenever he was notably displeased, which meant of course, that Grandfather was displeased with Father, and he was simply visiting that displeasure upon his daughters. To see the color shift in his irises was to witness the oncoming of a storm. Lily was no stranger to the cutting whim of his temper. She had learned to bear it with stoic defiance.

"Do not test me, daughter," he told her, his voice low. Betty studied the pattern of the carpet between her feet and did not move, much like a rabbit thinking to avoid the hawk's eye, Lily thought. "If you think you are able to push the limits I have set, you are sorely mistaken."

"Yes, Father." Lily's voice remained toneless. Both of them knew that it was Grandfather who set the limits, not her father. "I am sorry," she said. She wasn't, not really, but this was a game they played.

He could not have believed her less. For a few more long moments, he eyed her, and then he turned and stalked out. Lily watched him go. She reached under the pillow and pulled out her book.

"Do you know what Mother said?" Betty asked quietly. Some of the pep had left her manner.

"What did Mother say?" Lily thumbed through the pages, looking for the spot she had left. She braced herself to hear something else thoroughly unpleasant. Her mother had provided no defense thus far. She, too, desperately wanted Lily to be married. And in Lady Hanway's eyes, the viable window for Lily's nuptials was closing fast. Unlike her eldest daughter, Lady Hanway would do anything to keep the peace. She was much like Grace in that way.

"She claims not to know what she will do if you are not wed by the time I am introduced in court." Betty looked at her sister, uncharacteristic worry clouding her clear, pretty features. "That cannot happen, Lily. You would be—" Displaying the sort of grace and tact commonly lacked by their parents, Betty stopped herself before articulating Lily's worst possible fate.

"Would it bother you?" Lily inquired. "Tell me honestly." She flipped another page, though she had not read a word.

"Well, yes!" Betty burst out. "And I do not believe it would not bother *you*!" No sooner had the second sentence left her lips than she clapped a hand over her mouth, aware she had spoken too boldly.

"That is not for you to say." Lily responded. She concentrated on the page in front of her. She thought the strategy interesting and so committed the page to memory. "And my marital status is none of your concern. You have other things to worry about. Soon, the eyes of the ton will be watching you, not me." Even to her own ears, the words sounded disturbingly unconvincing. She could only imagine Mother's distress at the ultimate travesty of having a spinster daughter in attendance at Betty's debutante ball. What greater horror could befall an esteemed lady of the peerage? Did Mother truly have no knowledge of the world at large?

she wondered. Did she not know that the people were fighting for freedom on the continent?

"Do not despise me for saying so," Betty answered, "but I think I shall welcome them!" Her sunny, dreamy smile found its place once again on her lips.

"Welcome what?" Lily said distractedly. Her thoughts had been in the book in her lap and she was only partially attending her sister.

"Why, the balls of course! It's going to be so exciting and romantic. I cannot wait to attend parties to my heart's content!" She gasped. "Do you think I might find a secret lover, as Eleanor had Firthley? Soon it will be my turn to open Christmas gifts and Valentines at the breakfast table!"

Long fascinated by the ongoing struggles of people on the brink of revolution, Lily found such concerns insultingly shallow. She wished fervently that she could find a way to open her family's eyes to the type of world she saw, the one which those like Roger Montgomery worked tirelessly to bring justice. But then again, it pained her to think of crushing Betty's girlish dreams beneath an emotionless fist, whether that fist belong to a husband or her own grandfather. Why shouldn't her dear sisters be allowed to follow the paths that pleased them, if Lily was so determined to follow her own?

"Perhaps you ought to find this hypothetical young man first," she teased. "Although I suppose it would be exceedingly easy to hide a fictional love letter."

Betty huffed.

Smiling, Lily turned her attention back to the book languishing in her lap. She was chagrined to find that her appetite for reading had momentarily ebbed. All she could think about was her father's thinly veiled threat. Had he picked out a husband for her as they spoke? Was it truly Rumford, or was that simply a thinly veiled coercion? Was there someone different?

The very notion sent an unwelcome chill down her spine. Lily shuddered. Time was running out.

"What is the matter, Sister?" Betty touched her arm. "Suddenly you look unwell."

Lily shook her head. "It is nothing. I was just thinking…" Lili trailed off as her middle sister, Grace, entered the drawing room. She was carrying her embroidery and looking back over her shoulder. When she spoke to her sisters, her tone was hushed.

"Father is in a mood today," said Grace. She glanced at the other two. "Which one of you did it?"

"How do you know it was not you?" Lily retorted.

"Please." Betty giggled. "It is *never* Grace. And she never lets us forget it."

"That is untrue," Grace protested. She seated herself on Lily's other side, taking up her needle and thread. "I simply do not thrive on trouble like some others in this room." She looked down her fine, thin nose at the two of them.

"I cannot imagine whomever you might mean," Betty said innocently. "Surely not the oldest sister who refused to marry first."

The displeasure was writ large on Grace's face. She continued her sewing without looking at the stitches, preferring instead to pin her gaze on Lily. "Sister, you must give up this incessant battle. This is our home, not a battlefield. We are a family, not warring armies."

"No one said a thing about armies," Lily replied.

47

"After all, there is no army involved. I am alone on one side, and all of you are on the other."

"Do not say such sullen things." Grace had the tendency to sound like Mother when she admonished, and the similarity grated on Lily's nerves. She loved her sisters—honestly, she did—but no one knew better how to get under her skin. "It is hardly our intention to fight with you." Grace sighed. "I just do not think this tension is befitting of us. You must understand that, at least."

"Yes, I suppose so," Lily admitted. If she had thought the brewing conflict avoidable, she would have gladly steered clear. But there was no way to reconcile her personal, deeply held beliefs with the distasteful institution of arranged marriage to which their father would not stop alluding. He and Grandfather wanted to trap her in the safest kind of monied matrimony he could find, corner her like a wild animal in need of taming. Lily could not lie down and allow that to happen. She would not.

"Then why will you not do anything to resolve it?" Grace pleaded. "You are not the only one caught up in this web, Sister, no matter how you want to see it. Think of us, your sisters, who only want you to be happy. Think of Mother. You know she is frail."

Lily threw up her hands, annoyed at the tendrils of guilt slowly but surely creeping into her consciousness. Would that she could simply erase the specter of familial obligations from her conscience! But the part of her that remained grudgingly beholden to her family endured.

"Perhaps I shall escape to Gretna Green," she said. "Eleanor had the right of it," she muttered.

The scandalized looks on her sisters' faces gave her

pause. "All right, all right. You have made your point. Will it appease you if I promise to search for a potential suitor? I will not promise to take one, mind you. But I will make some effort."

"Do not be so stubborn, Lily!" Betty gushed. "Romance is beautiful! I can't wait to fall in love."

Grace smiled. "It is a start."

Lily frowned back at the two of them, but she didn't hold onto her gloominess for long. No matter how much they needled at one another, she could never stay truly angry with her sisters. She loved them both dearly, as well as Eleanor, the pariah, who had escaped with her secret love. But even as the conversation moved on to lighter, more mundane topics, Lily sat between Betty and Grace and wondered what exactly she was going to do.

# BROTHERLY LOVE

t was an uneventful morning at the Barton townhouse in London. Lord Reginald was enjoying some much-needed peace in his London townhome. Father had left for Lords earlier in the day, and his lady mother was having a lie in. No wonder after the late nights his sister and mother had spent lately clucking like hens. The siblings present in the house at that time were Reginald Barton, his married sister Patience, and his brother-in-law, Lord Percival Beresford, heir to the Earldom of Blackburn. The three young people were comfortably enjoying a nice cup of tea in the intimacy of the morning room while Reginald was reading the correspondence he had just received from their distinguished father saying that, due to the end of the war on the continent, Lords would continue to sit until they got the Corsican situation sorted. The window was open, but the morning was hot and still. It promised another scorching afternoon. Patience and Percival spoke of family matters.

"Papa will not be home for dinner," Reginald

explained as he looked up from the letter. "He is eating at the club after Lords. Something with procuring a conservative vote among these idiot left-leaning Whigs." He chuckled at something in his father's letter and folded the missive, commenting, "He also sent a private note to Mama. Is she awake?"

"I don't know," Patience said tucking back a bright red curl that had already begun to escape her maid's ministrations on her riotous locks. "I suppose so. Mama should be down directly. The sun is already high in the sky."

"And already hot as Hades," Reginald commented running a finger beneath his cravat.

"Reggie, please," Patience admonished her brother for his language as she pushed back the plate that had held the scones which had nothing but crumbs left on it.

A footman took the empty plate away. "Shall I bring more tea?" the footman asked.

Patience glanced at her brother and husband. "I think not," she said. "We will have a pot in the drawing room later when mother comes down."

"Very good, my Lady," said the footman with a slight bow to the family.

"You and Mother were up late last night," Reginald commented to his sister when the footman had left the room.

Patience nodded noncommittally, so Reginald did not push. He knew his mother and sister were talking about womanly matters, and it was unseemly to intrude, but he was concerned for his only sibling. She was nearly inconsolable when she lost the babe she carried, and so far, she had failed to quicken again. Of course, no one but the family knew of the loss, but Reginald could tell it weighed heavily on his elder sister.

Patience rose, and the gentlemen stood with her as she moved from the table. Presently, another letter arrived, taking the three of them by surprise. There was, after all, only the morning and evening post unless something was more dire. They lingered between the morning room and the drawing room.

"What is it?" Reginald asked, concerned. Although Wellington had snatched victory from the jaws of defeat at Waterloo, and the war with the colonies was finally settled, Reginald was so used to being on edge for bad news that he could not quite admit to himself that the conflict was over, as was his own part in war-time reconnaissance work. He could take a well-deserved holiday. He needed the quiet and relaxation. The sooner they could leave London the better. The memory of a dark-eyed temptress belayed that thought.

"I'm sorry, Sir," said the first footman, Grimes. "Nothing to concern yourself with. I accidentally took this up to the countess. It is your letter." For an instant, Reginald tensed. Grimes was usually more careful than that. Reginald's correspondence was private, sometimes direly so.

Oh, pish posh," said Patience unaware of Reginald's activities of late. "No harm done, Grimes."

His eyes strayed to Reginald as if seeking forgiveness. It was not forthcoming. Some of his letters had life or death secrets within them. Grimes and Helm were his confidants, and they knew better, but he could not speak to the man now.

"You know they are calling themselves America

now," Percy added as Reginald took the letter and glanced at the seal. Keegain.

Should he open it now, he wondered, with his sister at the table? He turned the missive over in his hand.

"They have been for quite some time," Percy finished.

Reginald shrugged. "Colonies or America, we have spent enough money on that godforsaken, savage-ridden land. We have troubles here at home with what to do with Bonaparte."

"Father said they decided to imprison him on the island of St. Helens," Percy said.

"Because that worked so well when he was on the island of Elba," Reginald replied dryly. "His followers will not admit defeat." Reginald wondered if he should speak to Mr. White about the problem. No. He deserved his holiday. He would only go to Mr. White if he was summoned.

"What would you have them do?" Percy asked. "If they execute him, he will just be made a martyr."

Patience laid a hand on her brother's arm, bringing the conversation away from the conflict. "Who is the letter from?" she asked. "That looks to be Lord Keegain's hand."

"It is," Reginald exclaimed, looking at the seal and then unfurling the elegant parchment. "The writing is unmistakably his neat script," he added. He began to read the even lettering.

"Keegain has the mark of most extraordinary penmanship," Patience said, effectively turning the conversation from talk of war and Napoleon.

"Yes. It's positively feminine," Reginald complained,

as his own writing was often marked with crossed out words when he misplaced letters in the words.

"I dare say I haven't heard from the Keenings for quite some time." Percy replied. He coughed, obviously avoiding the subject of penmanship. Percival's hand was neat and concise, much like the man himself. Keegain had a bolder hand, but still legible in every way. "Nothing dire, I hope," Percy said questioningly.

After all, the last letter Percy had from the Earl of Keegain boded ill for all involved.

"No, no," Reginald said as he read. This was a personal missive.

"Jane has been out of Society since Christmas last," Patience added with a soft look towards her husband. "First pending the birth of the Keening heir, and then with... home matters. Does he speak of Jane?"

Reginald shot his sister a look. Percival was a wonderful husband to his sister and friend to him, but Reginald often thought that just because Patience was quiet didn't mean she didn't occasionally crave adventure. Percy's involvement in politics often left his wife at home. Far be it from him in his bachelor state to make corrections in his sister's marriage, but he couldn't help but feel that Patience was restless. He wondered if he was having these thoughts because of his encounter with the Hawthorne girl last night. Obviously, that young woman was out seeking adventure in all the wrong places. He knew Patience would never be so bold, but still, he wondered if she craved some excitement. Did women crave excitement?

Truth be told, so did he. It bothered him more than he could say that Lady Hawthorne was out alone on the street and could have been seriously hurt by the rabble. Although the war was over, there was still tension in the masses. There would always be tension in the masses. He kept turning the thought over in his mind and could not think of a feasible reason why the lady would have been out at such an hour and in such a place. Was she meeting a lover?

As he absently scanned the letter in his hand, he mulled over taking the issue of her truancy to the girl's father, or would that be her grandfather? Gads! That thought made him hesitate. Everyone in the Ton knew that the old man was a sodding ass. His own grandson, Robert Hawthorne, had once bitterly said that he would never die. God didn't want him, and the devil was afraid he would take over. In any case, the man held onto his earldom and his children and grandchildren with an iron fist.

"Reggie! What does he say?" Patience persisted. "Does he mention Jane?"

Reginald's mind was brought back to the present, and he shoved the letter towards Percy, his brother by marriage, who read its contents aloud as they lingered outside of the morning room. Sun poured in through the colored panes of stained glass that topped the window making patterns on the parquet floor.

Patience's voice trailed off as she gazed absently towards the great oak tree just outside the window. It was apparent to her brother that she had drifted into private thoughts while contemplating some unhappy matters, as evidenced by the frown that appeared on her usually smiling face. She was soon brought back from her reverie and into the present moment by the touch of her husband's hand on hers.

Percy reached out and took his wife's hand and squeezed it gently. She smiled again. "I know you are missing seeing Jane and Julia in Bath this summer, but that is no reason for the long face," Percy said.

"No, it is not," Patience agreed, beaming up at her husband as he kissed her tenderly on the forehead.

Reggie shook his head. His sister and his friend were disgustingly in love. The only snag in their marriage was the fact that they had not announced the eminent arrival of a child, and of course, Percy as the heir to Blackthorn needed an heir himself. Percy's brother's wife already had an heir, and according to Patience, she was working on the spare, although that was a closely guarded secret. That fact was with Samuel being away at sea for months at a time. Reginald knew his sister fretted over the lack in her own life, but Percival did not seem concerned, although there seemed to be an abundance of new babies coming into the world. Reggie's mind on the subject of heirs and children brought his thoughts to how proud his friend, Keegain, was of his young son.

"How old must the boy be now? Do you think the lad is walking yet?" Reginald paced back to the table, lifted the teacup to his lips, realized it was empty, and put it back down.

"Who?" Percy asked, tucking some of Patience's riotous red hair beneath the cap she wore for propriety's sake. Honestly, thought Reginald, were either of them attending the conversation? "The Keening child," he said impatiently. They were all in the same room and yet all seemed in their own worlds.

"Oh, I doubt it," Patience added. "Babies are not born ready to frolic like some long-legged colt of yours, Reginald. Such things do take time." She exchanged a look with her husband, and Reggie glanced away. There was such pain in his sister's look. He wished he could offer some solace, but to even mention such a thing in mixed company was taboo. He loved his sister dearly. They were different as night and day, but one could expect that, he supposed, since she was a woman. She was soft and easily hurt. He lived to protect her, as a man was wont to do for the women he loved, but this was one hurt from which he could not protect her.

Her dearest friends, Jane and Amelia, had already given their husbands heirs, even though Amelia and Samuel were married nearly a year after Patience and Percy, due to the delay of their marriage because of the death of Amelia's father. However, Amelia and Samuel announced her pregnancy to the family nearly on the heels of the wedding.

As far as he knew, his sister was not in a family way, and she was anxious for it. He knew that was why she had chosen to have an extended visit here in Town with Mama. There were long and cloistered women's conversations the last few days. Father was able to escape to Lords, which was uncharacteristically still in session even though it was damnable hot in the city this late in the Season.

He had tried to pressure Percy into an outing while they were in Town, but the man stuck maddeningly by his wife's side when he was not on his own father's coattails. Reginald shrugged, trying to dispel the feeling of being left out of this undoubtedly private conversation occurring between his sister and his friend. "I may go for a ride myself this morning," Reginald said at last. "Will you come, Perce?" The ton frowned on racing through Hyde Park, but at a canter, there would at least be a breeze.

Hyde Park was certainly not his choice of riding places, but it was better than watching his friend and his sister gaze at one another in the cloying townhouse. Perhaps he would see Neville Collington, Earl of Wentwell, or Harry Westlake at Hyde Park. Being single, Harry was always up for an adventure; however, since he was not a peer, the man might have been able to escape the summer heat by going to Bath or the country. Harry's elder brother Andrew was still in Town. Of course, Harry and Andrew were both those horrid Whigs that his father abhorred. He smiled at the thought. Who else would do? Wentwell seemed a good choice. Neville's wife, Charity, was best friends with Keegain's sister by marriage, Julia Bellevue-Gruger, Baroness Falkland. It was likely the women were in Bath, but if not, perhaps he could cajole the man into having a dinner party whereby he could once again meet Lady Lillian Hawthorne under less suspicious circumstances than a Bonapartist's riot. It was a convoluted plan. Perhaps he should enlist his sister's help, or Percival's. "How about it, Percy?" Reginald repeated. "Are you up for a ride in Hyde Park?"

Percival shook his head. "I have some reading to get done," Percy said to his friend and then directed his gaze to his wife. "Would you like to sit in the garden or the drawing room? Perhaps it will be cooler out of doors."

Reginald hadn't really expected Percival to want to

ride this morning. He had always been better friends with Percy's younger brother Samuel, who surely would have raced with him, making the dowagers exclaim at their daring canter through Hyde Park, but most of his friends were leg-shackled now, and with their wives having babies, doubly so. They were not inclined to go off with their bachelor friends.

Presently, Samuel was at sea, somewhere in the Atlantic near the West Indies, he supposed. But with the war ended, perhaps he would be home soon. To hear Samuel tell of it, the very sun was an enemy of England in that part of the world, to say nothing of fever and insects, but at least the war there was over now. With luck, Samuel might be assigned on this side of the world. Undoubtedly, the Royal Navy would be called out to guard Bonaparte, and hopefully do a better job than last time.

Reginald shoved aside the thought of his friends Samuel and Jack and the Royal Navy. Instead, he declared to the under footman, "Have my horse saddled." And then to Patience, "Tell mother I've gone to Hyde Park to ride, will you?"

He thought most of the young ladies who frequented the park appreciated a moment of excitement in their decidedly boring days. It was unfortunate that most of his friends were now married. What was the off chance that he would see the lovely Lady Lillian Hawthorne? Unlikely.

"You do know, Regge, Hyde Park at this hour will be filled with young ladies looking for husbands," Patience said as they moved leisurely towards the drawing room. "I thought you wanted to avoid that rush. Unless you have changed your mind about marriage." She raised her eyebrows.

"Lud no," Reggie exclaimed. "But I will brave the matrimony mamas. With the summer heat blazing, I think the herd should be somewhat thinned. Only the staunchest of Lords and their families are still in Town." He had already mentally counted them, wondering who might want to have a dinner party to end the late season. "I feel like if I don't get some air, I shall pitch one of mama's glass figurines into the wall." He did not tell his sister that a dark-haired siren had so bedeviled him that he could barely sit still.

"By all means," Patience said waving a hand, dismissing him.

Reginald turned to go, but then Patience stopped him with a word. "Oh! Wait! What news in Keegain's letter?" she asked, as if she had just remembered the letter which had come with the morning post.

"It is an invitation to a fox hunt that is to be held at his country estate later in the summer, once the peers are released from Lords!" Reginald exclaimed with a fair amount of incredulity. "Apparently, the Keenings have decided to forgo Bath this summer."

Patience found even less to say about the matter than before. "How grand!" she replied in an even tone which dully contradicted her affirmation. She stood up slowly as the footman cleared the tea set. Percival kissed her on the cheek and took his leave. Patience walked towards the drawing room, and Reginald followed. Her needle-point awaited her hand on the window seat where the late morning sun was streaming into the drawing room. It was already a swelteringly hot day, and Reginald heartily wished for the country air. He ran a finger under his cravat.

Patience reached for the bit of fabric and settled herself on the window seat, needle in hand.

"You and Percy are invited to join as well, you know. I'm sure your invitation arrived at your townhouse this morning." Reginald turned to her, thinking that her lack of interest might have come from inferring that she was uninvited. That would certainly not be so.

"Whyever would Keegain be having a hunt?" she wondered as she punched the needle through the material. "I know they all like to ride, but I cannot see him and Jane chasing a poor fox about the wood." She shrugged as she looked up at her brother as her husband went to collect his books. "I shall attend, of course. I'm sure that Amelia and Samuel will be there if Samuel has leave. Perhaps Jack and Lavinia too. It will be marvelous to see them again, but I am also sure you or Percy will be capable of finding a perfectly fine excuse for me to not actually ride in such a tedious event. Do say so in writing your reply. I find hunting in general a rather frightening affair. I prefer to keep my feet, or at least my horse's hooves, firmly on the ground."

"Oh, I thought you would send my reply with yours and Percival's," Reginald said, grinning at her hopefully.

"Oh, very well." Patience paused. "It shall have to wait until we go home and I actually receive our invitation, of course."

"Of course," Reginald agreed.

Patience held her needle aloft, turning once more towards the vista of the rustling trees outside. The slight breeze outside had not made its way through the open window. "But I have no intention of riding in the hunt, Regge."

Reginald smiled, wondering if she was hoping to be enceinte by then.

"Well, I do believe the Poppys will be absolutely distraught when they find out you couldn't spare the time to ride with them." No doubt there would be all of the Poppys' squalling babies at the manor, he thought. He wondered which of the Poppys were still unmarried. There were such a lot of them. He would definitely be spending as much time outside as possible.

Patience turned to him abruptly. "You mentioned nothing of the Poppys coming along as well."

"Of course, they are. You know they are great friends of Jane and Julia. The whole lot of them will be there with all of their children. I have no doubt."

Patience laughed as she rearranged her needlepoint. "And remember, not all of the Poppy sisters are yet married, dear brother," she said. "Or for that matter, there are still unmarried Keening sisters. Lady Helen, I think," suggested Patience.

A picture of the stately blonde who reminded Reginald of an ice princess came to mind. "Lud! You shall have to run interference for me," Reginald begged.

"Ah, my friend. Being married is not a fate worse than death," said Percival as he reentered the room with a book and settled on the chair beside his wife. The scene was entirely too domestic.

Reginald shuddered. "I can think of nothing worse than being tied to some milksop."

"So, do not marry a milksop, brother dear," Patience said without looking up from her needlepoint.

Reginald was treated to a memory of the dark-haired woman with flashing eyes as she struck him for assuming she was a doxy. What else was he supposed to think? She was alone in a shady area of town. Just the thought of her stirred him.

"In any case," Percival added, "it shall be a rout. You know that the Keegains always throw a wonderful party."

"Yes," he said, and besides that, he had first met Lily Hawthorne at a Keegain party. Could he assume that she and her family would be invited to the fox hunt? Did she ride? It seemed likely. Perhaps he should reply to his own invitation and urge Keegain to invite the Hawthornes, even though there had been some kerfuffle with the Firthleys at the Christmas event, so the Keenings may avoid inviting either family. Oh, he certainly did not want to wait until the summer's end to see Lady Lillian again. There must be some event here in town where she would be in the near future.

The footman entered the room to announce that Reginald's horse was saddled and waiting for him.

"Enjoy your ride in Hyde Park," Patience said with a smile.

"You didn't even ask me who the rest of the party is, dear sister," Reginald replied, still smiling.

"I can imagine." She stretched herself in the sun and then turned back to needlepoint. "I am sure Percy and Samuel will be off with you and the other men, running around cross country, chasing some poor animal out of hiding for sport." She sighed and seated herself by the window once more.

"Oh, come, dearest sister." Reginald smiled. "Do not

be glum. I am certain you will find many ways to entertain yourself with the other ladies while we are out hunting. You need not soil your delicate sensibilities with the actual hunt."

"Humph," she said. "Jane and the Poppy sisters will ride; I am sure. So will Amelia and Charlotte. Perhaps Helen will stay in. Is Charity coming?" she asked. "She and Helen might keep me company. Do we know any of the other ladies attending?" she asked, a hopeful spark blooming in her tone.

"Not… precisely… Not that I recall." Reginald hesitated. "Keegain didn't exactly publish a guest list with our invitation, but we can assume. Still, wouldn't it be exciting to meet new people, to make new acquaintances and hopefully, new friends?"

"You know I find new crowds rather overwhelming. Whenever I am in a room full of new people, my first instinct is to find a quiet corner to avoid making polite conversation. Last time we went to a ball, mind you, I spent most of the time getting increasingly longer breaths of fresh air outside. Our hosts must have thought I found their company appalling," she replied, lowering her eyes. "I'm so glad all of the pomp of a Season is over now." She turned adoring eyes to her husband.

"Oh, Patience," her husband replied, leaning towards her from his chair. "Do it for me. You have been much too melancholy of late. There is going to be a nice picnic outside on the day of the hunt and a dance afterwards. When I think of how enjoyable all of it shall be, you know you will enjoy it."

Patience smiled shyly. "Of course, I shall," she

replied softly. "I just cannot like the reason for it. Poor fox."

"I suppose you shouldn't leave your brother unattended at such a populated event anyway," added Percival. "Why, if you're not there to keep a watchful eye on him, some devious lady might snatch him up!"

"Then I shall be thoroughly distracted!" Patience replied, and they both laughed. The pair had been matchmaking for too long.

Reginald snorted at their mirth and rolled his eyes skyward. He had been deftly avoiding both his mother's and his sister's attempts to find him a bride. He didn't intend to be leg-shackled any time soon.

"I'm off to Hyde Park to ride," he said at last. "Please send my acceptance with yours, Patience, dear." She liked that sort of thing and would dash off a letter in no time. Reginald knew that if he had to put pen to paper, he would spend the better part of an hour devising a response. Social correspondence confounded him. He preferred to deal in facts, and when possible, face to face. Besides, he revised his earlier thought, if he asked Keegain to invite the Hawthornes, he would seem much too interested in the dark-haired siren.

Reginald headed out the front door, leaving the saccharine domesticity behind him. Joyful as he was at the prospect of being invited to such a prestigious gathering, and having convinced his sister and Percival to join him, Reginald hated writing responses, elaborating on all the polite thanks dictated by such an occasion. His own writing, perhaps because it was often Crown business, tended to be brief to the point of terseness or convoluted with code and hidden meanings.

He told himself he was glad that Patience would send the letter with the footman directly, and she would make all the necessary preparations for their departure within a fortnight. There was some advantage to having a female relative to take care of such things, he thought. Now, if he could find Harry Westlake in town, he could ask if the Firthleys were invited to the Keening event, which would point to the likelihood of the Hawthornes being omitted, and he would not spill his secret longing to see Lady Lily Hawthorne. As a matter of fact, there should be any number of parties in town to celebrate the end of the war. He would just have to figure out which one the Hawthornes were planning to attend. His sister's friend Lavinia would know, and by association, Captain Jack.

# THE WENTWELL BALL

*L*ily stood her ground, hands clenched at her sides as her grandfather, the imposing Earl of Thornwood, bore down on her like a storm cloud. "Lord Rumford will be an esteemed guest at the Wentwell home," he thundered, his voice echoing through the ornate drawing room. "I expect you to be civil to him at the musicale tonight."

"Esteemed?" Lily scoffed, dark brown eyes flashing with defiance. "He's a pompous windbag who believes women are nothing more than decorative objects."

"You will not embarrass me in sight of the Earl of Wentwell," her eldest brother Robert added. "We are lucky to be invited."

Lily huffed. "They are people like any other." The only thing that kept Lily from refusing to go to the event at all was the fact that there would be other gentlemen in attendance, and she was aware of the ticking clock her grandfather had set. She had a month to find a suitor, or he would give her to Rumford.

"They are peers," her father added softly. "They deserve our respect."

"They are people, and respect should be earned," Lily muttered.

"Do have a care, Lily," her mother said, fluttering a handkerchief before her pale face. Lily was surprised she had not yet taken to her bed with vapors. That was her usual way of dealing with any disagreement.

"Enough of this insolence!" her grandfather roared, pounding his hand on the table. "You will attend the musicale and treat Mr. Rumford with respect, or you will remain here locked in your room until you learn your place."

"Locked in my room?" Lily repeated incredulously, her voice full of disgust. Then she countered with her trump card. "And how, pray tell, did that work out for Eleanor, Grandfather?" she asked, her voice turning saccharine with sarcasm.

Bringing up her younger sister's defiance was risky, but she felt invigorated. She clenched her fists at her side while the Earl of Thornwood looked ready to explode with ire. She did not care. She threw caution to the winds. "I will not abide by your archaic notions, Grandfather. I refuse to be cowed into submission by your outdated ideas of propriety. I am a person, not a dog that you can cage."

"That is not entirely so," Grandfather said. "If you keep acting as if you have lost your wits, Bedlam is a possibility."

Lily blanched, but in the next moment realized that having a crazy granddaughter would reflect badly on her grandfather. It was an idle threat.

"Please, both of you, let us not argue so," Lily's mother, Lady Hanway, implored weakly. She leaned against a silk-upholstered chair, her pale hand pressed to her forehead. "I can feel a megrim coming on from all this strife."

Her mother knew just the words to stop the argument. Lily loved her mother and would not willingly cause her pain, but that did not mean that Lily was beaten simply because she was willing to temporarily capitulate to her grandfather's demands.

"Very well," she said. "I will go the musicale, and I will speak to Lord Rumford," she conceded with a scowl. "That does not mean I will marry him," she shot back at her grandfather.

"But mark my words, Lily," added her grandfather, determined to land the final jab. "You will obey me. You will go where I say and when I say, or you will go nowhere!"

"Fine," Lily muttered, seething with anger. "I said I would go. I will even refrain from calling Lord Rumford a bore," she said sweetly.

Her Grandfather harrumphed as she added under her breath, "Even if he is a boar—a pig."

As her mother retreated to her room, seeking solace from the migraine that threatened, Lily retreated up the grand staircase to prepare for the dreaded event, but she did not go quietly. She stomped her slippered feet on every step.

In the bedchamber, Grace and Betty looked up from their needlework as Lily entered, her cheeks flushed with indignation. "What happened?" Grace asked, setting aside her embroidery hoop and moving to comfort her sister.

"Grandfather insists I be civil to that insufferable Mr. Rumford tonight," Lily fumed, pacing the room as Betty and Grace exchanged sympathetic glances.

"Perhaps you could find a way to avoid him?" Grace suggested gently, smoothing her light blue silk gown. "Mingle with the other guests, or engage in conversation with someone else whenever he approaches? Surely you can do that without much fuss."

"Maybe you can hide behind the potted plants," Betty offered jokingly. "He'll never find you there."

Lily snorted. "I would if I could smuggle a book in my reticule," she said. Her sisters could always make her smile. "Your suggestions are well-intended, but I must face him eventually." Lily sighed, resigned to her fate. "I vow, however, that I will not let Mr. Rumford dictate my evening. I will enjoy myself at the musicale, despite his presence. The music itself should be lovely."

Grace and Betty nodded, their faces full of sisterly support as they helped Lily dress for the impending event. Lily eschewed the corset, but the dress itself was binding.

The garment mother had chosen for the event was an elegant gown with an empire waist. It was a sheer confection the color of fresh melon with so much gold thread on the skirt that it felt like the weight of her responsibility was woven into the very fabric. This abundance of gold was not only to flaunt the earl's wealth but also to obscure the fact that the dress was so sheer that even with a petticoat, one could see the shadow of her limbs beneath the fabric. The thought of parading about before Lord Rumford in such a garment was sickening. This was exactly the decadence of the aristocracy that she hated, and yet she was required to wear the thing, to carry about the weight of the gold to show her worth, both in her form and her money. The stockings she wore were pink, giving an illusion of blushing legs. She wished she could wear her simple cotton dress. She felt so much more herself in it with the Bonapartists, but she had no choice in the matter—of attending or her dress.

Lily sighed as Grace and her maid helped her into the garment. The silk rustled, whispering across her skin, as Grace settled the fabric over her head and smoothed it over her body. The maid took charge of the numerous gold buttons that closed the back of the dress. The bodice was actually tasteful, with a scooped neckline and simple rouching on the sleeves.

"You look beautiful," Betty said, but Lily had her doubts. She was not the beautiful daughter. She was the intelligent one. Grace, on the other hand; she looked beautiful in a gown so pale it brought to mind summer clouds encrusted with pearls worked across the bodice. A double string of pearls graced her swan-like neck and more, held on pins, decorated her hair.

Lily was similarly decked out with gold. A single ruby the size of a baby's fist dipped just above her decolletage, drawing the eye to her bosom. Maggie, Lily's maid, clapped her hands with delight and declared her ready.

Ready for battle, Lily thought. She steeled herself for the challenge that lay ahead—navigating a treacherous landscape of societal expectations while attempting to remain true to her own convictions.

The musicale was held at the Earl of Wentwell's townhouse, and Lily could hardly contain her irritation as she entered the opulent drawing room. The windows were open, but the summer air was unrelenting, and the immediate scent of numerous varieties of costly perfume was overwhelming. Lily wished for a bit of country shade and a breeze, but there was neither. On the other hand, as long as they were in Town, she could look for another possible suitor. Once they retired to the country for the summer, that option would be lost.

The air was thick with gossip and laughter, as well as various fragrances covering the scent of perspiring bodies, as the impeccably dressed ladies and gentlemen mingled amongst one another. The countess, a buxom jovial woman, excused herself from her other guests and greeted Lily like an old friend. Some of Lily's pique melted away before her genuinely friendly manner. She fanned herself unrelentingly.

"I am about to melt," she confided to Lily's ears before addressing the Earl and her father. "The gentlemen have gone to the garden for cigars and brandy," the countess said wrinkling her nose. "And the Dowager Countess of Wentwell is speaking with the musicians, I believe." She glanced over her shoulder at the quartet. "They should be ready to start soon."

Lily's mother began to plot a path to the older ladies who were seated near the instruments. Father, Grandfather, and Robert nodded as if the countess was nothing but a servant, and with the direction of a footman, they made their way to the outdoor area that sufficed for a garden in town.

Once the gentlemen were out of earshot, the countess

confided to Lily and Grace. "I told my husband I would not have cigars in the house in this heat."

Grace just blinked in amazement at the audacity of the woman, but Lily had to speak. "You told your husband?"

"But he is the Earl of Wentwell," Grace said as if to confirm. "And you the countess?"

"Yes," the woman said.

"But it is his house, your ladyship," stuttered Grace.

"It is, but it is my house too, and do call me Charity." She looked from Grace to Lily as she wielded a feather fan with purpose. "We are of an age, I think, and share some friends, although we have not traveled in the same circles."

"Yes," Grace agreed, sharing their Christian names as well.

Lily pondered these thoughts as the countess recounted some of the gossip that was floating about London concerning the war and the officers coming home since Bonaparte was beaten. Lily bit her lip against saying the great man was hardly beaten, only temporarily delayed from his mission, but this was not the company in which to be sharing such things.

"Oh, wonderful," said Grace, clapping her gloved hands together. "See Lily, there will be other gentlemen about and you will be able to avoid Lord Rumford."

"Lord Rumford?" questioned the countess with a slight frown, which she immediately wiped from her face, presenting a placid aristocratic grace.

"Grandfather has chosen him as a possible suitor for Lily," Grace explained as they moved into the drawing room and found refreshments. Lily suppressed the urge to kick her well-meaning sister in the shin. She did not need gossips to learn that Grandfather had chosen him, nor that she was in such dire straits. It was bad enough that most of the Ton thought her a bluestocking and still twittered about Eleanor.

"Surely not," the countess said as she fanned herself unrelentingly. "The man is an old lecher who has buried three wives."

"So, I told my grandfather," Lily agreed.

"Well, I shall introduce you to my friend Lavinia," the countess said helpfully. "She is married to Captain Hartfield. I'm sure he can introduce you to some of the gentlemen home on leave who might be more to your liking."

"We know Lavinia well," Grace confided. "She is a good friend."

"Wonderful," said the countess, snapping her fan shut and clapping her hands.

"But do not tell Grandfather she is here," Lily added thinking of how Lavinia had been instrumental in Eleanor's escape. He could not abide the woman.

The countess nodded and said she hoped the musicians might be able to play something suitable for dancing. "This gathering was set up on rather short notice," she confided. "So, I'm not really sure if the musicians are prepared to play dance music. My husband decided just yesterday that we should have something to mark the end of the war and the end of this extended time in London." Her eyes strayed to the musicians tuning their instruments.

"Excuse me, please," she said and went to confer

with the musicians who had begun to play chamber music.

Lily stood uncertainly with her sister. They sipped their drinks. "Where is that potted plant?" Lily muttered, and Grace chuckled.

"It's not so bad as that."

"I'm surprised that this was a last-minute affair," Lily said, looking around at the opulence. "The servants must have been working long hours to pull it off." As she scanned the crowd for familiar faces, her eyes fell upon Lord Rumford, who was engaged in animated conversation with a group of equally pompous men. Sweat was pouring from his round, red face, and he looked ready to have an apoplexy. How could her grandfather think this man should be her husband?

Grace linked arms with her and followed her gaze. "So, how shall we discourage Lord Rumford?" She asked. "Shall we try to find you someone handsome and charming enough that Rumford will go away entirely?"

Lily couldn't help but laugh at her sisters' antics. "Very well, let us find this mythical gentleman who can save me from Mr. Rumford's clutches."

As they navigated through the throng of guests, Lily lost her sister to a conversation with Lord Andrew West-lake. She turned, hoping to find a corner where she could be her traditional wallflower self and literally hide behind a potted plant, when she suddenly noticed a newcomer to the party, Lord Reginald Barton.

She was not sure why her eyes were drawn to him. He was not a particularly handsome man, and yet, he had a presence about him that drew her eye. She had not realized how striking he was when she met him on the dark streets of London. His hair was the color of dark burnished copper. Nor had she realized how tall he was having, been seated in the carriage. The strands of his hair gleamed in the last rays of the summer sun that poured through the high windows and merged with his ruddy skin to cast a hue of golden sunshine over him, like copper in a forge. Around his broad shoulders, he wore a dark blue jacket. He paused in the doorway and tucked his striped waistcoat of cream and blue and russet in one long, slow motion, pulling the cotton snugly against his broad chest. His hazel eyes were intense as he gazed at the company. He was looking for someone. Then his eyes met hers, and his gaze softened. His lips turned up in a genuine smile. She felt the warmth of it.

Surely, he had not been looking for her?

She did not remember ever eliciting such a response from a man, and she noted his eyes stayed firmly on her face rather than her tantalizingly pink appendages which were nearly visible through her gown. It was a refreshing change, and yet a part of her wanted him to see her as a woman.

His words came back to her. *If you do not have a protector, I might be persuaded.*

Oh, well, that proved he did indeed see her as a woman, as all men did, she supposed, as a vessel for his own pleasure. She would not give him the time of day. She turned from him, giving him the cut direct, and she noticed coming from two different directions were two other gentlemen, the odious Lord Rumford and Lord Spencer. Drat! Lord Spencer was a known Bonaparte sympathizer, or at least he was known to Lily.

She had dodged him at the meetings when she could,

but here, he was a member of the aristocracy, and there was no way to avoid him. She hoped that he did not recognize her as the outspoken Miss Hawkins, but he seemed to not be looking at her face at all. She turned from Lord Spencer, hiding her face beneath her fan, although it was clear the man's eyes were scanning her appendages. She was nothing more than a pair of legs to him. That was certain.

Of course, at some point, she would have to speak to Lord Rumford. Grandfather demanded it. She might as well get it over with, she thought as the man approached.

"Lady Lillian," he said. "Might I offer you a refreshment?"

She gave him a tight smile, but before she could answer, Lord Reginald Burton was there at her side with his hazel eyes full of warmth. He held two glasses of lemon water and offered her one of them. She glanced from one man to the other as Lord Reginald deftly edged Lord Rumford away from her.

"Thank you," she said. She offered Lord Rumford a wry smile and turned back to Lord Burton.

"Lady Lillian," Reginald greeted her with a polite nod. "It is quite warm, is it not? We can expect an evening breeze, I hope, before the dancing begins."

"Yes," she agreed sipping the wine and making small talk with Lord Barton while Lord Rumford stood awkwardly at her side. Lord Spencer, still some distance away, ogled her until the orchestra struck up the first song appropriate for dancing.

"Might I have the pleasure of sharing a dance with you?" Lord Barton asked smartly.

"Of course, my lord," Lily replied, trying to mask

79

her surprise and delight since his offer took her away from Lord Rumford. She tossed the loathed man a brief smile as Lord Barton whisked her away. Lord Rumford was scowling at her. No doubt he would carry tales to her grandfather, but she would shrug. As a woman, how could she give such a personage as Lord Barton the cut? Grandfather had to understand that.

As they took their positions on the dance floor, she noticed Lord Spencer leering at her from across the room. Before she knew it, Lord Reginald had expertly maneuvered them away from Lord Spencer's predatory gaze, as if sensing her discomfort. Or perhaps he was just being possessive.

"Forgive me if I was forward," he said, "But it seemed that you did not want to dance with Lord Rumford."

"Thank you, Lord Barton, but I assure you, I did not need rescuing," Lily said with a wry smile.

"I did notice that about you," Reginald replied, attempting to lighten the mood with a mischievous grin. "You are one for adventure, and although Lord Rumford is harmless, I would suggest you avoid Lord Spencer."

Lord Barton was too observant by half, she thought. As much as Lord Spencer's leering annoyed her, Lily found Lord Barton's autocratic attitude just as off putting. "Lord Spencer and I are acquainted," she said, and Reginald raised an eyebrow. "He has some unsavory friends. Not the sort that would be advantageous for a young lady to cultivate," he said as if he expected to be obeyed.

She bristled but held her tongue. "Oh?" she teased,

laughing lightly. "Could you be jealous of the gentleman?"

"On the contrary, I am simply stating the obvious. He does not deserve the name of gentleman. Do not be lured onto the balcony with the man. He has not taken his eyes from you. I fear his intentions."

"Are you my Grandfather?" she asked, "that you should order me so?"

His hand tightened on hers for just a moment, and she realized that comparing him to her grandfather was the last thing he wanted her to do. Heat coursed through her, and her façade of politeness began to crumble as she remembered the blazing intimacy of their encounter in his carriage earlier in the week.

"For all that he is a peer, I repeat, he has some very unsavory friends," Lord Barton repeated haughtily. "It is best a lady avoid him."

Lily wondered if he would consider her one of those unsavory friends if he knew the truth about her. "I am aware," she said, and for a moment she felt as if his sharp eyes peered into her very soul. She was transported back to the moments in the carriage when he had held her captive by his gaze and his hand. An undefinable yearning curled up from her center, and she uncharacteristically lost her train of thought.

"Are you?" he said softly, his voice deep and penetrating.

Why did she feel as if she were melting in his arms? She was made of stronger stuff. "Am I what?" she asked, tossing back her curls in what she hoped was a coquettish movement. Her golden earrings bumped against her neck making her feel like nothing more than a setting for her grandfather's gold. The ruby felt cold between her breasts.

"Are you aware," he repeated as if she were somewhat slow.

She did not appreciate the patronizing attitude and could not keep the frown from her face.

"I think you are more naïve than you believe, Lady Lillian. I pray you, be cautious. There are unscrupulous characters in this world, even in the aristocracy."

"Especially in the aristocracy," she snapped and then realized she had spoken too freely. She bit her lip. This man was one with the aristocracy. He was no different than her own grandfather. He was even acquainted with her elder brother, Robert, who was but a younger copy of her grandfather. She should not have spoken.

"The commons are so anxious to find a new leader to get them out of poverty," he remarked, "they do not realize the sort of people most of the Bonapartists are. They speak a good talk, but sincerity is absent. What such men are seeking is not the betterment of the masses but power for themselves."

"And the aristocracy is different?" she asked, unable to control her bitterness.

"Often, the devil you know is better than the devil you don't know. Wouldn't you agree?"

Lily bristled at his words but clammed up, unwilling to betray her own sympathies for the Bonapartists in front of someone who clearly held conservative views. She had spoken too freely already, and her comment, combined with her outing to the Bonapartist meeting, left her exposed. She laughed lightly. "I haven't the vaguest," she said, smiling up at him with fake vapidness.

"I think you do," he said with all seriousness. "Do not play the coquette."

They danced for the next moments in silence. Surely, he did not think that she should be herself. How droll. She had always hidden among the aristocracy because she was nothing like the insipid creatures that the Ton adored. She wondered if he thought exactly that. She felt as if he wanted to strip the veneer from her, to see her. Really see her.

His hands were so warm upon her. They seemed to burn against the thin fabric that separated them, but perhaps that was just the heat of the summer evening. Despite the undeniable attraction between them, she knew that aligning herself with Lord Burton could be disastrous for her cause. She could not do it and remain true to her ideals. Grandfather would probably like him.

"Indeed, my lord," she replied coolly, refusing to take the bait. "It is fortunate, then, that we have such wise and noble aristocratic gentlemen to guide us through these perilous times."

Reginald raised an eyebrow at her sarcastic tone but said nothing, allowing them to finish the dance in tense silence. As the music came to an end, Lily couldn't help but wonder what lay beneath the polished exterior of the enigmatic Lord Reginald Burton. He bowed slightly as he returned her to her mother and the other matrons. He stood but a short distance away as if he was loathed to leave her side. His eyes seemed to burn a hole through the back of her neck, and shivers climbed up her spine.

The musicale buzzed with the news of Bonaparte's

recapture and the imminent return to normalcy. Ladies engaged in animated chatter, their faces aglow with the prospect of traveling to France once more, while gentlemen spoke of Waterloo and the Duke of Wellington's triumph.

"Can you imagine, Lady Lily," asked Mrs. Abigail Thompson, a notorious gossip, "how different our world shall be once we can travel freely to Paris again?" Her eyes sparkled with anticipation.

"Indeed, Mrs. Thompson," replied her dear friend Mrs. Sullivan. "I cannot wait to sip champagne again. It has been too long denied."

"I am sure that will be pleasant," said Lily, her voice carefully neutral as she weighed the political implications. She caught Lord Barton's gaze from a nearby group of cronies, his hazel eyes betraying a hint of concern as they rested upon her. She turned away. She did not need his scrutiny upon her, now of all times.

"Ah, Lord Barton," chimed in Lord Spencer who came between the two groups, joining them into one larger party. "I trust you are pleased with this news? A return to order and all that?" The groups shifted to include the gentlemen, much to Lily's dismay. She brought her fan up to partially hide her face in the off chance that Lord Spencer might actually see her. What would he think if he put two and two together and recognized her as Lily Hawkins from the Bonaparte meetings? Would that be a good thing or a disaster?

"Of course, Lord Spencer," replied Lord Barton smoothly, the corners of his mouth lifting into a polite smile. "But it is important to remember that change is never easy, and there are still many who might find fault with the way things stand. Still, tearing down the house seems counterproductive when a good scrubbing might achieve the same ends."

"What end is that?" asked Mrs. Thompson innocently.

"Getting rid of vermin," Lord Barton answered without looking at the lady.

Her mouth made a small O, and she hastened away.

"You mean outsiders," said Spencer.

The intensity behind Lord Barton's gaze spoke volumes. It was as if he were subtly warning her of the dangers of consorting with people like Spencer. Though she thought he might suspect her sympathies, due to her proximity to the meeting turned riot at their first meeting, she would not be so easily cowed.

"Perhaps, my lord," countered Lily, her voice as cold as ice, "the people I am most acquainted with are far worse than any outsider."

"Ah, but do the common people truly understand the nature of this Bonaparte movement?" Lord Spencer asked, looking directly at Lady Lillian now and obviously not connecting her at all with Miss Hawkins, the Bonapartist.

"*The movement*," Lord Barton said, "is dead now that their leader is indisposed."

"So, it was said when he was imprisoned on Elba," Lord Spencer said. "The man is notoriously slippery."

"Notorious," Lord Burton agreed sipping his wine.

"I wonder where they will send him this time," Lord Spencer added speculatively.

Lord Barton looked at him for a long moment before

sipping his wine. "Perhaps he will be hanged for treason," the gentleman said calmly.

Lily felt a shiver go up her spine. She noted that Lord Spencer's grip on his own wine glass tightened, and she was sure that Lord Barton noticed the reaction too.

"But treason against what country?" Lily put in, drawing Lord Barton's eyes from Lord Spencer as the man abruptly excused himself from their presence.

"Against all of Europe," Lord Barton replied.

"And yet many considered him a leader of the people," Lily said. "Some say he was beloved."

"The rabble may long for a new leader, my dear, yet remain ignorant of the true consequences of such an abrupt and foolhardy change."

The endearment annoyed her. Besides, who was he to say that the change would be foolhardy? "And you, Lord Barton, are an expert in such matters?" She arched a dark eyebrow, challenging him.

"As an aristocrat, I suppose I am. The responsibility lies with the aristocracy to maintain order."

"An order that keeps them in power," she retorted, her passion for freedom flaring. "The aristocracy will never willingly relinquish control. That is all they care about. Power and control."

"Speaking of the aristocracy," interrupted Lord Rumford, waddling onto the scene just in time to quell their heated debate. "I have just come from speaking with your grandfather, Lady Lillian. Might I have the pleasure of this dance?"

"Of course, my lord," she said through gritted teeth, allowing him to lead her away as she spared Lord Barton one last glance, torn between attraction and resistance. The air between them fairly crackled with unspoken tension, but was the tension due to their undeniable attraction or the heat of their political argument? She was uncertain.

As she and Lord Rumford danced, Lily caught a whiff of the stale odor that emanated from the man, inexpertly covered by his cologne. One dance, she vowed. She would not give him another, not for Grandfather or for all the jewels in the Crown.

Her thoughts went to Lord Barton. He was intriguing, but she would be no man's chattel. Even someone as captivating as Lord Barton would not turn her head. For now, she must focus on both resisting his charm and changing the oppressive society he represented. She had chosen her path, and it was with the Bonapartists.

After the dance ended, Lord Rumford led them to the table which held drinks. He was sweating profusely and obviously needed some hydration since a copious amount of liquid was dripping from the man's person. "May I offer you some refreshment, Lady Lillian?" he asked, his bulbous nose and ill-fitting suit only further highlighting the contrast between him and the athletic Lord Barton.

"Thank you, my lord," she replied, accepting the punch with a tight smile. She took a step back and wished for a wind to blow away the sour scent of the man, but not a ghost of a breeze came through the open windows. For a while, they talked of the weather and the Ton. As she sipped her punch and fanned herself, Lord Rumford droned on about the latest fashions. She wondered idly what he knew of fashion. It certainly was not evident in his dress or his hygiene.

He was utterly lacking the wit and charm that Lord Barton possessed, and yet, she knew that Lord Barton was dangerous to everything she held dear. Still, the more Lord Rumford spoke, the more she knew she could not marry this travesty of a man. Spittle collected in the corners of his mouth as he mopped his brow with his already sodden handkerchief. She shifted again, taking another slight step back, and threw a glance across the room to where Lord Barton stood speaking with the host and hostess and another couple. She thought the woman was his sister, Lady Patience Beresford. The woman was a tall prominent redhead. Another mark against the man, she thought. She had never found gingers attractive, she told herself, but Lord Barton was not strikingly so. His hair was darker than a true ginger, but the reddish high-lights were apparent in the flickering light of the many candles. It was like a dark fire burned within him. She was intrigued but also aware that such a fire was dangerous.

As Barton excused himself from the group, Lily could not help but follow him with her eyes. He cut a virile figure as he moved through the room, his broad shoulders commanding attention. She sighed inwardly, wondering how such an autocratic man could stir her emotions so. He would dominate her. He would demand her abject obedience. He would be a disaster. She could not even consider him.

Lily glanced up to see Reginald disappear into the garden, piquing her curiosity. She felt a pressing need for fresh air, and she was tiring of Rumford's monotonous prattle. Surely, she had endured enough to satisfy her grandfather.

"Excuse me, Lord Rumford," she murmured, setting down her empty punch glass on a footman's tray.

"Of course, Lady Lillian," he replied with a bow, granting her escape from his tedious company. She took a circuitous route to the doors that opened to the small town garden.

Once outside in the night air, Lily took several deep breaths, feeling the tension in her chest ease as she breathed the fresh scent of roses. It was still unseasonably hot, or perhaps not unseasonably hot for the city, she was not sure. She had never been in London this late in the summer. The family had always retired to the country, but the issues with Bonaparte kept Parliament seated late into the summer. Nonetheless, the out of doors was a respite from the close quarters of the ballroom. The fragrant floral scent which filled her nostrils as she wandered the moonlit path of the garden was a relief from the scent of cologne accentuated by the heat. She knew most ladies would not have ventured out alone, but she was not like most ladies. She needed this moment alone, this freedom. In the solitude, she could find herself.

Ahead, she caught sight of Lord Barton engaged in hushed conversation with another man – an aristocrat she did not recognize. They stood near a marble bench, partially obscured by shadows.

"…cannot be underestimated, Barton. If our suspicions are correct…" The other man's voice trailed off as he glanced around nervously. She realized she must have made some noise that alerted him, and she paused.

"Indeed, we must be vigilant," Lord Barton agreed, his tone serious.

Their words sparked intrigue within Lily. Was this political, or perhaps something more sinister? She crouched behind a rose bush, straining to hear what they were discussing. However, one of the many gold pieces on her skirt caught on a thorn, and the rustle of her gown as she tried to detach herself in the gloom betrayed her presence.

One man slipped away as she struggled with her gown, but Lord Barton stayed, watching and listening. "Who's there?" Lord Barton called out, his eyes sweeping across the garden.

Lily hesitated before emerging from her hiding spot, feeling unwise for eavesdropping in the first place. "It's only me, Lord Barton." She attempted to look the silly simpering fool, but she was not good at it.

"Ah, Lady Lillian," he said, his expression guarded. "What brings you to the garden… unescorted?" he added looking over her shoulder at the lack of chaperone.

"Merely seeking fresh air," she replied, feigning nonchalance. "The atmosphere inside was stifling."

"Indeed," he said, his eyes narrowing slightly. "And did the breeze carry any enlightening whispers your way?"

"Nothing I could make sense of," she admitted, her voice betraying a hint of defiance. "Though it seems you have interests beyond mere banter."

"Perhaps," he conceded, his gaze lingering on her face. "But some things are best left unheard."

"Is that a warning, Lord Barton?" she asked, raising an eyebrow.

"Merely a statement, Lady Lillian," he replied, his tone unreadable. "Not all secrets are meant to be uncovered, especially for lovely ladies." He smiled, but there was a seriousness in his words.

As their eyes locked, the air between them once again crackled with tension, and Lily was very much aware she was unchaperoned. For a moment, she wondered if he would reveal the truth about his clandestine conversation. But instead, he held her gaze, leaving her with questions unanswered and a heart yearning for adventure.

"Are you suggesting that I should not concern myself with such matters?" Lily challenged, her eyes flashing with indignation. "Because I am a woman?"

"Perhaps," Reginald replied, his gaze unwavering. "There are dangers in delving too deep into the affairs of others, especially when they involve... politics."

"Politics?" Lily echoed, her curiosity piqued despite herself. She wondered what he had intended to say before he changed the word to politics. "You seem to be quite well versed in the subject," she added.

"Only enough to be cautious," he admitted, his tone guarded. "And I would advise you to do the same, Lady Lillian. Shall I escort you back?"

She wanted to say she did not need an escort, but truth be told, she wanted to walk with him, and what harm would there be? They were in sight of the house. "I am not one to shy away from seeking the truth," she retorted, her chin lifting defiantly. "And I cannot help but wonder if your warning is genuinely for my safety or simply a means to keep me uninformed. After all, I am only a woman."

"Believe what you will," Reginald said, his expression inscrutable. "But know this—I do not think you are *only* anything, Lady Lillian. Nor do I think you see yourself as a victim; however, aligning oneself with suspected Bonapartists could lead to disastrous consequences."

She froze momentarily. No. He could not know. He was only guessing due to her presence at the meeting. True, it was not a far reach, but still... "That sounds like an accusation, Lord Barton," she said, taking a step closer to him, challenging him.

He paused, and the proximity between them only served to heighten the tension, their breaths mingling in the tepid night air. She could not help but notice the scent of clove on his breath—not tobacco nor alcohol, but cloves. In the midst of a party, he was fully in command of his senses. She found that interesting. Most of the Ton were already a bit tipsy.

"Consider it a friendly piece of advice," he replied, his voice low and steady. The timbre of it seemed to drill deep into her heart. "One must choose their allegiances carefully, lest they find themselves caught in a web of deceit and danger."

"Deceit," she mocked. "When I seek only the truth."

"Yes," he said. "The world is filled with liars and self-seeking men."

She laughed aloud. "Self-seeking men I believe," she said. "But I assure you, I am quite capable of looking after my own interests."

"Are you?"

"Your concern is touching," Lily scoffed, refusing to back down.

"Even when your own safety is at risk?" Reginald asked, his hazel eyes searching hers for any hint of doubt. He took a step closer. There was barely a breath between them.

"Especially then," she responded firmly, holding his gaze and refusing to step back. She would not give him the satisfaction. As the space between them shrank, Lily could feel the heat of his body and the intensity of his stare. It was both unnerving and exhilarating. She licked her lips, simultaneously wanting to best him and wanting him to take her in his arms and kiss her. She was acutely aware that they were alone in the garden with only a whisper of other couples some distance away. She could smell the roses and the tang of cloves strong in the summer heat. Would he taste of cloves? She wondered.

For a single instant, Lord Barton's eyes strayed to the sheer material of her skirt and the ruby between her breasts, and then he brought his gaze back to her face. "Very well," he conceded, his voice barely above a whisper. "But remember my words, Lady Lillian. Some paths are best left untraveled."

Was he still speaking of politics, she wondered, or something more personal? "Your warnings have been duly noted," she replied, her voice barely above a whisper, as their lips hovered mere inches apart. Her heart pounded in her chest, and perspiration trickled between her breasts as the heat threatened to overwhelm her. The temptation to close the distance between them was almost unbearable.

"Good," he murmured before abruptly stepping back, leaving Lily breathless and confused.

"Until we meet again, Lady Lillian," Lord Barton said with a slight bow. "Which I hope will be soon."

"Yes," she found herself saying. The word came out on a breathy sigh that was nothing like her logical self. It was almost as if another person entirely was speaking.

"Then I shall call upon you," he stated before disappearing into the shadows of the garden, leaving her standing alone amongst the roses, her thoughts tangled and her heart racing. She pressed a hand against her bosom, relieving the tickle of the perspiration but doing nothing to calm the rapid pounding of her heart. She had not just given him leave to pay court to her. She had not! Gads! How had that happened?

As the music from inside filtered through the night air, Lily wondered if her attraction to the enigmatic Lord Barton would truly lead her down a path fraught with danger and intrigue. But for now, she could only stand amidst the flowers, her mind filled with questions and her pulse thrumming with the memory of their heated exchange. Why hadn't he kissed her? Because she was not the beautiful sister, she berated herself. She was the intelligent one, and she had acted the ninny, betraying everything that she was.

Lily stood in the garden. The shadows enveloping her, shrouding her in darkness and secrecy, much like her clandestine dealings with the Bonapartists. Her breath came in short, sharp pants, and the scent of roses filled the air, displacing the scent of cloves. She felt a heat that she was not altogether sure was the summer night air. She struggled to come to her senses.

"Pull yourself together, Lily," she chastised herself,

taking a moment to press her hand against her heated cheek. "You must not let him affect you this way."

One thing was certain. Her grandfather would likely approve, but how could she encourage Lord Barton? It was clear he was everything that would enslave her. He had manipulated her into allowing him to call upon her, and he wasn't even her husband... or a suitor. No. She would not let this happen. She would not lose her freedom. She needed a weaker man, she deduced, but even as she thought it, she realized a weak man would not fulfill her, intellectually or physically.

Though she resolved to resist Lord Barton, his enigmatic charm and undeniable allure had shaken her to the core, and now, she had unwittingly invited him to call upon her. Drat!

She reentered the gayly lit ballroom, the music and laughter a stark contrast to the dark intrigue that lingered outside. It was time to find an alternative suitor, someone who could shield her from the oppressive weight of Lord Rumford's intentions—and Lord Barton's virility. Someone she could control.

"Ah, Lady Lillian!" a familiar voice called out. Lily turned to see Lord Spencer approaching her with glasses of punch in hand. His dark eyes gleamed with arrogance, and his cruel smile sent a shiver down her spine, but he did not seem to recognize that the gold clad debutante was the same woman who addressed the Bonapartists as Miss Hawkins. As a Bonapartist, she had avoided him. His sensibilities put her on edge. Yet, he was an influential member of the peerage, and more than that, he was a Bonapartist. They had the same political aspirations. Perhaps allying herself with him would be advantageous.

"Lord Spencer," she greeted, forcing a polite smile onto her face. "How kind of you to fetch me a drink. Refreshment is welcome in this heat."

"Anything for a lady as lovely as you," he replied smoothly, raising the glass to her lips. She took a small sip, her mind drifting back to her encounter with Lord Barton in the garden. Despite Lord Spencer's handsome features, he paled in comparison to the fiery intensity of Lord Barton's hazel eyes and the strength in his broad shoulders.

"Tell me, my lord, are you glad that the war is finally over?" Lily asked. Although she knew his stance on the matter, all anyone was talking about was the end of the war and Napoleon in chains. She hoped her bitterness was not apparent.

"Ah, the ever-changing landscape of politics," Lord Spencer mused, sipping his own drink and using the moment to ogle her over the rim of the glass. He did not seem to wonder at her comment. Indeed, she didn't think he saw her at all, except for the tantalizing suggestion of limbs beneath her skirts. "I believe we must adapt to the changes," he said. "Those in the forefront will be best suited to take advantage, but such a lovely lady cannot be interested in such a dull topic as politics."

"Of course not," she said laughing. "But the war is all anyone seems to be speaking of this evening. It is exceedingly dull," she lied.

"I hear that our hosts have a lovely garden," he said. "Perhaps a stroll out of doors would be a respite from the heat."

Lily felt a shiver go through her. How was it that she walked alone in the garden with Lord Barton without a care, but everything in her rebelled against walking with this man? With a carefully schooled expression she made her excuses. "I see my sister," she said. "I think she is looking for me."

He gave her a slight bow. "Lady Lillian."

As Lillian crossed the room to her sister, Grace, she couldn't help but steal glances across the room, searching for Lord Burton amidst the sea of elegantly dressed guests. Her attraction to him was undeniable, and yet she could not allow herself to become a pawn in his game—or anyone else's, for that matter.

There was still the annoying factor that her grandfather intended to marry her off and have the matter settled before they left London. With Parliament drawing to a close now that Bonaparte was caught, she had precious little time to deal with her suitors. Too soon they would be leaving London, and her grandfather would press Rumford's suit.

THE NIGHT AIR felt heavy as Lily returned to her family's townhouse, the weight of her conflicting emotions a burden upon her as much as the weight of her garments. As she stepped across the threshold with her sister, grandfather, father, and brother and into the candlelit drawing-room, she found her youngest sister, Betty, awaiting her arrival with eager anticipation. The gentlemen retired to the library, no doubt to smoke, since the habit was limited to the outdoors at the Wentwell estate.

"How was the musicale, Grace? Tell me everything,

Lily!" Betty exclaimed, her eyes wide with curiosity as she looked from one sister to the other. "Did you manage to avoid Mr. Rumford?"

Lily sighed, sinking gracefully onto the chaise lounge. "Mr. Rumford was, as expected, an unwelcome presence," she began, her voice tinged with annoyance. "But it was Lord Barton who truly caught my attention."

"Lord Barton?" Grace questioned, her brows furrowing in confusion. "I thought you disapproved of his aristocratic background and conservative views?"

"Indeed, I do," Lily admitted, her dark eyes betraying her inner turmoil. "Yet there is something about him that I cannot help but be drawn to despite our differences." She shoved away thoughts of the moment in the garden as she stood distractedly. She became aware of the wilted state of her clothing and the press of her stays. "Come. I want to get out of these clothes."

"Yes," Grace agreed. "My slippers have been pinching me all night." The ladies proceeded together towards the staircase. "Perhaps Lord Barton could serve as a suitable alternative to Mr. Rumford," Grace suggested innocently, only to be met by a sharp retort from Lily.

"Hardly," she scoffed, her voice laced with disdain as they mounted the stairs. "Marrying Lord Barton would be exchanging my grandfather's rule for his own. He is entirely too autocratic."

"Surely, Lily, you must admit he has some good qualities," Betty ventured timidly. "He is rich, after all."

"And heir to an earldom," Grace added as their maids came to divest them of their finery. "I did not see you dance with him."

"I did," Lily admitted the first dance. She did not tell them about the walk in the garden. "He has asked to call upon me."

"Oh, wonderful," said Grace. "He will give Lord Rumford some competition even in Grandfather's eyes."

"Yes," Lily said despondently.

"Do not look so glum. Surely, he is better than Lord Rumford," Betty urged. "He's young and handsome."

"Handsome, perhaps," Lily conceded reluctantly, "although I do not favor the spattering of freckles on his skin."

"You noticed his freckles?" Grace said surprised. "You must have obtained a close look at that!"

Lily ignored the implications. "Beauty alone does not make a man worthy of my affection." She paced the room, her steps echoing her swirling thoughts. "He may have charm and wit, yet beneath his polished exterior lies a firm belief in maintaining the status quo. He sees the common people as little more than pawns in a grand chess game, and I cannot abide such a view."

"Is there truly no hope for him to change, Lily?" Grace asked, her voice gentle. "People can grow and evolve, after all."

Lily laughed. "Oh, I do not think so." Her brow creased with uncertainty as she stood in her chemise, at last feeling some respite from the heat. "Consider it. Would Grandfather change? Would Robert?"

"Probably not," Grace agreed. "Do bring a basin of water to refresh us," Grace directed her maid.

"Exactly. And I certainly am not willing to stake my happiness on such a gamble," Lily said.

As the sisters continued their discussion late into the

night, the flickering candlelight casting shadows upon the walls, Lily could not help but feel torn between her desire for love and adventure and her commitment to her principles. She knew that a union with Lord Barton would be fraught with challenges and compromises, yet the moment in the garden engaged her fantasies and filled her with longing.

"Stay strong, Lily," she whispered into the darkness as she finally sought refuge in sleep. "For only then can you find the happiness and freedom you seek. Happiness is not in marriage with some gentleman, but in being true to yourself. Remember your ideals."

# PART II

# GENTLEMEN'S PLANS

*L*ord Reginald Barton stepped from the warm night into the dark confines of the gentleman's club, taking in the sights and sounds of his surroundings. Rich mahogany walls lined the room. The heat was oppressive, thick with cigar smoke and conversation, as members gathered around tables to discuss politics and other matters of import.

A long bar ran along one wall, where several men were already seated enjoying drinks. In one corner was a gaming table surrounded by young bucks eager to try their luck at cards or dice. At the far end was an ornate billiards table lit by the flickering candlelight of crystal chandeliers and attended by several finely dressed lords who had just entered the club in top hats and coats in spite of the warm weather. They spoke loudly, making Reginald think they were already in their cups although the night was young.

Reginald spotted Captain Samuel Beresford and Captain Jack Hartfield, newly ashore. They were speaking in low voices at a nearby table, their expressions grave. Cards were laid on the table, but Reginald doubted they were gaming. They were discussing the threat posed by Bonaparte's forces who might even now be building a plot to free the man from St. Helens. Lord Barton walked over to join them, feeling the weight of his responsibility press down on him more heavily with each step he took.

As he approached, their conversation stopped, and both men greeted him. "Barton," Captain Jack said. Jack gestured to the chair beside him while Samuel gathered the stray cards and reshuffled the deck, dealing Reginald into the game.

Reginald gave a curt nod and eyed them coolly before taking a seat. "Gentlemen, it's good to see you both again, hale and hearty. Are you glad the war is finally over?"

"Indeed," said Jack, "But I give it a month before someone gets a fart crossed, and we will be back at it."

Samuel chuckled. "It is good to be back on English soil, no matter how short the time."

"And I thought the sea was your first love," Reginald said, laughing, and then with more seriousness, he added. "Patience has spoken of how much Amelia misses you when you are at sea, Samuel," Reginald said.

"And I appreciate you opening your home to her," Samuel said taking a sip of brandy. "You and your sister. I hate for her to be alone."

"Especially now," Reginald added thinking of his sister's obsession with babies. He considered it likely Amelia was with child again.

Samuel paused, the glass halfway between the table

and his mouth. "Women have such loose lips," he said with a wry smile.

"Well, congratulations then," Reginald said.

"Oh, it is much too early for congratulations," Samuel said. "Amelia has only just informed me that she missed her courses this month, but come, on to other topics."

"Straight to business," said Jack.

"Well, I do have a wife to get home to," Samuel said taking a large sip from his glass.

"As do I," Jack added.

"But Lavinia is much more agreeable when you stumble in late than Amelia is," Samuel added. "So, now what news, Regge? Surely, all that is left is the mopping up now."

"I wish that were so," Reginald said.

The captains exchanged a look, the gravity of the situation settling over them like a heavy cloak. "What is it?" asked Jack.

"I know that Bonaparte has been seeking allies in England," Samuel said, his voice low.

"And, we have reason to believe he has met with sympathizers here before his capture and that Englishmen seek to free him." Reginald said. "We need to discover if the current intelligence is true."

"Englishmen?" Captain Jack's brow furrowed in concern. "Surely not. Why would men do that? It is treason."

Reginald shook his head in wonderment. "Why men would risk the drop for this man is beyond me. What has he given to the populous, even when he rose to power?

Nothing but heartache and war. I can hardly believe it is so."

"Even now," Samuel said, weighing his words carefully, "There are men who would see him restored to power. Those are dangerous men. They have nothing to lose at this point. They have moved past both sense and honor."

"We must certainly be vigilant," Jack said.

"And he was freed once. If he escapes again, the English Navy will be a laughingstock," Samuel added.

The captains nodded in agreement, and the conversation turned to specific matters of import. As Reginald sipped his brandy, his mind drifted back to Lily and their earlier conversation at Wentwell's ball. He wondered if she had any inkling of the danger they faced.

With a deep sigh, Reginald set his glass down and looked at his friends. He could not allow a woman to distract him. He had a duty to his country, and he would not rest until he had secured its safety. Whatever lay ahead, he was ready to face it head-on, with honor and valor as his guide.

"I thank you for your advice and your courage," Reginald said. "But I must put something else before you. There is an additional problem compounding the Bonaparte dilemma. Lady Lillian Hawthorne."

"How is she involved?" Captain Jack asked his brow furrowing with the question. "She is a lady; she should have no part in such rough dealings."

"Indeed, she shouldn't," Reginald said with a wry laugh, "But I took her home from a riot a week past, and at first, I thought it was just bad luck, but I have since revised my opinion."

The men stared at him.

"A riot?" Jack looked nonplussed.

"You believe she is a traitor?" Samuel said appalled at the thought. "A woman? A lady at that?"

Reginald ran a hand over his face. "I don't know what I believe," he said. "She was there at the Bonaparte meeting. I'm sure of it now. And at Lord Wentwell's musicale, she spoke with Lord Spencer. She knew him. They were... rather cozy."

"Spencer certainly has Bonapartist sympathies," Jack said, "but nothing has been proven. He is also a peer."

"And an arse and blackguard," Samuel interrupted before sitting his glass on the table with a clunk.

"She could just be unaware," Jack said.

"I know," Reginald said miserably. "I know. I told her that she should keep her distance, that I would keep her safe from such men, but I fear I may be failing her. I cannot tell her the particulars. More than that, she doesn't want my help, which may be because she is fiercely independent or because she is more involved with the Bonapartists than I care to know. If she were a man, I would have options to get to the truth, as it is—" He shrugged.

The captains exchanged sympathetic looks.

"How did you come to this belief?" Questioned Jack.

"Firstly, there was no reason for her to be in the vicinity of the riot, especially not alone. The longer I thought on it, the more I was convinced."

"Could she have been meeting someone?" Samuel asked.

"That was indeed my first thought, but I've watched her this past week, and she does not seem to be a woman of loose morals. On the contrary, she seems to hold very specific values, somewhat radical values. Let's just say I have reason to believe she is somehow involved with the Bonapartists. I cannot be sure, but I have a sense about such things, and I'm loathe to discount it."

"You shouldn't," Jack said. "That sense has kept you alive more than once in this business."

Reginald nodded. "I know. It is worrisome, but I have no real proof, except that a tongue such as hers on a gentleman would have him questioned, if not in irons. She talks most passionately, and her speech does not revere the aristocracy or the Crown."

"Have you met her grandfather?" Samuel dryly voiced the rhetorical question.

Reginald nodded. Of course, he had. The Earl of Thornwood was also a peer, and the man was a pain in the arse, but he was not a blackguard, and he certainly was not treasonous. On the contrary, the man was the most autocratic member of Lords that Reginald knew. He was staunchly against the catholic issue, and according to his own father had nearly come to blows over Pitt's Reform Bill of 1785. Each time the radical working-class campaign appeared in Parliament; Thornwood was the first to vote it down. He was of the opinion that only those who had a stake in the country should have a vote in it, and that meant the aristocracy alone. In his opinion, the entirety of the Commons was an abomination. Reginald thought the man would have been happy to have England regress to serfdom. And he still called Scotland and Ireland *those barbaric lands*, but Reginald couldn't debate that. The earl was not alone in that sentiment. There were a number who believed the same, though they may not be so vocal about their beliefs.

Even when the Reign of Terror prevailed in France, Thornwood's answer was to mow down the insurrection-ists with canon fire rather than give them bread. Of course, by that time, offering bread was too little too late. Probably half of the French aristocracy agreed with Thornwood's attitude, and the other half were dead.

But Reginald was not a violent man. He thought the whole issue could have been avoided if only the people with differing views sat down and had a civil discussion. The lack of communication and intolerance to others' opinions was exactly that kind of attitude that brought countries to the brink of war and beyond. Such things were always on a tinderbox, and the last thing he wanted to see was a woman hurt by the explosion, especially not Lady Lillian Hawthorne.

He had to admit, at least to himself, he had a tender-ness for her. If he voiced such sensibilities, she would probably laugh in his face, but it was the truth, and truth was something Lord Barton valued immensely, even as his work forced him to deal in lies. He prided himself in knowing the difference. "I would do everything in my power to protect Lady Lily, but I cannot jeopardize the mission," Reginald said at last.

The captains exchanged a look, understanding the implications of Reginald's words.

"It could be that she is simply naive," Samuel said, his tone gentle.

"Or she could be working for them," Jack chimed in, his voice hard. "Just because she is a woman, don't discount her deviousness. I love my own Lavinia, but she can be… quite resourceful when she doesn't get her way."

Samuel nodded in solidarity. "Amanda as well. What did Lady Lillian say to Spencer?" he asked.

"I don't know," Reginald said. "I was not close enough to hear, but they seemed to know one another well, at least from what I could see of Spencer's recollection."

"That man is a scourge upon the earth," spat Samuel. "You know, he was involved in the plot to kill Amelia's father. Nothing proven, but I am sure of his guilt. I'd like to gut him myself for the pain he has caused my wife."

Reginald nodded. "Well, I have to admit that would solve one problem, but I hardly think that murdering a member of the peerage would go well for you, Samuel."

The gentlemen sipped their drinks thoughtfully. Then, Reginald added, "I couldn't stand idly by while she spoke with Spencer, but she seemed to think my interference was because I was being jealous." Reginald shook his head, unwilling to believe that Lily would betray her country.

"No, I do not think she is working for them," he said as he continued to mull the matter over in his mind. "I can't believe that. At least not knowingly. But I cannot ignore the fact that she is involved in some way. I must speak with her and find out what she knows, but to do so could also compromise the mission. I wanted to let you know where things stood before I proceed."

"Be careful," Samuel cautioned. "You do not want to put her in danger, or worse, if she is in league with the Bonapartists—" He let the thought hang.

"I know. They would kill her as soon as look at her,

and she could put the whole mission in danger," Reginald said.

"She could put *you* in danger," Samuel added. "One mistake and you could easily end up dead. You would not be the first betrayed by a woman."

"I know. I know. You are telling me nothing I've not already told myself a hundred times over," Reginald said with a sigh. "I cannot let my feelings for her cloud my judgment. The safety of England must come first, but..."

"You love her," Samuel said softly.

Reluctantly, Reginald nodded and ran a hand through his dark auburn hair. "At the very least, I don't want to see her hurt."

"Or dead," Jack added. "But Reginald, you have to consider the risk to your own life. If you infiltrate and she is on the inside, and she outs you, you are dead. There is no way forward. No way we can help you. Her word will be your death."

"I don't think she would want me dead either," Reginald said softly. "At least, I hope she wouldn't."

"If she is truly loyal to the Bonaparte cause," Samuel warned, "you don't know what she would risk. They are crazy."

"And, as I said, you would not be the first man betrayed by a skirt," Jack said. "Tread cautiously, my friend."

Reginald shook his head violently. He had hoped his friends would calm his fears, but instead, he found himself more embroiled in doubt. "I know she is a risk, but I cannot just leave her there with these traitors and murderers. She cannot know what she is doing. Not really."

"It has been my experience," Samuel said thoughtfully, "that women know what they are doing as clearly as men."

"No!" Reginald shouted, losing patience with the whole situation. "She bloody well does not." He stood, drawing the attention of the club.

"Regge," Samuel said softly. He reached a hand out to his friend, and Reginald seated himself with an apologetic glance towards the other patrons. He spoke again with vehemence as the club returned to normal. His voice was low but emphatic. "She cannot. Because I am not ready to condemn her as a traitor to England, and if she knows what she is doing, she most surely is guilty of treason."

The three men fell silent, lost in their own thoughts.

"I will keep an eye on her," Samuel said firmly. "And if she proves to be a threat to our cause, we will deal with her accordingly." He threw a glance towards Jack for confirmation.

"Samuel," Reginald began, but Jack interrupted him.

"You are too close to this Reginald. Let us handle it. We will try not to hurt her. For your sake, and for the sake of the fact that she is a lady, I would hope that we need not interfere. But, if need be, we shall recommend that she come quietly. But if not, remember that I am captain of my own ship, Regge, as is Samuel. She will speak to no one once offshore. And she will be safe."

Reginald nodded, feeling a sense of relief wash over him. The burden of keeping Lily safe was a difficult task, especially if she was going into harm's way on her own volition, but with his trusted friends by his side, he felt more confident that he could face whatever lay ahead.

"Reginald, your concern for Lady Lily is admirable, but you must remember our mission. That is paramount. Bonaparte cannot be allowed to escape again," whispered Captain Samuel, glancing around to ensure they were not overheard even though he thought most in the club were loyal Englishmen. "We cannot let him get the slip on us a second time. We must not."

"And we are here to uncover the Bonapartists' plans," Captain Jack said, "not to play nursemaid to headstrong young ladies."

"Lady Lily is far too intelligent and involved for her own good. She could easily become entangled in something from which she cannot escape. She doesn't realize the seriousness of the situation," Reginald said. He knew he was belaboring the point, and perhaps he was just wishing it so. Was he blind to the truth?

Captain Jack chimed in, "Perhaps, if you reveal your true purpose to her grandfather—"

"No," Samuel interrupted. "The Earl of Thornwood is a bastard. If you do that, any affection she might have for you will be extinguished."

"This is an untenable situation," Reginald said, his voice tinged with desperation.

"Keep her close, but maintain your cover," Captain Samuel advised. "Ensure her safety, but do not let her suspect your true intentions. If you need us to remove her from the situation, we are here."

Reginald nodded grimly, the weight of his responsibility heavy on his broad shoulders.

"We have other news," Captain Jack confided. "We

have received word that a shipment is being smuggled into the country to arm the Bonapartists. It's due to arrive at the coast in two days' time. We believe it includes plans of some sort. I know this sounds crazy, but my contact tells me that it is a plan for a ship that sails under the sea."

"You are right. That sounds ridiculous. A fiction. Such a thing cannot exist. Nonetheless, we must intercept the plans and arrest those involved," Reginald replied, his mind racing with thoughts of the consequences should they fail.

"Perhaps we should let it play out," Samuel said. "Try to find the kingpins of the operation. This secret ship under the sea might be a trap. You are right. It doesn't sound real."

"Agreed," said Reginald.

"Have you heard of a man named Montgomery?" Jack asked. "I've heard his name bandied about recently."

Reginald shook his head. "French or Scottish?" he asked.

Jack shook his head. "From the Colonies, from what I could gather."

"I have contacts in Portsmouth who may be able to help us gather more information to see who this Mr. Montgomery is and his involvement," Samuel added.

"And bring him to justice before he causes further unrest," said Reginald. "Especially if he is the kingpin."

"But even if we arrest him, that's no guarantee that this plot will go away," Samuel said. "Do we have his Christian name?"

Jack shook his head. "It may be Roger, perhaps Robert. I'm unsure."

"Very well. I shall use my connections in Parliament to monitor any unusual activity," Reginald said. "If we can expose this Montgomery and dismantle his network, perhaps we can put an end to the threat," Reginald declared, determination clear in his voice. "After all, once Bonaparte is on the island and the Royal Navy is dispatched, I don't see how anyone would be able to infiltrate St. Helens."

"They did Elba," Jack reminded him.

Reginald sighed heavily and agreed.

"Fool me once," Samuel said with eyes narrowed, and the other men nodded.

After they fine-tuned their plans, Reginald's mind went back to the lovely Lady Lillian. He couldn't help but think of Lily and the danger she might face if she continued her clandestine meetings. He knew he couldn't reveal the truth to her grandfather, but how could he protect her without betraying his duty? He couldn't trust her with his own involvement, though perhaps he would have to do so to keep her safe... but at what cost to his own safety? As much as he juggled the possibilities in his own mind, he could come up with no sure answer to the dilemma.

# WALTZING WITH THE ENEMY

*A*t the ball hosted by Lord and Lady Blackburn, Lily began to be quite certain that Lord Barton was dogging her every step. He had called at her home. He appeared at every gathering, every ball, every musicale, and every dinner party she frequented, and now, he was ever at the edge of her sight. It could not be a coincidence. Did this mean that he had an entendre for her, or did it just mean that he was concerned about her Bonapartist sensibilities? Did he want to use her to gain access to them? That was a horrid thought. She had been too open with him. She had forgotten how dangerous that information might be in the hands of a conservative like Lord Barton. It was a mistake she would not repeat. She hoped it was not already too late.

Lily watched as Reginald's hazel eyes narrowed at Lord Spencer and Mr. Nesbit, his lips pressed into a thin line. She knew the two men were sympathizers with Napoleon, but Lord Barton could not know that. She could not fathom why Reginald seemed so intent on keeping her from speaking to them. His tall, athletic frame blocked her path, and Lily stared up at him in frustration.

"Lord Barton," she said, dark brown eyes flashing indignantly.

"Lady Lillian." He gave a small bow with a condescending smile, and she decided to attack the issue with her usual forthrightness.

"You need not protect me from every man who crosses my path, Lord Barton."

"Forgive me, Lady Lillian, but I cannot stand idly by while questionable individuals attempt to ingratiate themselves with you," he replied, his voice low and tense.

"Of whom do you speak?" she said, feigning innocence. She opened her eyes wide as if in surprise at the possibility of such scoundrels attending an event of such high standing.

His eyes narrowed, and he took a deep breath through his nose but said nothing.

She wondered what secret he was keeping from her, but then, men always kept women in the dark. Perhaps it was because her mind listed towards politics, but she wondered if his interest was entirely her association with the Bonapartists. A random thought crossed her mind, and for a moment, she dismissed it. Could it be jealousy that motivated him? The thought sent a rush of desire through her veins. She decided to test the waters. "Jealousy does not become you, Lord Reginald," she chided, snapping her fan shut and attempting to step around him.

"Jealousy?" Reginald's eyes widened in surprise before he composed himself. "It is not jealousy, Lady, but concern for your well-being that drives me."

So, it was her Bonapartist leanings and not simple romance that put her in his crosshairs. Lord save me from interfering aristocrats, Lily thought. Don't I have enough of that nonsense with my grandfather? She began to turn away from him, but he most rudely caught her arm. "Dance with me," he said.

"I beg your pardon," she answered. She would not kowtow to his domineering attitude. Now, she wouldn't dance with him even if he asked politely—as a gentleman should—but he had taken two steps towards the dance floor with her in tow. She could not pull from his grasp without making a scene. "It is customary to ask for a dance," she sneered.

Lord Barton did not answer. He only smiled at her as they joined Lavinia and Captain Jack Hartfield in the square. Belatedly, she made note that Lord Spencer had been coming her way. Lily could not continue to be churlish, although she certainly felt that way. She had dealt with her grandfather's autocratic attitude for days on end and certainly didn't want to keep company with another so like him.

The dance brought them together for a moment, and Lord Barton held her masterfully. She could not fault the perfection of his steps or the unwelcome comfort she found in his arms. For an instant, she forgot everything but his hand on hers. Then, the moment was lost as the dance took them apart. She was partnered by Lavinia's husband, Captain Jack. "Lavinia tells me that there are quite the number of officers of the Royal Navy in town," she said hoping to find an alternative suitor to Lord Rumford and perhaps set some obstacles for Lord Barton.

"There are," Captain Jack agreed, but he did not follow with an offer to introduce her to any of the gentlemen. She thought that was ungallant of him, but then the dance took them apart and she was partnered with Lord Barton once again. His hand was so warm on hers, warm and possessive. His eyes seemed to look into her soul.

"I am warning you," he said. "Lord Spencer and Mr. Nesbit are scoundrels. Stay away from them."

She laughed lightly. "Are you my keeper?" she asked.

"Someone has to be," he muttered.

Their conversation continued to be snippets of orders and countermeasures, which made Lily angrier by the moment, and when the dance was done, she barely waited for Lord Barton to thank her for the set before she stalked away from him. He was entirely the cad, and she would have nothing to do with him. No matter that he made her heart sing.

---

The evening wore on, and Reginald found himself drawn back to Lady Lillian's side. He attempted to engage her in conversation, subtly probing her knowledge of the ongoing political turmoil. He hoped to glean some insight into how involved she might be without arousing her suspicion, but she was sharp.

"Lord Reginald, you seem quite preoccupied with politics tonight," Lily noted, her dark eyes narrowing slightly. "Is there something you want to tell me?"

For a moment, he was tempted, but it was just too much. He knew she was involved with the Bonapartists. He knew it with every ounce of intuition that had ever kept him safe in his work. How could he trust her with his secrets... with his life... with the future of England?

He could not. At least, not yet. "Forgive me, Lady Lillian," Reginald replied, struggling to maintain his composure. He had never cared so much what a contact thought of him. Because, he reminded himself, she was more than a contact. He was in unclear waters. "After your outing of the previous evening, I merely wish to ensure your safety and well-being," he said with all of his gentlemanly charm.

"Your concern is touching," Lily retorted, her pride apparently wounded by his patronizing tone. "I am perfectly capable of taking care of myself, and I have no interest in becoming embroiled in your political machinations. In case you haven't noticed, we do not really agree politically or about the governance of the poor."

"Nevertheless," Reginald persisted, "I would advise you to exercise caution around certain individuals."

"So you have said," she replied. "You do not need to repeat yourself."

"I do if you continue to ignore me," he snapped and then sighed. "I do apologize," he said in a more moderate tone. It would not do to antagonize her, but the woman was utterly exasperating. He tried to explain, to appeal to her obvious intelligence. "There are many who would seek to exploit your cleverness and convictions for their own ends."

She paused for just a moment, her eyebrow arched in surprise. "Never has a gentleman commented upon my acumen except to point it out as a short-coming," she said. "Nonetheless, I am not sure your words are complementary. It is clear that you think yourself cleverer than I, and therefore, of a mind to steer me from my error."

"That is the hope," he admitted.

"Your warning is duly noted, Lord Reginald." Lily's tone was frosty, her displeasure evident.

This was not going in any way shape or form in the direction he wanted it to go. Reginald knew he had to tread carefully, lest he push her further away. He felt like he could only repeat his previous warnings, and she kept deflecting them. He longed to keep her safe from the coming storm, but without revealing his true purpose, he feared he might lose her trust entirely, either because she didn't trust him or because she was hurt or dead or branded a traitor.

None of the options before him seemed a good choice, and he did not know how to alleviate the animosity between them, except to exploit the obvious sexual tension between them. He could not be sure, but he thought she was fighting the same attraction that he felt. With that in mind, he went to the refreshment table to garner two glasses of lemon water. He waited until Lady Lillian had finished dancing with Lord Spencer with plans to waylay her, but no sooner had the dance ended than Lord Rumford caught the lady's attention. Bloody bad luck, he thought as he drank both of the glasses of liquid himself.

~

LILY GRACEFULLY SPUN around the room, her silken skirts rustling as she moved even though the material was weighed down with gold. All around her, the guests of the dinner party laughed and chatted, their polite conversation punctuated by the lively music of the orchestra. She felt Lord Spencer's fingers press into her skin as he clasped her hand too tightly during a turn, his eyes searching hers with an almost predatory hunger, but she could think of nothing but Lord Barton.

At last, the dance ended, and Lily quickly stepped away from her partner. Suddenly, she felt a heavy hand on her shoulder and saw Lord Rumford standing beside her, beckoning for her to follow him out onto the terrace. Panic rose in Lily's chest—what did he want with her? Surely, he did not think to propose? Dread must have filled her eyes, followed almost immediately by a faint glimmer of hope as she spotted Lord Barton across the room. As much as she resented his high-handed attitude, he was welcome in the moment. She smiled at him brilliantly, and he excused himself from their hosts and strode towards them, cutting off Lord Rumford mid-sentence.

"Ah, there you are, Lady Lillian," he said smoothly, extending his arm for her to take. "This is our dance, I believe."

Though she knew full well it was not, she gratefully accepted his intervention. She did not want to speak with Lord Rumford, and although Lord Spencer was also approaching, Lord Barton gave her a ready excuse to avoid both.

Lord Rumford looked muddled but gave up her company.

Lord Spencer turned to another lady.

Lady Lillian allowed Lord Barton to lead her back into the throng of dancers before she realized it was a waltz. Oh, this was much too intimate a dance to share with him! He held her hand loosely, but his opposite hand, which nearly spanned her waist, was hot as a branding iron upon her. As they began to dance, Reginald leaned in close, and she caught a whiff of clove. His voice was barely audible above the music. "I apologize if I overstepped my boundaries earlier, Lady Lillian. It was not my intention to bring you any distress."

"Apology accepted," she replied softly, the heat of his body and the scent of his cologne making her head spin. She tried to focus on anything other than the strong arm encircling her waist and the giddy sensation each touch brought. She reminded herself that she did not like this man.

"I did not mean to upset you," he said, "but Lord Spencer associates with some of the rougher men about town. Most notable is a certain Mr. Montgomery," he said.

"How do you know of Mr. Montgomery?" she ventured, hoping to distract herself from the desire that threatened to overwhelm her.

Reginald hesitated, his hazel eyes searching hers and his hand tightening momentarily on hers and then relaxing as he brought her into a spin. She could see the struggle within him, the knowledge that he held some secret but was unwilling to share it with her. Frustrated, she sighed, feeling as though her own curiosity was thwarted once again simply because she was a woman.

"Montgomery is known to some of my naval

friends," Lord Barton said at last, "but he is not the sort of man with whom a lady should associate. He has an association with Lord Spencer... business dealings perhaps. Montgomery has a rougher sensibility than a gentleman might have, but coming from the Colonies, I suppose that is to be expected. Boston, I think."

"Virginia," Lady Lillian said automatically, and Lord Barton seemed to concentrate wholly on the dance after that. Lily could not complain. The gentleman was an excellent dancer, and for a few moments, she was transported. As long as the man didn't open his mouth to castigate her, she was perfectly happy in his arms.

As the waltz came to an end, Lord Rumford reappeared by Lily's side, his pudgy fingers reaching for her hand. Reginald reluctantly released her, his gaze lingering on her face even as she was led away. She still felt the hot imprint of his hand upon her, and her heart still raced with excitement. The scent of cloves and cologne was in sharp contrast to Lord Rumford's ripe odor.

"Until we meet again, Lady Lillian," Lord Barton murmured, and she knew that beneath the layers of secrets and deception, there lay a connection between them—one that neither could deny.


REGINALD STOOD FROZEN, the blood draining from his face as Lily's mention of Montgomery hung in the air between them. He watched her being led away by Lord Rumford, and a cold dread settled in his chest. He knew now that Lily was in far deeper than he had ever suspected, and it terrified him.

Reginald lurked in the shadows, consumed by a potent mix of rage and protectiveness. He was well aware of the dangers posed by the Bonapartists and the precariousness of her situation. He knew others loyal to the Crown were tracking the Bonapartists. They would be stopped, and she would be in the middle of it. He tried to protect her, but she refused to listen to any warnings he gave her. How could he keep her safe when she refused to acknowledge that there was even a threat? How could he tell her how great the threat was when he had to keep his mission secret? On top of all of that was the fact that the majority of the Bonapartists were ruffians who had no business being in contact with a lady.

Lost in thought, it took him some time to realize that the music had ended and yet another partner had taken possession of Lady Lily's hand. His chest burned as he witnessed her laughing carefree in the arms of another man, seemingly unaware of the perils lurking.

His vow echoed in his head—no matter what obstacles lay ahead, he would shield her from being swept away into this treacherous world into which she had so naively stepped. He would not fail in protecting her. She may hate him, he decided, but she would be alive.

"Reginald, you look like you've seen a ghost," Captain Jack remarked, clapping a hand on his shoulder. "What's wrong?"

"Nothing," Reginald muttered, shaking off his concerns with a forced smile. "I've had enough dancing for one evening. Care for a game of cards?"

Captain Samuel nodded in agreement, and the three men made their way to a quieter corner of the ballroom where several card tables had been set up for those seeking respite from the festivities. Reginald's mind, however, was anything but at ease. Images of Lily in danger swirled through his thoughts, making it impossible for him to focus on the game at hand. Unsurprisingly, he lost hand after hand, much to the amusement of his fellow players.

"Seems your luck has run out tonight, old chap," Captain Jack teased, raking in another pile of chips.

"Indeed," Reginald agreed absently, his gaze flicking back towards Lady Lillian, who was dancing with carefree abandon. His heart ached to protect her, to keep her safe from the treacherous world she had unknowingly entered. He needed to find a way to get her out of this mess without betraying her trust or revealing his own secrets. But how?

"Lady Lillian seems quite taken with you," Samuel observed, following his friend's gaze. "Perhaps you might consider discussing your shared interests with her. Make a plan of how much to reveal. She may understand more than you think she will, and your honesty may bring you closer together. Perhaps then you can convince her to have a care."

Reginald frowned, remembering the waltz they had just shared and the questions she had asked. She was right. They both wanted a better world, though their methods of achieving it were vastly different. He wondered if there was a way to bridge that gap, to make her understand the dangers she faced without compromising his mission.

"Perhaps you're right," he conceded, rising from the card table and making his way back towards Lady

Lillian. As he re-entered the ballroom, he saw her in conversation once again with Lord Spencer, her dark eyes flashing with passion as she argued her case for a more equitable society. Lord Barton started to bear down upon them, but at that moment, the orchestra struck up another waltz and Lady Lily and Lord Spencer were quickly swept away in each other's arms. The couples began to twirl around the floor, Reginald watched with dismay, his fists balled at his sides as he felt a surge of such violent emotion. He could not name it. Certainly anger, and a potent rush of fear mixed with dismay, and possibly jealousy.

Lord Spencer was no gentleman although he was a peer. Even if he was not a Bonapartist, Lord Barton had every reason to fear for Lady Lillian's safety. But he believed that Lord Spencer was a supporter of Napoleon, and seeing Lady Lily within his grasp made his blood boil. Watching their heads bowed close in quiet conversation, he became more certain than ever that Lady Lily was more involved in Bonaparte's plot than she should be.

When the dance was over, Spencer deposited the lady near the refreshment table, where they both took drinks, and then they parted ways. In a few moments, Reginald noted that Lady Lillian had slipped out of doors.

Perfect, he thought. He followed her.

Following the rose garden path, he found her only a few yards from the doorway. She stood sipping her drink; lemon water, he observed. The flickering candle-light from the doorway illuminated the glittering gold on her ball gown, which was scandalously sheer. He took a moment to admire her. She was lovely.

"Lady Lillian," he said, bowing formally.

"Are you following me?" she asked with eyes narrowed. She took a step back, the shadow of rose bushes obscuring the view of her person which the ballroom light had illuminated.

"I am glad to have a moment to speak with you in private," he said.

She raised an eyebrow. "Do tell."

"It has come to my attention that you are associating with the most unsavory of characters," he said.

"This again," she scoffed and turned away.

He stood between her and the door, intercepting her path. "Listen to me. I tell you this at great peril to myself and perhaps England," he prefaced his remarks.

"Oh, you are the arrogant one," she said, eyebrow raised.

Reginald decided to get right to the point. "I am fairly certain you were not meeting a lover when I found you at the crux of the Bonapartist riot."

"How dare you!"

"I do dare," he said. "I care for your safety, Lady Lillian. Things are happening that you know nothing about. Promise me you will stay away from the meetings," Reginald implored, his voice laced with urgency as he clasped her wrist. He could feel her pulse fluttering madly before she yanked her hand away from his grasp. Her nostrils flared and she looked like a spirited filly about to bolt. He had touched a nerve there. He was sure of it.

"Lord Reginald, you have no right to make such a

demand. You are not my father nor my grandfather." Lily's eyes flashed with defiance. Her color was high. It was clear that she was angry, but he had to press on.

"Your safety is at stake!" he exclaimed, his frustration evident as he hinted awareness of her activities. "If your grandfather knew what you were involved in..."

"You wouldn't dare tell him," she whispered, her voice trembling with fury.

No, he wouldn't, but he should. The man would be horrified to think of the danger with which his granddaughter was flirting. "Surely you can see, I only want what is best for you," Reginald pleaded, his voice breaking, filled with concern.

"Then trust me to know what is best for myself." With that, she turned on her heel, and Reginald knew he could not let her leave like this. He snatched her hand and pulled her towards him.

Her step faltered, and for one heartbeat, she was right there, against his chest, warm and quaking with passion. Was it anger or desire, he wondered, as she tilted her head up to him. Her gaze was dark and liquid like the deepest depths of night and infinitely beautiful.

He looked at her, giving her a beat to pull away, but she didn't.

Instead, her eyes fluttered shut, her long dark lashes like soot on her flushed cheeks.

She was so soft, so vulnerable, so exquisite. He was overcome with a single thought, and before he could think twice about it, he kissed her with all the longing within his soul. For one blissful moment, she melted against him, opening to him, and making tiny mewling sounds that stoked the fire in his veins. Just as quickly as it started, however, she pulled away and her gloved hand came up to strike his cheek.

"How dare you!" she snapped and stalked away, leaving Reginald to watch her retreating form as desire thrummed through him in hot waves. He watched helplessly, as he thought she was paving a path to hell, and he could not save her.

## INTRIGUE AND INFLUENCE

The moment Lily stepped into her family's grand estate, she was greeted by the formidable figure of her grandfather, the Earl of Thornwood. His piercing gaze bore into her as he inquired about her evening.

"Rumford seemed quite taken with you, my dear," he said with a hint of satisfaction. "But who was that other young man? The one you waltzed with?"

Lily feigned ignorance, her cheeks warming at the memory of Reginald's strong arms around her. "I'm not certain, Grandfather. There was so many new faces tonight." It could have been Lord Spencer or Lord Barton. She had waltzed most scandalously with both.

"Your mother should not have allowed you to dance the waltz," he said.

"If I am to be married within the month, I cannot see the difference a dance might make," she said feeling churlish.

"Mind your cheek," Grandfather said, "and tell your

mother I wish to speak with her. That young man held you far too close for propriety's sake." Lily wondered if there was any way she might discern which of her partners her grandfather was aware of.

"Of course, Grandfather," Lily replied, her heart fluttering at the thought that for Lord Barton, it had not been close enough, and then there was the moment in the rose garden. She had been kissed, and it had been nothing like she had imagined a kiss might be, a sloppy and awkward endeavor. No. This was bliss. It set her soul afire, and for a moment there was nothing in the world but his touch.

"You are flushed," Grandfather noted.

"In case you hadn't noticed, the weather is entirely too hot," she said as she excused herself and hastened up the stairs, eager to escape his watchful eye.

Upon entering her room, Lily found her sisters awaiting her arrival, their excited chatter filling the air. Grace was already regaling Betty with her own adventures, and Betty was eager to hear every detail of the night's events from both of her elder sisters.

"Tell me everything!" Betty, the romantic one, implored as she clasped her hands together.

Lily hesitated before sharing her thoughts about Lord Barton, her voice tinged with frustration. "He's heir to an earldom, but he's just like Grandfather – a controlling tyrant."

"Are you sure?" Grace chimed in. "He doesn't look the part. And if he is indeed the heir to an earldom, surely Grandfather would have no objections. This could get you out of the marriage to Rumford, you know."

"Out of the frying pan and into the fire," Lily grumbled.

"Does he know about your secret meetings?" Grace asked, her eyes wide with curiosity.

"Of course not!" Lily snapped, irritated by their prying questions. The sisters exchanged knowing glances.

"I only thought you might have told him when you took your walk in the rose garden," Grace said, and Lily hissed with displeasure. She didn't think anyone witnessed that.

"I told him nothing," Lily said in a low growl. "He deserves nothing."

"Come Betty," said Grace. "I think Lily has had enough of us."

Her sister was not wrong. "I'm sorry. Good night," Lily said as her sisters retired to their own rooms, leaving Lily feeling churlish and alone with her thoughts.

As she lay in bed, she couldn't help but fantasize about Lord Barton—Reginald. The warmth of his body as they danced together, the intensity of his gaze, and the kiss. Oh, the kiss. She rolled over, hugging her pillow. If only he were not so authoritarian, she mused, her heart aching despite her best efforts to resist him. But it didn't matter—it was Rumford she needed to worry about, the man Grandfather had chosen.

As Lily drifted off to sleep, the lingering memory of Lord Barton's kiss melded into his whispered plea. The deep timbre of his voice echoed through her mind: "Stay safe, Lady Lillian." And she vowed that she would, no matter the cost.

. . .

THE FOLLOWING EVENING, Lily arrived early to the dimly lit room where the leaders of the Bonapartists met with whispered conversations and the quiet rustle of papers. She was early, as she had planned. She needed to speak with Mr. Montgomery.

The meeting was held in a small, hidden chamber, accessed through a concealed door behind a bookcase in an unassuming townhouse. Shadows flickered on the walls, cast by candles tucked into every crevice to provide some semblance of light. The basement room beneath the abandoned London townhouse was a far cry from the lavish ballrooms Lady Lillian typically frequented, but she was not Lady Lillian. Not here. Here she was only Miss Hawkins, attending another one of her secret meetings, where like-minded individuals discussed the political climate and their desire for change. The air was thick with the smell of damp earth and conspiracy, but she had a different agenda at the moment. Her heart raced with anticipation and anxiety as she approached Mr. Roger Montgomery, the charismatic leader whose speeches had drawn her into this world of subterfuge.

"Ah, Miss Hawkins," Montgomery greeted her warmly, his eyes sparkling with intrigue. "I'm glad to see you again."

"Mr. Montgomery," Lily replied, her voice steady despite the fluttering in her chest. "I needed to speak with you about Lord Rumford. My grandfather is pushing me towards marriage with him, and I must find a way out."

Montgomery leaned in closer, his gaze intense. "That's quite an unfortunate situation, my dear. But what makes you think I can assist you?"

"Because," Lily said, lowering her voice, "you have connections and influence that could help me."

"But why would I?" he asked.

"Because we share the same cause," she said, as if it were obvious.

"A cause that is greater than both of us. We all must make sacrifices," he said as he turned to greet Lord Spencer as he came through the door with some other men, and she was summarily ignored.

She had expected better from Mongomery, but he was as arrogant as the aristocracy. His attitude grated on her.

MORE PEOPLE WERE COMING into the basement room now. Among the crowd were men and women from various walks of life, united by their shared vision for a world where people were truly equal. She moved away from the front of the room and brushed perspiration from her brow. Montgomery's lack of empathy was a blow. She had actually expected him to help her. Weren't they friends of a sort? Compatriots in their shared cause?

Roger Montgomery called the meeting to order with a clap of hands. His forceful voice carried in the small room.

"Friends," began Mr. Montgomery, his dark eyes cold and piercing as they scanned the crowd. "We gather here tonight to discuss our plans for the future—a future that belongs to Napoleon Bonaparte and those who support him. We will no longer be beholden to the whims of the aristocracy or the oppression of the English government. Like our brothers and sisters in America, we choose freedom—freedom from want, freedom from tyranny, and freedom from the aristocracy. No man should be raised above another."

No man, thought Lily, but what about women? Where did women fit in this rebellion? And didn't they stand in solidarity with the Emperor Napoleon Bonaparte? Wasn't he above other men as their emperor?

"We stand together as one," Montgomery said. "We must seize the opportunity before us."


THE DAMP AIR clung to her skin as she listened to the impassioned speeches echoing through the room. One after the other spoke. She knew she too could take the stage, but somehow, Montgomery's rejection of her request had dimmed her vigor.

The room erupted in cheers and applause as the members rallied around their shared cause. Lily clapped along with them, feeling both exhilarated and terrified by what lay ahead. Her heart pounded in her chest. No matter the shortcomings of the cause, she was in the right place. She felt as if she were on the verge of history.

Freedom from want.

Freedom from tyranny.

Freedom from the aristocracy.

All were good things; things she believed in wholeheartedly.

Lord Spencer spoke from the front row. "Our

contacts have informed us that there are many within the government who secretly share our cause, waiting for the opportune moment to strike. We are governed by a mad man and a spendthrift. How long will the populous cry for bread while Prinny ignores the crisis?"

"While Prinny feasts," someone called from the back of the room.

There was a general murmuring of agreement.

"It is time for strong men to take action." Lord Spencer continued, detailing clandestine meetings, ciphers, and secret rendezvous points which were coming together for the common good. Lily took issue with Lord Spencer's comment about strong men, but she couldn't help but feel a thrill in being part of something so much larger than herself. She let herself be carried away by the exhilaration of being part of the greater good.

Her heart raced as she took in the magnitude of their plan, acutely aware of the danger surrounding her. Her agile mind listed and codified the words as Lord Spencer spoke them, and yet she could not help but notice there were some things that did not fit. Where was the gold promised from the Americas? How would these grand plans come to fruition? There seemed to be missing pieces in this proposal, and all must work together for good. If there were discrepancies, it would be dangerous for all. She felt called to point them out so that they could be corrected.

The room erupted into applause again, interrupting her words.

Montgomery began speaking again, and the crowd was growing rowdy, filled with excitement. They were anxious to press forward willy-nilly, and yet, Lily knew that if discovered, any who supported Napoleon would be branded a traitor and face dire consequences. There could be no loose ends. There could be no mistakes. Yet she could not ignore the allure of the cause, the promise of freedom and equality for all. This was how all people should live, in freedom, not under the thumb of a man like her grandfather.

As the speeches continued, saying much the same thing, Lily found her thoughts drifting away from the fervor of the moment. The problem of her marriage to Rumford was a niggling thorn in the back of her mind. She brought her thoughts back to the present. It was important that she understand this strategy. Something was not right with it.

She tried again to piece together the full plan and came up short, but perhaps she had been left out of some of it. She was, after all, a woman. Her conversation with Mongomery had just recently made that abundantly clear.

She would speak to Montgomery afterwards, she promised herself, even though he had dismissed her request earlier, which brought her back to her own personal problem. Her normally keen focus on the meeting was at risk of wavering. She couldn't shake the thought of her grandfather and the threat of being forced to marry Lord Rumford, a man who represented every-thing she despised. This distraction threatened her concentration, but she knew she must remain vigilant. She needed all of her wits about her. She brought her mind back to the present.

"Finally," Lord Spencer concluded, "we have

received word that Bonaparte himself is aware of our efforts and has expressed his gratitude for our unwavering support. We shall free him, no matter the cost!"

"How?" someone shouted.

"A ship that sails, not on the sea," Spencer said enigmatically, "but under it."

Murmurs of astonishment spread through the crowd. Lily's heart quickened, though she couldn't shake the undercurrent of trepidation. The room was filled with fervent whispers as the members exchanged thoughts and opinions and voiced their amazement. Lily wanted to know how this ship could be. She didn't trust things she didn't understand. The idea of an underwater ship was ludicrous, of course, but if such a think existed, it was so fantastical that she could not quite comprehend it.

The more she tried to imagine such a thing, the more her personal plight seemed to eclipse matters at hand, making it difficult for her to concentrate on the impassioned words of her fellow Bonapartists and the plan at large.

Her mind wandered back to the looming threat of her marriage to Lord Rumford—a fate she would do anything to avoid. In her desperation, she wondered if she could find a suitor among these rebels, or even a pretend one, just to escape her grandfather's iron grip.

The room echoed with applause, but Lily's mind was elsewhere, enmired in her own problems. She scanned the faces around her, trying to discern if any of these men could be her salvation, even if it meant venturing further into the shadows.

Montgomery was finishing up his speech now. "Remember," he declared, his voice steely with determination, "we must remain vigilant, for the enemy is always watching. We have come too far and sacrificed too much to be deterred now."

He was right, of course.

JUST AS THE applause was dying down, a sudden commotion at the top of the stairs jerked Lily from her reverie. The disruption interrupted the fervent atmosphere, and some dashed for shadowy corners. Her heart raced with apprehension as she realized that someone was attempting to infiltrate their secret meeting. Whispers and hurried footsteps reached Lily's ears, her heart pounding as she stiffened with anxiety. Were they discovered by Bow Street Runners or some member of the Crown's forces? The members of the group were on high alert, and anxiety spread through the room like wildfire. She noted some sprinted for the back entrance, including Lord Spencer, but she was too far from the door.

The door burst open. Two of the men standing guard at the top of the stairs dragged a gentleman down the steps and into the room. He looked to have been knocked silly. The Bonapartists ceased their murmurs and stared at the intruder.

As the gentleman was brought into the dimly lit chamber, Lily's eyes widened in shock as she realized the newcomer was Lord Reginald Barton. His face was flushed, and the darkening of a bruise was already beginning under one eye. Although the man was an opponent of everything she held dear, he was also a man she had kissed. The thought caused her heart to beat fast. She stared at him, trying to make sense of his presence, but her thoughts were interrupted when Montgomery demanded, "Who is this?" His voice was cold and menacing.

"I caught him snooping around. Says he's here to join up," said one of the men holding Lord Barton.

One of the group members declared, "He's dressed commonly, but look at his 'ands—all pink and pretty. He ain't never done a day's work in his life," said the other.

"This man is no loyal Bonapartist!" Came a voice from the crowd. "We should dispose of him immediately!"

"A spy!" another shouted.

"What say you?" demanded Montgomery.

Lily's breath caught in her throat as she wondered what she could do. What was that fool doing here? He would ruin everything! Her mind raced, grasping for some way to salvage the situation that wouldn't expose them both as the group moved with menacing intent.

# CAUGHT

*L*ord Barton attempted to speak, but his words came out in a mumbled stammer as he licked blood from his lip. The suspicion in the room grew palpable. Lily realized that this would go very badly for him if they believed he was an enemy to the cause, and what else could they believe? Lily knew that if she didn't act quickly, Reginald would be killed. Despite her anger towards him, she couldn't bear the thought of his life being snuffed out so brutally. She jumped to her feet, words on her lips before she really considered her actions.

"Wait!" she cried, drawing all eyes to her.

The group held, waiting for her words, her sanction. It was one thing to die for her cause and quite another to stay silent in the murder of another, and yet what was she doing? By drawing attention to herself in this moment, she was aligning herself with a man she knew to be diametrically opposed to all they believed. She wavered only a moment before she spoke. "I know this man," she said.

The crowd waited, the tension palpable. "He's my cousin."

The alarm in the room eased slightly, but Montgomery's gaze remained locked on Reginald before glancing back toward Lily. "And you vouch for his loyalty?" He asked Lily, his eyes hard upon her.

Lily hesitated, knowing Reginald held views contrary to the Bonapartist goals. Her mind raced, searching for a way to save him without jeopardizing her own position in the group. "Yes," she said finally, her voice firm and confident. "He may be misguided, but he is no threat to us." The men looked skeptical, and the crowd shifted nervously.

"Misguided how?" murmured someone in the crowd.

"He has been a quiet supporter of our cause," she added. "He came to take me home last week when there was trouble." That much was true. He did take her home, much as she had not wanted his assistance.

"Aye," called a man in the crowd, collaborating her story. She didn't know the man but searched out his face. He was a thin balding sailor, a wiry fellow she had seen on occasion. "I saw her get into his fancy carriage when things turned ugly. Carried her off, he did."

Montgomery stepped forward, his eyes narrowing as he searched Lord Barton's face.

"Weren't you with Miss Hawkins? Arguing with her about being here, in fact. And now you want to join us? Why should we believe anything you say?" another asked.

Several men murmured in agreement, glaring at

Reginald. "Yes, I brought my cousin here, but I did not want to leave her here alone. I had another engagement that day. I wanted her to stay at home."

The room fell silent as everyone turned to look at her. Some nodded in agreement, knowing that family connections often played a crucial role in their covert operations, and surely a man should protect his female family. Others, however, remained skeptical, still eyeing Reginald with suspicion and disdain.

I say we kill 'em and throw him in the Thames," someone shouted.

"You would throw Miss Hawkins' cousin in the Thames?" asked Montgomery with an eyebrow raised.

Some of the group began to settle, and although there were still murmurs, no one else advocated killing him, at least not at the moment.

"He's telling the truth," Lily said. "This is my cousin, Reginald. I have been trying to make him understand—"

"Then he is not convinced," Montgomery interrupted in a hard voice.

"No. No. That is not it," Lily said. "It's only, he only thinks that women should be safe in their homes. He agrees in principle. He does not agree *with me* being here."

Some of the gathering nodded. She knew very well that most of the men in the room agreed with that sentiment. This was no place for a woman. She took the thought and ran with it.

She turned towards Reginald, fire in her eyes as she laid into him. "You don't accept my autonomy, do you? You came here to check on me. Admit it. You think I don't have a brain and that I'm only good for bearing children! Freedom and equality are only for men, right?" Her words rang true with her passion, echoing the sentiments that had been too long constrained in polite society.

Reginald stared at her.

Lily forced a laugh, filling the silence, her heart pounding in her chest. She was not sure if the origin was passion or fear, but the words poured from her. "Yes, my dear cousin Reginald is indeed a Bonapartist," she declared. "But he believes that these meetings are not the place for women." She turned to face him, a fervor in her dark eyes, and unleashed the torrent that had been bubbling within her since their last encounter. "He doesn't think women should have a passion."

Something like a flash of fire passed through his eyes, but he said nothing, and Lily continued unabated. "He thinks I have no business being here, that I don't possess the intellect to understand the intricacies of politics or perhaps the desire for freedom, but I know what it is like to not be free. I know what it is like to have my life ordered by circumstance." Her voice trembled with indignation as she thought of Lord Barton, Lord Rumford, and her own grandfather. Rage against the injustice filled her heart. "Like most aristocrats," she spat, "he thinks, I, and women like me, are nothing but broodmares."

"It's not..." Lord Barton interrupted her. "Women... having children," he began but hesitated, perhaps considering his situation, but he continued anyway. "It is a woman's gift. God's gift. Life-giving..." He shook his head, and would have continued, but Lily glared at him, finally growling, "Aragh!"

The men in the room began to laugh at the encounter. They poked one another, taking her outburst in good humor.

She wondered if the blows the men had rained upon Lord Barton had befuddled him. If so, they were both lost. At length, he spoke.

"Yes, of course," he said through gritted teeth. "My fair cousin has opened my eyes. I see that all people, men and women alike, must be free. I stand corrected." He gave her a brief nod.

"Very well," Montgomery said, still eyeing Reginald with suspicion. "You may stay, but do not think we will hesitate to deal with any disloyalty." Montgomery nodded for the men to release him, and they shoved him aside.

"Understood," Reginald murmured to Montgomery while straightening his clothing. He recovered himself and stuck out a hand. "So, you are the famed Montgomery my cousin has spoken of. Pleased to meet you, Sir."

"I am," Montgomery said taking Lord Barton's hand.

While he shook it up and down, Lord Barton sent a thankful glance towards Lily.

Lily let out a small sigh of relief. She was nearly certain that most of the crowd would abide by Montgomery's word, although she was not sure. Most especially, she was concerned about Lord Spencer, who might recognize her in association with Lord Barton. Surely, he would recognize Lord Barton, but as she looked around the room, she realized he had truly slipped out the door earlier. He was no longer in attendance. He had taken his leave when Lord Barton entered.

It was, of course, true that Lord Barton would recognize him as easily as the reverse, and without Lord Spencer in attendance, there was no one to connect her cousin with Lord Barton. But what would happen when Lord Spencer returned?

She would think of it later. She breathed a sigh of relief in the moment. Now that the immediate danger was over, she realized how angry she was. Inwardly, she was seething. Her whole body was shaking in reaction to the stress of the past few minutes.

Lily was feeling anything but magnanimous. She shot Reginald a venomous look. She would have words with him later. For now, she had to maintain this charade, though it galled her to vouch for such an infuriating, arrogant man.

With that, the meeting resumed. But as Lily listened to the continued discussions, she was consumed by a mixture of relief, confusion, and antagonism towards Lord Barton. Her mind was churning as she evaluated the last few minutes. She had saved Reginald's life, but in doing so had put her own position at risk.

What was he doing here, she wondered, when he held such conservative beliefs? The only answer that came to mind was that he was, as the others assumed, a spy. He must be here as a spy, hoping to uncover traitorous plots. The thought made Lily bristle. And how foolish she had been. She had vouched for him and let him into her world.

No. He had entered her world uninvited and put everything she believed in at risk, including his own life. Lily seethed. Why else was Reginald here, when he was so opposed to everything she held dear? How dare he intrude on her cause? And she had been forced to implicate herself to save his life. He kept telling her to avoid the meetings! It was he who should avoid the meetings. He must go home after this and stay out of her life. He could not come to another meeting. She would not stand for it.

She tried to push aside her anger as the meeting continued, focusing on the discussions at hand. Later, she would confront him, but for now, she had to play her role and maintain the façade of solidarity.

REGINALD, for his part, couldn't help but be grateful for Lily's intervention. He knew he owed her a debt. There was a charged moment there. Still, now he knew for a fact who the elusive Mr. Montgomery was, and more than that, he knew Lady Lillian's part in this was not miniscule as he had hoped. Montgomery had heeded her, and although he was glad of her assistance, he couldn't shake the feeling of unease that came with being in this room. He needed to find a way to gather information without revealing his true intentions, all while keeping Lady Lillian safe from harm. He had told her to stay home, but he was cognizant of the fact that if she had not been here, his own situation might have been much worse. On the other hand, if he hadn't been distracted by worry for her, would he have been more careful? He supposed he would never know the answer to that, and as one learned in this business, forward motion was often needed to release oneself from the mire.

Reginald stood stiffly, his aching jaw clenched, as he

listened intently to the proceedings. As he concentrated on remembering the plans of the Bonapartist group, he couldn't help but feel a mix of repulsion and admiration. He abhorred their cause, but their passion and dedication were undeniable. He knew he had to be careful; one false move could mean his life. And now that Lily had vouched for him, her life was on the line as well. He was well aware that he had put her in more danger, not less, and it pained him.

If only the woman would stay home where she belonged, and yet the fire and passion with which she had defended him made him see her in a different light. The woman was magnificent. She had thought on her feet with all the verve that ever was expected of an intelligence worker. He knew there were women in the Crown's employ, but he had never agreed with the practice of putting women in harm's way. Even now, he did not agree, and Lily was not a spy for the Crown. She was deeply embroiled in the countermovement. A traitor. He understood her yearning for freedom, but these people were not in business to procure freedom for the masses. What they wanted was power, and what they were dealing with was treason. Although the Crown generally did not hang women, the thought made his mouth dry.

Still, she was a woman among women. There was so much more to her than a pretty face and a well-turned leg. He could not help but admire her. In his heart, he vowed to protect her with his life, even as he knew she would not wish it so.

With that thought, he attended to the words of the speaker more fully. It was paramount that he should discern the time and place of the rescue attempt. Bonaparte could not be released upon the people again. He would end this, and the quicker, the better.

AT LAST, the meeting concluded, and Lily wondered if she should again approach Montgomery with the problem of her impending marriage to Rumford if her grandfather had anything to do with it. She knew she could attend these meetings because Grandfather generally retired early, and no one really kept a close watch upon her. As a wife, the dynamic would change, and she would be subject to a husband's whims. It could not happen. She would not allow it.

As the men filed out, Reginald approached Lily. "Allow me to escort you home, cousin," he said with false charm. His hazel eyes betrayed no sign of the tension between them. If anything, he looked at her with admiration.

"Fine," Lily snapped, realizing that declining would only cast suspicion on their hastily constructed cover story. Refusing now would seem odd after her impassioned defense of him. Although sitting in a carriage with this man was the last thing she wanted, she couldn't refuse without undermining all she had said about her *cousin*. Her previous anger was reignited.

Lily suppressed a scowl. She wanted nothing more than to flee from him. Instead, she pasted a smile upon her face. "That would be lovely," she forced out, taking his proffered arm. "Thank you, cousin."

Once they were alone in the carriage and underway, Lily confronted Reginald. She rounded on him spitting in anger. "Just what do you think you're doing coming here? You lied to me earlier, and now you've inserted yourself into my life, causing a dangerous situation. Why were you there if you don't agree with Bonaparte? Was it just to spy on me?"

Reginald tried to smooth over the issue, but she was having none of it.

"You are right," he said. "I have been keeping things from you, but not because you are a woman. It is for your safety."

"Lies!" she accused.

"And perhaps my own," he added. As the carriage hit a rut in the unkept road, it lurched forward, and she was pushed bodily against him. His arm shot out to steady her. She slapped it away even as she wanted to melt into his arms. The evening had been trying, and now that the adrenaline rushed out of her system, she felt like she wanted to wilt on the spot.

Squashing down the obvious physical attraction between them, she pulled herself to the other side of the carriage and barreled on. "You lied to me. I cannot abide a liar, Lord Barton. You're no supporter of Napoleon. You're here spying, putting us all in danger. Why? Why were you there?" She knew he did not just happen to this part of town. He had to be following her. "Tell me the truth," she demanded.

"I was there for reasons beyond my control, but I assure you it was not just to spy on you."

"Beyond your control?" Lily scoffed. "You are making excuses, Lord Barton. "That is a lie. Is it that you just can't bear the thought of a woman being involved in such matters? Or is it impossible for you to just tell the truth?"

"*This is true.* I cannot abide the thought of you attending those meetings," he said evasively, his jaw clenching. He reached up to rub it.

She noted that his jaw was probably hurting from the beating he took, and like her, now that they were out of immediate danger, all of those little things crowded in. Her feet hurt. She felt sticky with sweat. His jaw was probably throbbing. She would not allow herself to feel sorry for him. He had brought this upon himself. She turned from him.

REGINALD CONSIDERED how to speak to her to make her see the error of her ways. "You must understand, Lady Lillian, the danger you put yourself in by attending those meetings is far greater than you realize," he said. "I cannot allow you to continue down this path."

"You cannot allow me?" Lily's voice trembled with anger, her eyes narrowing. "*You?* You have no authority over my life, Lord Barton. It is not your place to dictate my actions."

Reginald implored her, reaching out to take her hand in his, to turn her to listen to him. She could literally feel the pulse in his wrist pounding as he placed her hand in his and laid his other hand over hers. "This is a matter of life and death. I won't stand idly by while you risk everything."

"Risk everything?" Lily echoed, her voice dripping with sarcasm. She yanked her hand away from him. "I am a grown woman, Lord Barton, capable of taking care of myself and making my own decisions. I will not be coddled or controlled by you or anyone else!"

Reginald tried another tact. "Please," he said gently. "You are flirting with death. What you are doing is treason! You are fighting a war that cannot be won, and the Crown will not allow this. You are an English subject. You must bow to the Crown."

"The American Colonists took their independence," she spat.

"The Americans were an ocean away from the Crown," Reginald interrupted. "And they were men of substance." He knew she would take exception the moment the words were out of his mouth. What he meant was that the Americans, for the most part, were merchants and men of money. Having seen this group of Bonapartists, he was more frightened for her than previously. They were for the most part a band of rabble.

She spoke angrily. "Men!"

"These are ruffians and scoundrels, not men of honor. I will take your place."

Lily sputtered, too angry to even speak.

"Lady Lillian, you have to agree this is dangerous. You are not that stupid." Lily lifted her chin. What sort of backhanded compliment was that? she wondered. Acknowledging her intelligence while telling her that she was stupid? "I'll do as I please. If my grandfather cannot stop me, then I am certain you cannot."

She crossed her arms over her chest and looked determinedly out of the window into the night.

He couldn't help but feel the weight of their unspoken desires and unresolved tensions pressing in on them. And with each passing moment, the danger they faced grew more palpable and urgent, and not all of that danger was in association with Bonaparte.

JUST LIKE A MAN, she thought—bark orders and expect obedience. Well, she was not one to kowtow to her grandfather. She would do no less for Lord Barton. Instead of obedience, his words ignited a spark of defiance within her, fueled by the lingering resentment she felt toward him. "I don't care what you said, Lord Barton. You have no right to give me orders." she hissed. "I will not be controlled by a man who would see my freedoms suppressed. I. Will. Not."

A second bump in the road caused them both to attend to their placement on the carriage seat. As the conveyance swayed, their bodies brushed against one another, the friction igniting an undercurrent of tension that neither could ignore. They stared at each other, their anger blurring into passion as they were reminded of the undeniable connection between them. She could feel the heat of their proximity, the tension between them crackling like lightning in the hot air.

"Is that all you think of me?" he asked, his voice gruff, barely above a whisper. "As someone who wants to control you?"

"Isn't it true?" Lily challenged, her heart pounding in her chest. And for a moment, as they stared into each other's eyes, it seemed as though the world had fallen away, leaving only the two of them and the battle of wills that raged between them. "Or do you even know what truth is?"

Reginald held up a hand. "Then, let me explain..."

"Please do," she snapped. "And do not excuse your lies with platitudes. The truth this time." She crossed her arms over her chest. "Truth."

"I had to protect you," Reginald insisted. "These are dangerous men."

Lily let out a bitter laugh. "Oh yes, you want to protect the poor, helpless woman. I don't need your protection! How many times do I need to say it before it sinks into your thick neanderthal skull?" Her eyes flashed with defiance. "I make my own choices. I don't need a man, least of all you, controlling my fate. I have had enough of that from my grandfather. I won't take it from him, and I won't take it from you. I control my fate. Me and me alone."

Reginald stared at her, frustration simmering beneath the surface. "But do you?" he asked. "Or do those ruffians control your fate?" Reginald said, his voice low and intense. "I want you to know this, Lady Lillian: I will do whatever it takes to keep you safe, even if that means going against your wishes."

"Your chivalry is sorely misplaced, Lord Barton," Lily retorted, her cheeks flushed with emotion as she retreated into the persona of a lady. "Now let us speak no more of this tonight. I have had enough of secrets and lies for one evening." She turned to look out of the window at the night, her hands folded primly in her lap like the lady she was.

~

Reginald clenched his fists, fighting the urge to protect Lily from the dangers that surrounded her. "The thought of a hangman's noose around your neck—" he muttered under his breath. The thought filled him with fear, although it was likely as a lady, she would be deported not killed, but still, a lady—*this lady* crowded onto a prison ship was more than he could bear.

He knew she would never accept his help willingly, but the thought of her being caught up in this web of intrigue and deception was almost too much for him. The tension between them crackled like lightning before a storm, creating a charged atmosphere that seemed to spark with every heated word exchanged. He wanted to shake some sense into her. He wanted to protect her. He wanted to touch her.

The realization that the only way he might be able to do that was with his name came to him. If she was his wife, he wouldn't have to involve her grandfather. She would be his to protect. The thought stirred him more than it should.

Still, the notion of locking her in a room—preferably a bedroom—for the immediate future was not an ill-fated conception. His body whole-heartedly agreed with that thought. In fact, being locked in said room with this firebrand seemed a blissful way to spend the next few weeks. She would not agree, but he would protect her. In some primal part of his being, he knew she was his, as irrevocably as his own heart was in her traitorous hands.

"Very well," he said, finally breaking the silence. "As I have declared, Lady Lillian, I will do whatever it takes to keep you safe, even if that means going against your wishes."

"And as I said, your gallantry is misplaced, Lord Barton," she retorted, her eyes flashing with defiance. "It appears we are at an impasse."

Perhaps that was true, but he did not want to slay this dragon. He wanted to make her purr with contentment. He wondered if she had ever felt true contentment in her short life. Considering who her grandfather was, he thought she must have come from the womb fighting for her autonomy and her identity. He didn't want to break her. He wanted to give her a moment of rest. And peace. And passion. He wanted to put aside all of the politics and hold her close.

"Just take me home," she said with a sigh.

That is exactly what he wanted to do. Take her home. To his home. Instead, he gave Helms the order to continue to Hawthorne House.

They sat in tense silence as the carriage rumbled down the darkened streets, the air fairly crackling between them. The silence between them grew heavy with unspoken words and unresolved sexual tension.

Reginald struggled to rein in his temper and his desire. This obstinate woman vexed him as much as she intrigued him. As much as he wanted to shake some sense into her, a part of him thrilled at her fiery spirit. He wanted to know if that passion would translate to more intimate endeavors.

Marriage with her would never be dull. No. What an adventure that would be with this vixen! His imagination took flight. What would she do if he pulled her into an embrace just now? Slap his face, no doubt, and yet it was worth the risk. Before she slapped him, would she melt in his arms like she did the last time he kissed her? That kiss had haunted him, and he wondered, would he have that single moment of bliss before she came to her senses? His desire, driven by a mixture of fear for her safety and longing for her person, nearly overcame his control, but he was an agent of the Crown and used to keeping his passions in check. There would be time to court this firebrand once she was safe. First, she needed to be safe. He tamped down his desire and tried to reason with her one last time.

"Look, Lady Lillian. Lily..." Reginald began, his voice strained with emotion.

She raised an eyebrow.

He liked the way her Chistian name fell from his tongue. They were in a life and death battle, and it seemed that calling her by the feminine flower name would remind him of her delicate nature, and he needed reminding. For all her bravado, she was still a woman. "I know you're upset with me, but this isn't just about politics anymore; this is about your safety. We need to come up with a plan now that I am in the persona of your cousin. No one will expect you to arrive alone to the meetings now." He knew he could no longer insist that she stay at home. It galled him to say it, but say it he did. "We shall need to arrive together."

"That is true," she agreed.

He took her hand in his, and before she could object, he leaned in and pressed his lips against her gloved hand, driven by a mixture of fear and longing. "Trust me," he said. His voice was rough with desire.

"How can I when you have done nothing but lie?" Lily said, her eyes glistening with some unnamed emotion. Her words were filled with less fire, but no less conviction. "I am capable of making my own decisions."

"I believe you," he said. "And I will tell you the truth. As much as I am able." Her defense of him had gained that much, he thought. "We need to form a plan together, for both of our safety. Please, visit my sister Patience tomorrow. We must talk further."

Lily hesitated for a moment, her eyes narrowing suspiciously. "There will be no more lies between us," she said.

He nodded his agreement. "No more lies," he said, but he also knew, even as he said the words, he could not tell her the complete truth.

Lily wavered, then gave a curt nod relenting. "I cannot abide a liar," she said softly.

And, Reginald thought, he was a professional liar. That was what it took to be an intelligence agent for the Crown. They would have a rocky road ahead of them, but oh what a ride, he thought.

They sat in prickly silence as the carriage rolled on into the night.

The rhythmic clopping of the horse's hooves against cobblestones filled the air as the carriage lurched forward. The dim glow from the gas lamps lining the streets as they moved to a better district cast flickering shadows on Lily's face, her dark eyes thoughtful.

As the carriage pulled up to the Hawthorne townhouse, Reginald helped Lily down from the vehicle. The moment their hands touched, a current passed between them, igniting a fire that threatened to consume them both. They stood there for a moment, neither willing to acknowledge or break the unspoken connection that bound them together.

"Goodnight, Lord Barton," Lily whispered at last as she turned away towards the house.

"Goodnight, Lady Lillian," he replied softly, watching her take the servants' stairs into the grand house. "Be safe, my Lily," he whispered to himself. At least, he thought, she was safe for the night. Who knew what the morrow would bring.

# AN UNWELCOME VISITOR

*W*hen Lily arrived home, she was dismayed to find Lord Rumford visiting in spite of the late hour. She attempted to slip upstairs, but such a surreptitious move was not to be. Lord Rumford was sitting in the drawing room, engaged in animated conversation with her grandfather, and Lily knew she was caught out. As the door closed behind her, all eyes turned towards Lily, and she felt the weight of their disapproval bearing down on her. A hand went to her stark braid and simple dress. She suppressed the desire to curse.

She realized that her grandfather had summoned her, and although her sisters would have tried to cover for her, they were not able to do so. Now, it was late, and more concerning than Rumford's presence was the fact that Grandfather knew of her absence.

Her grandfather's eyes narrowed, clearly not satisfied with her explanation of a simple walk, but he said nothing further on the matter. At least not yet. After all,

Lord Rumford was a guest in the house. She could hope that Grandfather would not speak harshly to her in front of a guest, but she held no illusions that this was over.

"AH, Lady Lily, so good of you to grace us with your presence at last," Lord Rumford commented icily. "Your grandfather has been quite concerned about your whereabouts."

"Apologies, Grandfather," Lily lied through gritted teeth. "I went for a walk. It is so hot, and the confines of these walls were beginning to suffocate me."

"Your sisters attempted to explain your absence, but their efforts were in vain," her grandfather said sternly. "And why are you dressed like a commoner?"

"I thought it best upon the street," she said. "I did not want to be recognized as quality."

"Well, you wouldn't be," Lord Rumford said most ungallantly. "You look like a maid."

Grandfather gave the man a stern look, which Lily was glad of, but then Grandfather turned his ire on her. "You must learn to take your responsibilities as a young lady more seriously, Lily. You will not go out without a maid and a footman in attendance. You know better than that."

"Yes, Grandfather," she said. That was not a terrible hardship. There were several servants that would help her. Could it be that grandfather was so convinced that women were incapable of independent thought that he did not actually know she was gone from the grounds? Bless small favors, she thought.

. . .

"INDEED," Lord Rumford added with a smug smile. "It would be most unbecoming for my future wife to shirk her duties so carelessly."

LILY GLARED at the portly man who sought to control her life. The thought of being bound to him made her want to vomit. She would not do it. But she knew better than to voice any displeasure in front of her grandfather.

"OF COURSE, Lord Rumford. I assure you it won't happen again." The words tasted bitter on her tongue, but she swallowed her pride for the sake of her family, while thinking she had to escape this inane existence.

"Sit," Grandfather ordered.

"I am not dressed for company," Lily said unnecessarily.

"So, we see," Grandfather said. "Sit."

She was forced to sit and entertain Lord Rumford, whom she was coming to despise more and more by the day. She could not help but compare the man to Lord Barton. In every way, he came up short. And the visit, though short due to the hour, was entirely too long in Lily's estimation.

THE MOMENT LORD Rumford had taken his leave, her grandfather turned on her. The flickering candlelight cast ominous shadows on his aging features, emphasizing the displeasure that was evident in every line of his face.

She tried to maintain her composure under his gaze, but her fingers trembled ever so slightly, and her heart raced as her grandfather's narrowed eyes bore into her.

"Where were you?" he demanded.

"I told you," she began, but he interrupted.

"A walk! At this hour?" he demanded, his voice low and dangerous. "You expect me to believe you were simply out for a walk? Do you take me for a fool?"

"Of course not, Grandfather," Lily replied, forcing herself to meet his gaze. "I assure you, my intentions were innocent. I did not know that Lord Rumford would be calling this evening."

"TELL ME WHO YOU WERE WITH," her grandfather ordered, his voice like ice.

"NO ONE," she lied, feeling the weight of her deception bearing down on her. "I sometimes just like to be alone with my thoughts."

"Liar," her grandfather growled. "Is it even possible for a woman to be truthful?" he asked. "All men's problems began with Eve." Her grandfather stared at her for a moment longer before releasing a heavy sigh, disappointment etched on his face. "You are an odd one," he said. "Regardless, your actions tonight have proven you are no better than the wildest hoyden. I expect more from you, Lily. You are to be married soon, and I will not tolerate such reckless behavior. If this keeps up, it is likely Lord Rumford will not have you."

Oh, praise heaven, she thought, but Grandfather kept

right on talking, castigating her for her absence and her bookishness.

"It was enough getting him to look past your blue-stocking ways. After all, I convinced him intelligence in a son is a good thing, and even your distinctive features would not go wrong in a son."

That thought brought a renewed wave of nausea, but it would be a certain thing that any children would not be obtaining brains from their father. On the other hand, she had considered that pulling the wool over Rumford's eyes would not be too difficult, but the reality crashed down on her. The thought of letting that man have access to her body, to bearing his children, was beyond loathsome. She would not do it. She had to find another way. For a brief instant, the chiding face of Lord Barton appeared in her mind's eye—children with his distinctive hazel eyes.

"Do you understand?" her grandfather snapped as he caught her wool-gathering.

"I understand, Grandfather," Lily murmured, though her thoughts screamed in defiance. She couldn't reveal the truth—that she had been attending a secret meeting of the Bonapartist group, trying to find a way out of the marriage Lord Rumford threatened to force upon her. Lord Barton's unexpected appearance and her loyalty to their cause had only further complicated matters. As easy as Lord Rumford was to deceive, Lord Barton was not.

She was certain she would get nothing past that man. Marriage to him simply would not work. But her heart leaped with the thought, and her midsection felt like melted chocolate. He could give her everything except what mattered most, her freedom.

"See that you do," her grandfather warned before turning away, leaving Lily to stew in her tangled web of lies and emotions.

"Grandfather?" she said.

He turned.

"Lady Patience Beresford invited me to tea on the morrow. I don't want you to think I am disappearing unbeknownst to you."

He nodded. "Blackburn is a good man," he said referencing Lady Patience's father-in-law. "Bring your sister with you. Grace will keep you out of trouble," he said.

Before she could object that Lady Patience nor Lord Barton had invited Grace, Grandfather had stalked away, wielding his cane like a club.

She hurried down the hallway, her skirts rustling softly against the cold marble floor, desperately seeking the sanctuary of her bedchamber. She wanted to be alone. Mostly, she wanted to be out of this house.

The air was suffocating, and she did not think the miasma was only due to the summer heat. Shadows fell about her soul like the thick velvet curtains that lined the walls of Thornwood Manor.

"Lady Lily," called a hushed voice as she passed by the footman, Angley, who stood guard near the entrance hall. He was one of her favorite servants.

"Yes, Angley?" she said.

He glanced around furtively before leaning in closer. "Begging your pardon, my lady, but a footman saw you alight from a carriage earlier. I can only assume your grandfather knows, or will know, you were with someone."

Lily stopped abruptly, her heart hammering in her chest. The walls seemed to close in around her, their gilded frames and intricately carved moldings bearing witness to her deception.

BETRAYED BY A MERE FOOTMAN. Not Angley, but someone. Certainly, Grandfather wasn't gazing out of the window for her return. That was almost laughable. But the reality of the situation was far from amusing. Her position was even more precarious than she had realized. If her secret activities were exposed, the consequences would be disastrous, not only for herself but also for those she sought to protect.

Grandfather would seek to badger Grace into betraying her. She had to warn her sister and come up with a plan. In the meantime, the only reason Grandfather had not confronted her was because he wanted to see if the carriage driver was someone he could force into marriage if he thought Lily was ruined. Lily groaned. Lord Barton would certainly be a catch in her grandfather's eyes, and he would take her freedom as surely as her grandfather, perhaps moreso. At least, she managed to escape her grandfather's thumb. As much as the man thought he was next to the Lord Almighty, he was old, and Lily was not.

. . .

"THANK YOU, ANGLEY," she whispered tersely, her eyes narrowing at the footman. "Your loyalty is commendable."

THE FOOTMAN BOWED SLIGHTLY, his eyes filled with regret. "I'm sorry, Lady Lily. I only thought you should know."

"Do you know which footman it was?" she asked.

"Yes, it was—" But she held up a hand to forestall the answer. She didn't want to know. If she knew, she would surely treat the servant differently. She wanted to dismiss him out of hand, but of course, she couldn't do that. In the end, all of the servants were in her grandfather's employ. This reminded her that she could trust no one, not even her own maid.

"Shall I speak to him?" Angley asked.

She shook her head. "No. After all he is in Grandfather's employ," she said. "And he was doing my grandfather's bidding."

"I'm sorry," said Angley.

"So am I," she muttered, turning on her heel and continuing down the hallway.

LILY'S EYES flashed with anger as she stormed through the hallway, the footman's words ringing in her ears like an ominous portent. She paced the floorboards like a caged animal, muttering. "Bloody hell!" she hissed under her breath, her hands clenched into tight fists at her side.

As Lily climbed the grand staircase, her thoughts

churned with the tumultuous events of the evening. The Bonapartist meeting, Reginald's unexpected arrival, and their tense escape—it all seemed like the stuff of thrilling adventure novels. But this was no fictional tale; real lives were at stake, including her own.

As she reached her bedchamber, Lily quickly closed the door behind her, taking a deep breath as she leaned against it for support. She knew that her secret was hanging by a thread, and she couldn't afford to let her guard down for even a moment.

Her heart raced with fear and frustration. She paced back and forth, wringing her hands together as she contemplated her next move. She couldn't abandon the cause or her allies, but now, things had changed. Drastically. What if Lord Barton had the lot of them arrested? She knew he did not agree with their persuasion. What if Montgomery decided to have Lord Barton killed? It was a close call this evening. Would the next evening and the next be less fraught with turmoil? What was Lord Barton really doing there? Had he followed her because he fancied her, or was he there for some nefarious purpose and just using her for his own ends?

LILY'S THOUGHTS were consumed by the events of the evening and the dangerous game she now found herself playing. She couldn't help but wonder if Lord Barton's presence at the meeting was a blessing or a curse.

SHE FELT the pressure of her secrets and desires pressing in around her, threatening to suffocate her. She had no one she could trust. Not really. Sure, her sisters loved her, but they would be appalled, and the servants all valued their employ. She paced the room, her mind reeling with the implications of the evening's events. How could she protect her family and continue her involvement with the Bonapartists without revealing her true motives, and now, how could she not when Lord Baron's life depended upon her part in this play? And what of Lord Barton—the man whose presence simultaneously infuriated and captivated her? His very presence filled her with an explosive combination of frustration and anger, and yes, she must admit, passion. She paused, bringing her fingers to her lips in remembrance, and her whole body seemed to revel in the emotion.

Lily threw herself onto the bed with a huff and hugged a pillow. She had to admit, their near discovery at the meeting had rattled her. Perhaps Reginald's presence wasn't entirely unwelcome... but she'd never tell him that.

She screamed her frustration into the pillow as she had done as a child, but she was a child no longer.

"BLOODY HELL," she muttered to herself again, her frustration boiling over. "Why must he be so insufferable yet so... enthralling?" And because the swear words felt so liberating, she spoke them again to the stark walls of her gilded cage. They were not ladylike, and she did not care.

"My Lady?" said her maid, Maggie, with censure as she entered the room to prepare her for bed.

"It has been an awful day," Lily told her as she rolled over on the bed and looked up at the woman.

She nodded. "Lord Rumford," she said, the older woman's face softening. "You do not favor him."

"I do not," Lily agreed while the maid unbuttoned her clothing and helped her into her nightgown.

"It is a woman's lot in life," the maid said, rambling on about duty and femininity as she gathered Lily's soiled clothing.

Not her lot, surely, Lily thought. She would not have it. She let her mind wander, her thoughts consumed by the dangerous game she was playing and the dangerous man who had become her cohort. Their interactions this night had been fraught with peril and excitement, and she had never felt more alive, but beneath it all lay something far more troubling—a connection that threatened to consume them both. As much as she tried to deny it, she couldn't escape the pull Lord Barton held over her.

"Shall I brush your hair?" the maid asked.

Lily shook her head. "I'll do it," she said. "That will be all, Maggie. Thank you."

When the maid had left, Lily bolted the door. Lord Barton—Reginald—was so charming and honorable. He made her feel cherished. She paused in the brushing as she thought of him.

"OH! DAMN HIS CHARM AND CHIVALRY," she muttered, her fingers absently braiding her hair. "Curse his audacity. He has no place in this treacherous game," she whispered fiercely, her heart pounding in her chest at the memory of his touch. "He has no place in my life. I cannot let him distract me from my purpose. Not now. Not ever."

But deep down, she knew that it was already too late for such resolutions. Despite her best efforts to maintain her composure, she felt herself being drawn inexorably towards Lord Barton no matter how dangerous that attraction might be to her autonomy. One thing was increasingly clear as she considered the events of the evening: the stakes had never been higher, for their country or for each of them personally, and neither of them could afford to falter.

She fluffed her pillow trying to get comfortable. She picked at the fine embroidery on the pillowcase. She stared at the ceiling. The shadows cast by the flickering candlelight seemed to taunt her with their silent accusations. She knew she couldn't continue down this path forever—something had to give. But for now, all she could do was hold her secrets close and pray that her actions would not lead to disaster.

Perhaps on the morrow, Lord Barton would have some insights. Tomorrow she would speak with Reginald and his sister Patience. Perhaps together they could find a solution, one that freed Bonaparte and didn't involve her marrying the odious Lord Rumford.

She had to retain her freedom, no matter what the cost. She would not, could not, succumb to a marriage like her mother had, a marriage that diminished her into the shadow woman she now was. She feared her attraction to Lord Barton, and yet she could not deny that she was looking forward to the visit with him in more ways than one. She blew out the candle and for a moment blinked at the darkness.

The room seemed to close in on her, trapping her within its confines. She swore under her breath and tried to order her troubled thoughts, which were swirling like a whirlwind around her. She rolled over, hugging her pillow, and tried to find rest, but her mind would not still. It was determined to process everything that had transpired this evening. From the life and death stakes of the Bonapartist meeting to Lord Rumford's petty advances, her life felt like a never-ending maze of danger and deception. And Lord Barton—dear, maddening Reginald—was at the center of it all, caught between his duty and… what? His desire? Did he desire her? And did it matter?

"Can I truly trust him?" Lily wondered, clenching her fists as her mind raced with uncertainty. "Or will he betray me in the end? As all men do in their own selfish endeavors?"

# PART III

# DOUBT AND DECEIT

*R*eginald paced the length of his study, the flickering candlelight casting shadows on the walls. He had removed his jacket and waistcoat. His shirt—due in no small part to the anxiety of the evening, as well as the summer heat—clung to his chest. His cravat was tossed across one of the wingback chairs beside the other clothing. He knew he had to maintain his cover as a loyal Bonapartist in order to protect Lady Lillian and gather enough information to bring down Montgomery and Spencer.

It was a delicate balance, one that would require both cunning and an understanding of the political landscape. Normally, he was up to the task, but Lady Lillian, his Lily, added a new variable he thought, as he restlessly paced his study, the image of Lily's fiery dark gaze seared into his memory. More than anything, he needed Lily's assistance to make it work.

He wanted to be able to send her home, or barring

that, send her to Samuel or Jack's ship for safekeeping, but that no longer seemed the best way forward. Doing so would wreck the mission and alert the Bonapartists. She was too much a part of the conspiracy. Dear God, how had that happened?

Opening a hidden compartment in his desk, he replaced his pistol in its box and retrieved a small book filled with notes and details about the Bonapartists. He began to study it, at last putting names and faces to the words written on the page. He went over the information he had learned by heart—the key players within the group, their goals and methods, and any recent developments.

As much as he disagreed with their cause, he had to immerse himself in their world to play his part convincingly, and moreso, to convince Lady Lillian to play her part. He wanted desperately to send her safely home, but that was no longer an option. For better or for worse, when she spoke in his defense, she had tied her fate with his. For better or for worse, he thought, thinking the words were apropos. She had unwittingly agreed to this marriage, this partnership of risk and danger.

His own life had many times been at risk, and the other patriots who worked with him and the Crown may have also been in danger, but nothing in his past compared to what he had to do in the next few hours, days, or weeks. Never had his actions held such import. Nothing had so unnerved him as the realization that she was in danger, and although he turned the matter over and over in his mind, he knew he could do nothing to lessen that fact. He had studied the situation in the hopes of finding a different plan, a new option that might keep her safe. There was none. They were in this together and must let it play out no matter the consequences. His mouth felt dry with fear for her.

He considered what he should tell her and what would mitigate the danger. He knew that he had crossed a line by attending the meeting, but he had hoped that she had followed his advice and stayed home. Still, if she had stayed home, what would have happened this evening? Perhaps he would have been killed. Perhaps the Crown forces would have rushed the traitorous group and killed the ringleaders.

For a moment tonight, he had considered calling out, yelling for the reinforcements who waited. But how would he have saved her, if not from death itself, from being branded a traitor? Bullets could go astray, but even if she had survived the evening, how would she survive the aftermath? In that moment, when he weighed the consequences, she surprised him and came to his rescue like a fiery chariot.

The thought of her being involved with such dangerous men drove him to distraction. And now, he found himself torn between his duty to his country and the undeniable connection that had formed between them. He had to convince her to the side of the Crown, but even as he thought of this, he knew it would not be an easy task.

Why was the woman so stubborn? Why Bonaparte? The man was a demon. How could she side with him? Or was it the people? What difference could a few of the unwashed masses really mean to her? They died every day from one malady or another. No matter how diligent one was, you could not save them all, nor in truth did he want to.

"DAMNATION," he muttered, running a hand through his disheveled hair. Why must everything be so devilishly complicated? He couldn't deny the surge of protectiveness that had washed over him when he saw her in that dimly lit room—her slender form standing out like a beacon in the darkness. But he also knew that he had placed her in even greater danger by doing his duty to the Crown and involving himself in the meeting, and the weight of that responsibility weighed heavily on his conscience. His personal choices should not matter, but they did. He was a man of the Crown, but first, he was a man.

"PERHAPS I CAN USE this to our advantage," he mused, his mind racing with possibilities as he tried to come up with a plan for their meeting on the morrow. If he could just convince Lily to work with him, they could bring Montgomery and Spencer to justice without jeopardizing their own safety. But first, he needed to make her see the truth about the Bonapartists and find a way to earn her trust—a task that seemed more daunting than any mission he'd ever faced.

"Heaven help me," Reginald muttered, his resolve hardening with each passing moment. "I will protect her, even if it costs me everything."

As the shadows deepened, Reginald found his bed. He was no further towards a decision, but he was determined to stay true to his honor as it concerned his country and the lovely Lady Lillian. He also knew he was on the brink of a precipice—a point of no return that would change both their lives forever. He could only hope that change was not a disaster.

LILY AWOKE the next morning feeling refreshed and determined. As she brushed her hair, there was a knock at her door.

"Come in," she called, expecting her maid.

Instead, the footman Angley paused at her door. "Pardon me, milady, but your grandfather insists on seeing you."

Lily sighed. No doubt the old man wanted to chastise her further for last night's escapade. "Very well. Please inform my grandfather I will be down shortly."

Angley hesitated. "There is one other thing, milady. Your grandfather has been advised that you arrived home in a carriage last night. He knows you were out with someone."

Lily froze. So, the cat was truly out of the bag. Her mind raced, trying to think of some plausible explanation, but nothing came.

She tried out her most demure attitude. "I... I don't know what you mean," she stammered. "I went for a walk to clear my head and got lost. I caught a public carriage home."

Even to her own ears, the excuse sounded feeble.

Angley gave her a knowing look. "You best come up

with a better tale than that for his lordship, milady, or there'll be the devil to pay."

With that ominous warning, he took his leave. Lily's thoughts chased each other in panicked circles as she finished dressing. What was she going to tell her grandfather? The truth was out of the question. She'd just have to brazen it out as best she could.

Squaring her shoulders, Lily headed downstairs to face the inquisition. She could only pray her quick wits would find a way to satisfy her grandfather's questions without revealing too much about her actual whereabouts. The game was afoot.

Lily descended the grand staircase, each step feeling like she was approaching the gallows. Her stomach churned with anxiety.

She paused outside the breakfast room door, taking a deep breath to steel her nerves before entering.

Her grandfather sat at the head of the long mahogany table, silver hair gleaming in the morning light. He peered at her over his teacup. No one else sat with him, which did not bode well. It meant that everyone had fled his ire this morning.

"Good morning, Grandfather," Lily said brightly, hoping her cheer sounded natural.

"Hmph. What's good about it?" He stabbed his fork into a sausage with unnecessary force. "Now, in the light of day, the time for mendacity is past. Perhaps you can enlighten me as to where you were gallivanting about last night?"

Lily busied herself preparing a plate from the sideboard, avoiding his shrewd gaze. "I've already told you; I simply went for a walk to clear my head."

"Do not take me for a fool, girl!" her grandfather thundered, banging his fist on the table. The dishes rattled, and the servants cowered. "You think I don't know when my own granddaughter is lying to me?"

Lily winced, nearly dropping her teacup. This was not going well at all. Time for a different tactic.

"Very well. I was not planning to go far," she said carefully. "I was thinking and went further than I had planned. I did not wish to worry you over a small matter. I'm sorry for deceiving you."

Her grandfather's eyes bored into her. "Who were you with? I'll have a name."

Lily's thoughts raced wildly. She couldn't give Reginald's name; that would only lead to more questions. Inspiration struck.

"Lord Spencer," she blurted out. "And his mother. They were coming home from some gala, and we... we met by chance, and they were kind enough to see me home safely."

It was a risky gamble, but she knew her grandfather approved of the handsome lord. Surely, he wouldn't suspect she was truly out with Spencer plotting treason.

Her grandfather studied her a moment longer before giving a curt nod.

"Next time you go haring off, you will inform me first," he growled. "No more sneaking about like a thief in the night." And you will take your sister with you." His eyes narrowed. "Do not cross me."

"Yes, Grandfather," Lily murmured demurely, relief flooding through her. Crisis averted, for now at least. How she was going to take her sister with her was another hurdle that must be crossed, but that would be a future problem.

As she sipped her tea, Lily pondered how to handle her meddlesome grandfather in the upcoming days. The stakes were getting higher, and she would need to take greater care. For the sake of the cause, she could not afford to trip up again.

# SISTERS, SECRETS AND SURPRISES

*L*ily attempted to escape without Grace, but that was not to be. She clenched her fists as her grandfather, the Earl of Thornwood, delivered his decree. "From now on, you will take your sister Grace with you every time you leave your room," he commanded, his voice cold and unyielding.

"Grandfather, this is not fair to Grace!" Lily protested, her dark eyes flashing with anger and regret. She had hoped to keep her innocent younger sister out of the dangerous web in which she found herself. How could she continue attending meetings with the Bonapartists now?

A part of her wondered if revealing that Lord Barton's carriage would be arriving soon would somehow extricate her from the situation with Lord Rumford. However, she didn't want to marry at all, and involving Lord Barton would only complicate matters further. Grandfather would question Lord Barton about his intensions, and it was best that her family thought she was visiting with Lady Patience instead of her brother. She could only hope that Grace would keep her secrets and that Lady Patience would understand. This tangle was becoming unmanageable.

As much as she despised admitting it, even to herself, Lily harbored a strange affection for Lord Barton, despite his brusque manner. There was something about him—an underlying sense of honor, perhaps —that intrigued her, as well as the physical attraction that she was determined to fight.

"Enough, Lily," her grandfather snapped, ending any further discussion. With a frustrated sigh, Lily acquiesced, knowing better than to challenge him further.

Later, the sisters climbed into Lord Barton's carriage, Grace's innocent excitement a stark contrast to Lily's stormy demeanor. As soon as they were alone in the carriage, Lily divulged the details of their predicament to Lord Barton. His expression grew serious.

"I expected that you would be accompanied. By your maid or your sister," he said, smiling at Grace. "As much as you manage to find yourself alone in the most compromising predicaments, I could not think that was with your family's approval."

"No," she agreed, smoothing her dress and looking straight forward. She was not sure how this meeting would go, but she hoped that she and Lord Barton could formulate a plan. How they would do that with Grace in their company was going to be difficult unless she was willing to divulge the entirety to her sister.

Lord Barton continued. "So, as I told you, we will go to my sister's home. We will tell Patience and her husband—"

"Wait. Wait. Wait." Lily said, unhappy with the idea of involving more people in their dangerous mission. Nevertheless, Lord Barton directed the carriage toward his sister's house, determined to follow through with his plan.

"Tell her what?" Grace piped up, and they both grew quiet, unwilling to embroil Grace in the dilemma.

"How much does your sister know about your nocturnal activities?" Lord Barton inquired.

"A little," Lily said enigmatically.

"I know she goes to meetings for women to have more freedom. I don't really know much more about it," Grace said. "Only that I worry about her going out so late at night. I'm glad that you are here Lord Barton, and perhaps can act as her protector."

"I don't need a protector," Lily snapped, but she could not meet Lord Barton's eyes over her sister's head. She knew she had not told Grace the whole truth, and now Lord Barton knew too. She felt the warmth of a blush filling her face. How much would she be forced to divulge now, and how would Grace act when she found out the truth? It was one thing for her sister to keep her comings and goings secret when Grace thought they were meetings of other women and quite another to learn what Lily was actually doing.

Lord Barton said nothing, but Lily could almost hear his thoughts berating her for her blatant lies to her sister.

After a few minutes, Lily voiced her question. "Are you certain it's wise to involve your sister and her husband in this? I would not wish to endanger—" She broke off aware of her sister's presence.

Grace frowned.

"Prudence and Percy are loyal to England above all else," Lord Barton replied, his voice filled with conviction. "Their desire for justice is as strong as our own."

Grace looked from one to the other in confusion. Lily supposed that she must be told something, but for the life of her, she couldn't imagine how to broach the topic.

Momentarily, they arrived at the grand residence of Lord Percival Beresford, the eldest son of the Earl of Blackburn, Lord Barton's friend and husband to his sister, Patience. As they departed from the carriage, Lord Barton held onto Lily a moment longer than necessary, the warmth of his touch sending a shiver down her spine. She wanted to lean into him, but she did not. She would not be made weak.

The edifice loomed large, and Grace commented upon the architecture, but Lily was silent, wondering how and what they would explain to Grace to keep her from telling Grandfather the whole plot, and how they would continue to attend the Bonepart meetings together when it was clear to Lily that Lord Barton was no friend of Boneparte.

Upon entering the home, Lily paused. The foyer was decorated with a mixture of gold and white, light oak and silk, polished and shining. An ornate crystal chandelier hung from the center of the ceiling, and brocade draperies were pulled back from the large windows. Wood carvings scattered the walls, and a golden trim lined the beams and moldings. Artwork depicting the Beresford family hung throughout the room. The house was the epitome of aristocratic opulence.

"Lady Beresford is in the drawing room," the butler announced.

Lord Barton nodded his thanks and led the way.

Fine paintings in gilded frames were hung on the walls along the corridor, depicting scenes of the country-side. Lily could not help but think that, just like her own home, the paintings alone could have fed a village.

The butler opened the door to the drawing room, a room full of fine furniture with rich, sturdy wood positioned about the room in a way that invited conversation. The Persian carpets beneath felt soft and luxurious even through Lily's slippers. The floor-to-ceiling windows were thrown wide open, allowing in a slight summer breeze.

A lady with bright red hair, who must be Lord Barton's married sister, Lady Beresford, laid aside her embroidery, and stood to greet them. "Regge," she said pleasantly, and then turned to Lily and Grace. "You must be the Hawthorne ladies my brother has been speaking so highly of," she said brightly, welcoming them to the room. She glanced towards the door where the butler still stood. "Have some tea brought to the drawing room," she said. "I told Molly to keep the kettle hot."

The butler nodded. "Very good, my lady," he said. "Will his lordship be joining you?"

"In due time," she answered.

Outside, Lily could hear bits of conversation from the gardeners, the occasional bird chirping, and footsteps echoing down the hall, no doubt the steps of servants. The large edifice must have many, but at present, the meeting was private.

Once the butler vacated the room, Lord Barton turned to his sister. "Percy is not at home?" he asked.

"No," she said. "His brother, Samuel, had some issue that needed his brother's expertise," she said, "But he should be home directly, and Lady Amelia has come for a visit."

A beautiful woman with silver blonde hair and blue eyes laid aside her needlepoint to acknowledge the newcomers.

"This is my dear friend, Lady Amelia," Lady Beresford said. "She is married to my husband's younger brother, Captain Samuel Beresford, but we were like sisters long before we made the relationship official. I trust her implicitly."

As introductions were made, Lily thought that this was entirely too many people to know about their business. Nonetheless, Lord Barton took it all in stride.

As they sat together in the elegant drawing room, Lily fretted, uncomfortable even in the opulence that should have been the epitome of luxury. The velvet fabric of the seats caressed the skin, the smooth swirls of honeyed oak and the fine weave of the tapestries all gave evidence of safety, and yet Lily did not feel safe. She clenched her hands on her lap.

Instead of keeping their secrets, Lord Barton launched right into a discussion of what had happened the previous night. Lily had to be grateful that he did not share all of the dangers, but nonetheless, Grace gave a small gasp, and her dark eyes went wide with horror. Lily knew that she would have to do damage control before they got back home, or Grace would not be able to keep her mouth shut, and Grandfather would know all. She wondered if that had been Lord Barton's plan all along, to out her to her grandfather.

There was a moment of silence as a footman brought tea and cakes, but then the conversation went right back to the Bonapartists, each of her hosts wondering how anyone could turncoat on their gracious monarch and the jovial Regent. Mentally, Lily replaced their officious words with 'mad monarch' and 'spendthrift son.'

As the day progressed, Lady Amelia shared a story of traitors causing her father's death, which resonated deeply with Lily. For all that her grandfather held her captive, her father was a sweet man when not guided by his father, and Lily loved him dearly. She loved all of her family, even when she did not agree with them. She could not imagine life without her father. "And then, of course, the blackguards kidnapped my friend," Amelia added.

"How awful," Grace interjected. "I have heard tell of ladies kidnapped for ransom," she ventured, and Lily wondered when and where she heard such a thing. She had thought her younger sister was perpetually sheltered from such things. "I, for one, am eternally grateful that Wellington has at last put an end to all that nonsense," Grace added.

Only Grace would call the greatest battle of the war nonsense. "But I do not see how you are involved in all this, Lily?" Her voice rose on a question, and Lily knew she had to answer, but she had no words.

Lord Barton broke in then with some hesitancy. "Lady Lillian has been a great help in infiltrating a group of second sons," he said.

"May they all burn in hell." Amelia spoke with vehemence, and Grace opened her eyes wide.

"Sorry," said Amelia, her hand going to her stomach unconsciously. "I suppose my language has suffered somewhat being married to a sailor." Her face softened at the thought of her husband.

"No one can blame you," Lady Patience said. "Not after what happened to your father."

Amelia smiled, a humorless turning of her lips, and Lord Barton continued. "Anyway, I may have been lost if Lady Lillian had not vouched for me, at her own peril."

"Oh, Regge!" exclaimed Lady Patience. Grace's eyes were wide as saucers. Lily did not like the way this conversation was going at all, but like a runaway stallion, it just seemed to barrel onwards. Lily imagined the upcoming cliff.

"Anyway, it is best you do not know the details, sister dear," Lord Barton said, including Grace in his look and then turning back to his own sister. "But we need your help, Patience. Lady Lillian does not want her grandfather to know the particulars, but he has become suspicious of her travels and is restricting her movements, most especially in requiring her sister, Lady Grace, to accompany her. Obviously, we do not want to put Lady Grace in danger."

"Oh," Lady Patience broke in, obviously seeing the problem. "Lady Grace must stay here with me," she said.

"That would be a great help," Lord Barton said. "Obviously, I trust your discretion in this, Patience."

"Lily, I don't like this," Grace added in a worried tone.

"Unfortunately, the mission has gone beyond what any of us can alter now," Lord Barton said, directing his serious gaze to Grace.

"Perhaps the ladies, Lillian and Grace, should visit more often," Lady Amelia added, and Lady Patience nodded. She suggested the same, hoping to ease the worries about her grandfather's demands. "I will write a letter to your mother," she said. "That way, your grandfather won't constantly worry about your whereabouts. It is perfectly acceptable for you and your sister to visit a married lady."

Lily hesitated, her thoughts racing. She appreciated the offer but knew that her grandfather would never relent so easily. He would have questions, and she wasn't sure that Grace could navigate those troubled waters. Nevertheless, she nodded slowly, agreeing to consider the idea.

"Thank you, Lady Patience," she murmured.

"Regge, should we invite them to stay now? Several days perhaps."

"That might be wise," Lord Barton said. "And now, we must make plans." Lord Barton stood and offered his hand to Lily. With a quick glance at her sister, Lily stood to accompany Lord Barton.

Her mind was racing at the thought of staying the night with Lord Barton's sister and her husband, if not tonight, then in the near future. Things had moved so swiftly, but it was after all, essential that she and Lord Barton speak in private to make plans for the next meeting of the Bonapartists. They could not think all would go well proceeding willy-nilly as they had on yestereve. She hesitated, uncertain how she could stop the runaway progress of this plan.

"Lord Barton is the most justice-minded man I know," Lady Amelia said, her eyes shining with admiration. "With exception, of course, of my Samuel." Lily couldn't help but feel her anger towards Lord Barton's involvement dissipate as she listened to Amelia's praise as the young woman soothed Grace's worries. Lily knew she would have to offer some additional information to her sister, but for now, Grace seemed satisfied by Lady Amelia and Lady Patience's words. They were so very proper as they sipped tea amidst the turmoil.

"Shall we?" Lord Barton asked, and Lily was hard pressed to disagree. They did need to make plans for the next Bonaparte meeting, and she certainly did not want Grace to be privy to the details.

Later, as they took Lord Barton's carriage home to Hawthorne house, Grace turned to the man himself, her eyes serious. "Lord Barton," she said, "ladies Amelia and Patience spoke of your honor and bravery, but Lady Patience is your sister. She must speak so of a brother she loves. I do not know you, and you are asking me to keep silent and allow my sister to accompany you, and—"

"No one is *allowing me*," Lily interrupted.

"Please, Lily," Grace said in her soft yet unyielding voice. She turned back to Lord Barton. "If I am not mistaken, there is some danger."

"There is," he agreed.

Grace sucked in a slow breath. "I ask something then, to keep my silence."

"Grace…" Lily began. She certainly did not want her

sister matchmaking her with this gentleman. Things were complicated enough already.

"Name it," said Lord Barton.

"I ask that you keep her safe, Lord Barton," Grace said. "I will have your promise as a gentleman of honor."

"I will protect her with my life," Lord Barton promised.

"I am my own person," Lily objected. "I do not need—"

"She may not like it," Grace interrupted.

"I'm sure she won't," Lord Barton said, grinning at Lily, who glared back at him.

"But I expect you to keep your promise."

"I shall," he said, holding out a hand to Grace and shaking it as if they had made a gentleman's agreement.

The carriage stopped in front of Hawthorne House. "If you two are done ordering my life," Lily said. "We have arrived home."

Lily controlled the desire to leap from the carriage. That would likely only land her on her face in the street. Instead, with all the dignity she could muster, she took Lord Barton's aid. He walked them to the door, and Grace invited him in, which meant that Grandfather would quiz him on his politics and his intentions. So be it, thought Lily. He was a grown man. She would not try to shield him from Grandfather's interrogation.

She picked up her needlework and acted the lady while Grandfather cloistered Lord Barton in his study.

When the inquisition was over and the ladies had gone to their own rooms, Grace said to Lily. "You could do worse than Lord Barton, you know."

Lily was sure that Lord Barton had answered all of Grandfather's questions without giving up a smidge of real information. As far as Grandfather was concerned, they were just visiting Lady Patience, and yet, Lily thought, Grandfather was probably weighing Lord Barton against Lord Rumford as a marriage prospect.

"We are visiting Lady Patience," Lily said firmly. "Not Lord Barton."

Grace smiled a knowing smile. "There is only one reason a man swears to protect a woman with his life, Lily. He wants to keep her by his side."

The thought made Lily's heart sing. "Nonsense," she said.

# FORGING FORWARD

*T*he next day, Reginald stood by the window, watching as a carriage bearing his Lily approached his home. He scowled at the sunshine.

"Come and sit, Regge," said Patience. "Your glowering will not change the situation."

The sun cast long shadows across the manicured lawn, providing a stark contrast between the beauty of the day and the tension he felt in his chest.

"My Lord… Lady," said a footman who nodded to both Reginald and Patience. "Lady Lillian Hawthorne and her sister Lady Grace Hawthorne have arrived for their visit," he announced.

"Grace, again," muttered Reginald thinking this was an unwelcome addition to the pot of stew. He had hoped that Lily would be able to visit his sister alone, which would allow them more freedom to talk, but there was no help for it. He had impressed upon her grandfather that his sister would be present, obviously, since Lily was visiting her house, but apparently Lord Thornwood was unconvinced.

"Do bring them in," Patience said as she cast a glance at her brother. The footman bowed, and a moment later, he ushered the women into the drawing room where Reginald and Patience were waiting. Another footman appeared to carry their belongings to the rooms they would use while visiting.

"Lady Lillian, Lady Grace," Reginald greeted the women formally, rising to his feet. Lily's sister's presence made any discussion that much more difficult but not impossible.

An awkward pause descended as Lily and Reginald regarded each other warily across the room. Patience glanced between them, then tactfully addressed Grace. "I am so happy to have you visit," she said.

"Thank you for inviting us," Grace, ever cordial, said.

Silence ensued.

Reginald looked at Grace. "How much do you know about—" Reginald began.

"Nothing," Lily interrupted.

"Well," said Patience as she laid aside her embroidery and addressed the ladies, most particularly Lady Grace. "I would love to show you our garden. Shall we go for a walk? I'll have the staff bring us tea outside. Perhaps there will be a bit of a breeze." She nodded towards the footman who had remained at the door to be available. Patience came forward and linked arms with Grace, allowing Reginald to hang back to speak with Lily. Bless you, dear sister, he thought.

"Shall we give my brother and your sister a bit of

privacy?" she whispered conspiratorially to Grace, and he had to smile. No doubt Grace would assume that he and Lily were romantically involved, especially after his long talk with her grandfather. In the long run, that was not a bad thing for her sister to assume.

Reginald smiled at Lily, who was wearing her perpetual frown. He longed to see a smile on her face. He wanted to fill her life with happiness. She seemed to have already been subjected to enough gloom for a lifetime.

Grace glanced at her sister, but Lady Patience was surprisingly forceful as she led her into the garden. "We have quite a growth of lavender," she confided. "It helps with sleep. Did you know?"

"It does have a soothing scent," Lady Grace agreed.

Reginald held out an arm to Lily, and she somewhat reluctantly took it. They followed Patience and Grace at a distance. "I'm sorry," she said as Patience and Grace pulled ahead of them. "My grandfather insisted that I may not go out alone."

"Well, I must say, the man has finally come to his senses." Reginald couldn't help himself. "The truth is, you should not have been out alone in the first place! You are a woman and ought to be safe at home, tending to more suitable activities than conspiring with..."

Lily yanked her arm from his grasp. "Suitable?" Lily scoffed, her voice rising in pitch. "I am no fragile flower, Lord Reginald, and I will not be relegated to embroidery while men like you decide matters that affect us all. Decide badly, I might add."

His eyes were twinkling, and he was fighting a smile.

If finally dawned on her that he was baiting her. "I do not appreciate your humor, Lord Barton," she said stiffly, drawing in a sharp breath and the smell of lavender and summer roses. It was quite different from the smell of filth and squalor in the lower town. It was actually quite lovely considering that the unfavorable scent of town rose precipitously as the heat bore down upon it. The small town garden was very welcome indeed.

Reginald rubbed a hand over his face and finally said, "I only meant I expected such a development before this, considering what I know of your grandfather. But now, I'm afraid you will not be able to give up your excursions without causing a great deal of difficulty, so we needed to give your grandfather reason to allow you that freedom."

Stepping forward with an air of calm authority, he took her arm again and placed it most firmly on the crook of his elbow. It felt good there. "Your visit here allows that. We are both aware of the danger this situation presents, and arguing will not help us find a solution. Regardless of our individual beliefs, we must find some common ground here. Let us walk."

Lily looked up at him, her dark brows furrowed, but eventually, her expression softened slightly. They both knew they had to work together if they were to navigate the treacherous path ahead.

"Very well," she conceded, taking a deep breath. "But you must admit your actions last night were rash."

"I had hoped you would heed my advice and stay home," he said as he led her along the path.

"I told you I would not."

He nodded. "So you did. I should have listened to you."

Surprise rushed across her face, and she paused.

She was very easy to read, he thought. All the more reason why he had to be careful what he told her. Still, he had to tell her something. "Perhaps it is time we learn to trust one another," suggested Reginald. "I think we both want the same thing: to protect our country and expose those who would see it fall."

"You work for the Crown," she accused.

"I do."

"And you want to imprison Napoleon Bonaparte."

"I do," Reginald agreed. "And I need your help."

Lily stood shaking her head emphatically. "No. I believe in his cause. He deserves his freedom. He only wanted to help the people. That is a noble cause."

Reginald paused, his hazel eyes meeting hers with a newfound determination. He did not agree with some of the aristocracy who felt the man was literally the antichrist, but he did note that Boneparte did nothing but wreak havoc. Still, Reginald held his tongue. He had not arrived at this place in life and with the Crown by having a loose tongue or by being foolhardy. "Perhaps," he said. "Perhaps his cause is even just, but it is too late for him, and the cause of the brigands at the meetings you attend is not so noble as Bonaparte's."

"You think his ends noble?" she asked, confused.

"No."

"But then—"

"If he had stayed in France alone, perhaps," Reginald said rubbing a hand over his face.

"England financed Louis," she snapped.

205

"True," he agreed.

"They had no right!"

They had every right, Reginald thought. Louis was the King. Keeping peace in France protected England, he could argue. Bonaparte was quite frankly a despot intent upon conquering the continent with eyes to England next, but arguing would not gain him the direction he wanted.

Instead, Reginald held up a hand. "But let us not argue about the past. Let us go forth together for the future. Perhaps we can find common ground. I hope that together we can find the evidence needed to bring Montgomery and Spencer to justice for the crime of treason. But we must tread carefully, for any misstep could prove disastrous. We could both lose our lives."

"Treason? You think it is treason then that they speak out against injustice?" She shook her head violently. "No!"

He could see she would not agree with this. How to proceed to make her see sense…

"They are not speaking out against injustice. They are speaking out against the King and the Regent. By definition, that is treason."

"Bonaparte only wanted what was best for the people," Lily argued. "In America—"

"We are NOT in America," he interrupted, losing patience. He didn't give a damn about what happened in America. He cared about England. "But perhaps," he continued more softly. "Perhaps if Bonaparte had stayed in France, France alone would have had the need to decide what should be done, given their national sovereignty," he said. "But when he took money from other nations, when he *invaded* other nations, when he attacked other sovereign lands, he gave up the right to be called a savior to the people and became a conqueror. I —and the Crown—will not allow him to conquer England."

"But England supported Louis."

"He is the King," Reginald added in a remarkably even voice all the while thinking that there were those in government who funded both sides of the revolution, hedging their bets on human life and profiting from the war. Her dear friend, Lord Spencer, was one of those. Reginald thought the practice was reprehensible, perhaps even moreso than the bloodshed perpetrated by Bonaparte or the rabid populous in France. He did not voice this fact, however. He wanted to keep Lily on track to support his ends with the Bonapartists, and if he muddied the waters, she would be more sure than ever all aristocrats were demons. Instead, he commented on the situation in France. "Changing the government by beheading the royals is not a choice the people should have made if they wanted the world to respect them."

"The people screamed for bread while the rich had lavish parties, and the Austrian…" She closed her mouth over the hot retort. He could see the tenseness of her shoulders as if she bore the weight of the world. "The queen," she began again, "is rumored to have said 'let them eat cake.' Either she was cruel or daft. Either way, she should not have treated them so. The French people did not need the world's respect. They had fear."

"Exactly," Reginald said. "The world feared them, like one might fear a thief in the night. Is fear a way to effect change?"

"But do you truly think that there is another way to effect change?" she asked. "Who listens to the cries of the poor?"

"Certainly not men like Spencer. He's voted against the bill that would broaden the vote in Commons for men of property."

"He—what?" Lily frowned.

"He is speaking of freedom to the Bonapartists while collecting bribes from the French, all the while voting in congress against the very legislation which would allow those not born to the aristocracy to have more say in the government. This is the type of man you are following. His sins are egregious. He has no honor. He takes from the very people he proposes to help."

Lily sank down on one of the garden benches. "I... didn't know," she said.

"How could you know?" Reginald asked. "Women are generally not included in such discussions of politics."

"And that is the problem."

"I agree," Reginald said. "I think women, if they were taught and understood the intricacies of the government, would lend a softer more moderate opinion, but we are far from allowing women to vote. Too many think it is radical. That women would vote with their hearts instead of their heads."

"Perhaps they should," she muttered. "We need more heart in government, more kindness, more equity."

"Nonetheless, it will not be discussed."

She sighed, disheartened.

"Not yet," Reginald continued laying a hand on her

arm. "But men of wealth instead of simply men of property—"

Lily was stuck on what he had said earlier. "Women voting? You have thought about this? You think it is possible?"

"I have," he agreed. "And I do, but not in our generation. Perhaps our children or grandchildren."

The words brought a flush to her cheeks, but he continued unabated. "But I think the vote will go for common men first. It's been brought up in Parliament. As you might expect, your grandfather is violently opposed."

"And you? Are you opposed?" Lily raised an eyebrow and turned bright eyes to him. She was listening now. Truly listening.

He tried to talk with her like an equal, a rare thing indeed for a man to do, and yet it felt right. He found he liked speaking to her in such a way. It was freeing not to have to mince words or dumb down his thoughts for a woman who was uneducated, not by her own volition, but nonetheless, uninformed. "Not entirely," he said. "I do think people who vote must be taught. We can't give the vote to all willy-nilly. The poor will vote for anyone who gives them a loaf of bread, which means votes could be bought."

She nodded. "Like in France. The reign of terror might have been avoided with bread that cost the aristocracy pennies." She paused in thought. "But votes are always bought. Isn't that already happening in the rotten boroughs?" she asked.

He had somehow not expected her to be so well informed about politics, but she continued to surprise him. She only nodded at her own words and continued. "They spoke of education in the Colonies," she added.

"In such a barbaric land?" He was surprised.

"Yes. They said it was the prime focus of reading— that is teaching the people to read."

Not reading the Bible, Reginald thought. Well, that didn't bode well for the Colonies, he was sure. A moral compass was an integral part of the good of humanity.

Lady Lillian closed her eyes, remembering what she had read, and then recited apparently by rote. "In the Colony of Massa—Massachusetts, a law was made to have schools to make certain their charges could read and understand the principles of religion and the laws of the Commonwealth." She continued, reciting some of the laws the colonists had enacted.

Reginald was impressed. He knew of few men with such recall and those practiced for years to perfect the art. Many were known for their skill in espionage since they could memorize plans at a single glance.

"Laws of the Commonwealth," Reginald repeated. "So, they intend to educate the masses?"

She nodded. "It fell short of funding though," she added. "So, I doubt there will be immediate change, but the Colonies—the Americas," she corrected, "Are not hamstrung with antiquated notions of aristocracy and Divine Right."

"Perhaps not," he said. "But they are like every nation, I think, hamstrung by greed. Consider, do you not think they could have found the money to build schools if they really wanted to do so? Instead, I'm sure the gold lined greedy men's pockets."

"I suppose so," she said thoughtfully. "So, can it be

fixed, do you suppose, or will greed always ruin it?"

"*Greed is* one of the seven deadly sins," Reginald said. "I don't think it will disappear on the morrow, but as long as good men—"

"And women," she added.

"And women," he repeated, "do their part to oust the ones intent upon evil, I think God will take care of our country. I think eventually, the aristocracy in England will have to bend, but I promise you, Lady Lillian, it can be done without courting treason."

"What do you mean?" she asked.

"Change is coming," Reginald said.

He paused to gather his thoughts. He wanted to shout praise to God. She was actually listening to him instead of just berating his ideas. It seemed strange that a woman who was so angered by men silencing her was so prone to silencing others—disinclined to listen to others —and yet it was clear that was what she herself had been taught. She could not be blamed for that.

Perhaps if he had asked Patience to put forth these thoughts, they would have had more appeal. Lady Lillian seemed to distrust him, and perhaps all men on sight, but considering who her grandfather was, he could understand her hesitancy. The man was a tyrant, and his grandson was not much different. Perhaps, since that was what she saw, she knew of nothing else. But she was intelligent. He hoped his explanation would help her to see that he was not her enemy, but instead, men like Spencer who found truth an anathema would betray her trust and the trust of the people he urged to support him.

"Since the printing press and the jacquard loom," he continued, "it is clear change is coming. Men are

211

moving their families to the city for work, and with that, they are not tied to the land. The productivity of the land is changing. It is not only landowners who will hold the purse strings. Merchants and tradesmen are becoming more prominent too, due to the money made in trade with the new machines. It will soon be impossible to keep them out of government. It is not the aristocracy that runs the country," he said. "Money runs the government."

"The root of all evil," she murmured.

"Ah, yes. The *love of money* is the root of all evil, but we can appeal to a person's better nature. And so, we must teach the merchants and tradesmen to understand the workings of government so they can take their part as honorable men."

"And women," Lily interrupted.

Reginald nodded. "And women," he agreed. "I know patience is hard, but things are changing, and to push change too fast only leads to war and bloodshed as people more stubbornly stick to their own agendas. It is putting the cart before the horse."

"Like in France," Lily said.

"And in the Colonies," said Reginald.

"I see that the French were hasty in their choice of bloodshed, but America? I see their point. They were not represented in Parliament."

Reginald was hesitant to say that most of the commons was not represented in Parliament, so he simply nodded, wondering where she would take the conversation.

"Do you think if King George had offered the colonists titles," she wondered aloud, "would it have made a difference? If they had representation in Parliament? That was their complaint, after all."

"Lud," he said stunned. "Like thirteen dukedoms?" He laughed aloud. "The colonists might have agreed, but Parliament certainly would not, and I can't imagine the King would either. Imagine raising commons to such a height."

"It's a thought I've been entertaining," she said, screwing up her face with concentration.

He chuckled again. "It takes an age to get anything done in Parliament now. Imagine if they had to send letters across an ocean for a quorum." He seemed to find the notion hilarious.

"I had no one to discuss it with," she added. "It seemed that the late King did not seriously consider their grievances."

It was on the tip of his tongue to say, *and why should he? He was the King,* but he did not. He did not point out that the colonists were his subjects, and it was the prerogative of a King to do as he wished. Instead, he said, "You can always discuss such things with me," he promised. "No matter how outlandish."

"I suppose such a thing could only be effected if we had much faster ships."

"With faster ships," Reginald surmised, "the greedy would just fill their pockets faster, and the wheels of government would still turn slowly for the common people."

"Like Spencer," she said.

"Yes."

"So, Spencer is on the take," she mused after a few moments. "I've always had a bad feeling about him."

"You have good instincts."

"What about Nesbit?" she asked. Reginald opened his mouth and closed it. The Baronet Nesbit was a whiny little man, but not even on his list of possible traitors. He had fallen below Reginald's purview."

"He's such a miserable man," Lady Lillian said. "But he seems to have come into a bit of money. He said his aunt died—"

That was something Reginald could check. Deaths were recorded in the parishes. He had found that following the money usually upended the traitors. He had ceased believing the words of their mouths, but he did believe the coin in their purse.

"Surely, some of the men who want to free Bonaparte want to free him for the sake of freedom itself," she added. "Should they be lumped together with those corrupt men taking bribes and selling freedom to the highest bidder?"

"Perhaps they shouldn't," Reginald agreed, "But when a man—or a woman," he added with a raised eyebrow, "goes against the Crown, there must be consequences. Without consequences, there would be anarchy."

"Then how do you suppose the Americas will manage it?" she wondered aloud.

"Oh, I think the whole experiment will fall apart in a few years. With the aristocracy, we have a chosen hierarchy. Without that, it will be a free-for-all. Watch and see. This common election they have will not work. Whoever pays the most bribes or has the most blackmail threats on his opponent will win and be their ruler. This vote they think they have will never be clean and fair. What leader they obtain from such an election will undoubtedly be a despot, an evil man paying for the privilege of rule. That is the nature of man. Didn't your own Napoleon say it matters not who votes, only who counts?"

"There are rumors that he did say that," Lily agreed. "But he did not say he would be the one counting. I do not think he is so corrupt. I think he believes in his vision even if others don't."

"Don't be naïve," Reginald said. "Station doesn't just hold the commons where they are. It is the same for aristocrats. Although there are some with honor, many I warrant; what holds some of the less honorable aristocrats at their station is that they can never *be King*. With the current situation of the mad king, think what might happen if all the dukes had a chance at the Crown. Well. I would not like the chances that our civilization would come through intact. Laws keep greedy men from being despots. Even bad laws executed by good people."

"I see your point. I don't like it, but I see it. It seems there are too few good people."

"Yes. When bad men combine, the good must associate, else they will fall, one by one, an unpitied sacrifice in a contemptible struggle," Reginald said quoting Edmund Burke. "In essence, all that is necessary for evil to triumph is for good men to do nothing. *Good people*," he corrected, and she smiled.

She had a lovely smile. He saw it way too rarely.

"Let us associate and forge ahead then," said Lily, extending her hand to Reginald like a gentleman. "As allies, if not friends, to root out the scoundrels in this group, but I will have your promise, Lord Barton." She held his hand tight.

"What promise is that?"

"That the men who are only seeking succor from their ills will be treated fairly by the Crown."

"I cannot speak for the Crown," he said, but she interrupted. "Of course, you can. Were you not at the very meeting *speaking* for the Crown?"

He supposed that was true. Reginald considered her hand, feeling the warmth of her fingers through her gloves, and he did not want to lie to her, but his stock in trade for his work for the Crown was steeped in lies. There would be little if anything he could do for any caught out as traitors. Perhaps he could argue for deportation instead of hanging, but even that was unlikely. He felt soiled as they shook hands. He knew he could not fulfill that promise, but he wanted to. Lord knew he wanted to give her the world she wished existed, no matter how fanciful it was.

And as he touched her, Reginald couldn't help but wonder if there was more than just anger and frustration that fueled the heat between them, but they had more than that passion at this moment. They had a pact to have each other's backs in the fray ahead. That much he could do. He may not be able to protect all of her friends, but he could protect her. "Very well," he agreed, releasing her hand. "But first, let us plan our next move. We cannot afford to make any more mistakes or have unplanned situations catch us unawares."

After nearly an hour of hashing out plans, Lily and Reginald rejoined Patience and Grace, who were having tea and discussing the latest fashions. Patience called for a fresh pot and looked up as they entered, her gaze darting between them. "Have you two come to an under-standing?" she asked delicately.

The tension in the room was palpable. "We have," Reginald said enigmatically, and Patience deftly changed the subject. They visited for several hours, talking about nothing more important than the weather, the fashions, and general gossip until it was time to retire.

Once back in their room, Grace turned on Lily, face aglow with excitement. "Well?" she demanded.

"Well, what?" Lily asked.

"Well, did he ask you to marry him?" she said, her voice filled with scorn. "What did you say?"

Lily blinked. She supposed she should have expected this reaction. She had no idea nor inclination of what to tell her sister about what transpired between her and Lord Barton. She retreated into her usual taciturn demeanor, and Grace eventually let the matter drop.

THE NEXT DAY, while Reginald took Lily for a carriage ride in Hyde Park, she told him about the conversation she had with her sister and what Grace had assumed.

He smiled bemusedly. So, she was thinking of marriage, he surmised. He nodded thoughtfully. "What did you tell her?" he finally asked.

"I told her you proposed," she said, throwing her hands aloft. "What else could I say?"

He chuckled. The thought struck him as funny. She seemed so out of sorts. He pressed his advantage. "And did you tell her your answer?" he asked.

"Of course not! She knows I do not want to marry."

"I see," he said. "Still, it might give us more cover."

"A false engagement?" she said.

Well, he thought, since as of yet, you do not want a real engagement. "As you wish."

"I don't wish an engagement at all," she said, confirming his belief. "False or otherwise." Nonetheless, her cheeks turned pink with the words, and her already mysteriously dark eyes turned dark as burning coals. He thought perhaps she was not as averse to the idea as she would have him believe.

TRUTHFULLY, Lily found that after her conversation with her sister, she had spent the night thinking about the possibility of being engaged to this man, but of course that was impossible. He was impossible.

Lily held up a hand to forestall Lord Barton. "Let's not rehash this. We have more important matters before us."

Reginald looked mildly surprised but nodded. "Of course. The mission must come first."

Lily shuffled on the seat of the carriage and folded her hands primly in her lap. She needed to remain cool. She would not think about the fact that they were a man and a woman alone in a carriage driving in Hyde Park as if they were a couple. With her nervousness, her voice became sharp. "Remember what I told you about maintaining your cover with the Bonapartists? They're a suspicious lot, and we can't afford any more missteps."

"I remember," he said. "I may not have your eidetic memory, but I do understand the importance of secrecy, and actually, I've been doing this longer than you have, my dear. I've prepared a thorough background story to share at the meeting. My cousin's role as a long-standing supporter of the cause, familial ties in France, financial interests connected to Napoleon's success." He rattled a purse.

"Financial?" she said.

"Nothing speaks like money," he replied. "Montgomery has already mentioned that I may be able to find a way to exonerate one of his compatriots."

"Well, if the man is innocent..."

"He is not."

"Oh. Was this a bribe, then?" she said, surprised. "Montgomery attempted to bribe you?"

"He did."

"What are you going to do?"

"See if I can get the man released," Lord Barton said with a shrug. "I have already put out some feelers. "It will do much to strengthen our cover."

"Oh." Lily sat for a moment, thoughtful. "But if the man is guilty... What is he guilty of?"

"Murder," Lord Barton said, "and impersonating a Queen's guard, which is perhaps more troubling."

She opened her mouth in a small O. "More troubling than murder?" she voiced.

"*Treason is* more troubling than murder," he said. He did not think she agreed with him, but he tried to impress upon her that the murder of the Queen was not the same as the murder of a commoner, no matter how regrettable that might be. Still, he was certain that although released, the man would not go far without his shadows from the Crown.

She did not think that would be an easy task to recapture the man and said so, even as misgivings filled her.

"Don't worry," Lord Barton said. "We will catch him again."

"Good." Lily paused, and a long silence ensued. "I wish you wouldn't have to accept a bribe or release a murderer," she said. "I can vouch for you again if needed. Though I wish you hadn't infiltrated at all."

"Ah, if wishes were coin," he joked.

"It's true," she insisted. "You were reckless."

Reginald's jaw tightened. It was a rather fine jaw, she thought. He had left a shadow of ruddy whiskers upon it, and she found she had an urge to pull off her glove and put her hand on the roughness of his cheek. Ridiculous!

"Reckless or not, I'm committed now. Too much is at stake." He leaned forward intently. "And I still wish you could stop attending the meetings."

Lily bristled. "Absolutely not. My access is invaluable."

"It is. But as wishes go, we are both foiled. I just wish we could minimize the danger," Reginald insisted. "As a woman..."

"I can handle myself," Lily cut him off sharply. This was an argument that she felt secure in waging. "I won't be cowed and sent tamely home to embroidery. I intend to find out who among the Bonapartists are loyal and who is there solely for profit. Only then will I agree to your exercising your... your..." She waved a hand about distractedly. She didn't want to think too much about what she was doing. It felt like betrayal. No matter which way she turned, she was betraying someone.

"Arrests?" Reginald supplied.

"Yes," she said at last, clearly not happy with the word. "But I will not see my friends arrested for wanting freedom. For wanting to feed their families."

"I TRUST murder and bribery are crimes for which you think people should be punished," he said. "Or would you allow all manner of rabble to run free?"

"Of course not," she snapped. "I do not condone murder, or bribery for that matter." She could not argue that fact, but she would not see people jailed for following their belief to see Bonaparte freed. She would not. But she did not voice that thought. If she had, she was certain that Lord Barton would find some way to leave her behind.

Reginald's expression was unreadable, but he gave a single nod. "We shall proceed together as we planned, but if things go awry, promise me, you will make your escape."

Lily nodded. It was the best compromise she could hope for, but she had no intention of leaving. No matter what Lord Barton thought, she would see Bonaparte freed if it was within her power. She had to do so without endangering Lord Barton, and that made the work so much more dangerous, but she trusted that the gentleman's skills would keep him from harm. And with her determination to find the truth, she was sure she could help to free Bonaparte—and Lord Barton. What exactly did she want to do with him?

Dangerous work lay ahead. Personal feelings would have to wait.

# PART IV

# SEARCH FOR TRUTH

*L*ily stood outside the entrance to the secret meeting location, her heart pounding in her chest. She knew she couldn't afford a mistake tonight. Reginald's life, as well as her own, depended on her ability to vouch for him and maintain his cover as a fellow Bonapartist. The thought of Reginald being discovered and executed as a traitor sent a shiver down her spine. As much as she did not agree with his politics, she did not want to see him hurt. The thought of him dead brought an unaccustomed tightness to her chest and a hollowness that bordered on pain.

"Deep breaths, Lily," she told herself, trying to calm her racing thoughts. "You can do this."

As she led Reginald into the dimly lit room where the meeting was taking place, she could feel her hands trembling slightly. She clenched them into fists, willing herself to appear composed and confident.

Lily glanced at Lord Barton, noting how he held himself with an air of quiet confidence. She couldn't help but admire his determination, even as she knew what a dangerous game they were playing.

"Very well," said Montgomery, his gaze lingering on Reginald for a moment longer before turning back to the group. "Let us proceed."

As the meeting continued, Lily couldn't help but fidget with the fabric of her gown. Every time she caught herself, she forced her hands into her lap, trying to keep her nerves under control. The weight of their mission pressed down on her, and she knew she couldn't afford to show any signs of the changes that had recently taken place in her heart. She still believed in Bonaparte's grand plan for the world, but her understanding of those in charge of this particular plan were somewhat tarnished.

At one point, Reginald reached over and placed his hand over hers, stilling her movements. She looked at him, startled by the warmth of his touch, but unaccountably grateful for the steadying presence he provided. She had not previously realized how alone she really was in this group.

"Thank you," she whispered, hoping that together they could navigate the treacherous waters of intrigue and deception and emerge unscathed on the other side. For tonight, they were allies in a dangerous dance, and the stakes had never been higher.

A HEATED CONVERSATION had developed in a corner of the room, and the duo approached a group of men engaged in the discussion about Napoleon's military strategy. Reginald listened intently before offering his own insights, drawing on the knowledge he had painstakingly acquired in preparation for this very moment. As he spoke, the men looked at him with growing respect and interest.

"Ah, Cousin Reginald, you have certainly studied the subject well," one man remarked, clapping him on the back. "It's no wonder Miss Lily vouches for you. I'm sure you will be an asset."

"Yes, I've taken great pains to learn all I can," Reginald said, smiling thinly. "After all, the cause of freeing the emperor is too important to take lightly."

As they continued their conversation, Reginald deftly steered the topic towards their plans to liberate the former emperor. He was careful not to push too hard, lest he arouse suspicion, but his questions were probing enough to elicit valuable information about their methods and contacts.

"Tell me, Lord Spencer," Reginald ventured, turning to the dark-eyed nobleman. "What do you believe will be the key to Napoleon's successful return to power?"

Spencer's cold eyes gleamed with ambition as he leaned in closer. "Patience, careful planning, and coin, Lord Reginald," he hissed. "We must strike when the time is right, and not a moment sooner. Our allies in France are growing bolder, and soon, they will be ready to act."

"Is there enough money?" Reginald asked, his mind racing with the implications of what he had just learned.

"Is there ever? You are inciteful," Spencer said. "But we must wait for the right moment."

"And how do you intend to ensure that we are prepared for that moment?"

"Ah, now that would be telling," Spencer said, smirking as he glanced around the room. "But rest assured, we have our ways."

Lord Barton gave the man a thin smile. It was galling to play the part of a nobleman who was as corrupt as Spencer himself to make this mission work.

"MISS HAWTHORNE," came a sudden whisper, causing Lily to startle. It was Montgomery, pulling her away from Lord Barton's side with his query. "Pray tell me, how long has your cousin been sympathetic to our cause?"

"Long enough," Lily replied coolly, her voice steady despite the alarm bells ringing in her head. She glanced around the room, ensuring that no one else seemed to be paying them any attention, but in the group, Montgomery's word was law. If he suspected Lord Barton of a nefarious purpose, their plan was ended. "My cousin is a man who prefers to keep his involvement... discreet."

"Indeed," Montgomery murmured, clearly unconvinced. His gaze shifted to Reginald, narrowing as he assessed the man who claimed to be a loyal Bonapartist. "One can never be too careful when it comes to matters of loyalty, Miss Hawkins."

"Quite," Lily agreed, refusing to be intimidated. "And I trust my cousin implicitly. He is as dedicated to our cause as anyone here." With a moment of inspiration, she added, "He has preferred to support with coin instead of brawn."

"Ah." Montgomery held her gaze for a moment longer before finally nodding, seemingly appeased. "Very well," he said, relinquishing his scrutiny. "I shall leave you to your discretion, Miss Hawkins. We shall see if your cousin proves himself worthy of our trust."

As the man walked away, Lily exhaled slowly, her heart pounding within her chest. It was a close call, but she had managed to deflect any suspicion—for now. Lord Barton was right. Coin greased the palms of these men and allayed their misgivings, or perhaps they were just too greedy to dismiss the gold. The thought gave her pause.

The meeting progressed, with the members discussing their latest machinations and plans for the future. Lily paid close attention, making mental notes of who seemed loyal and true and who might have more dishonorable attentions. Since Lord Barton had spoken to her about bribes and violent activities, she was looking at her fellow compatriots with a different eye. Could any of these actually be so base? How could she have been so mistaken about their true intentions?

Her mouth went dry as she watched Montgomery take the purse that Lord Barton offered. He had told her that his purse would speak to Montgomery, but she had not believed him entirely. Now, seeing the money exchange hands, she wondered what other favors were being exchanged. Was any of this actually for the common man's good?

But as she stood there observing the gathered conspirators and trying to think of a good reason for the exchange of the purse, an unexpected commotion caught her attention. A man stumbled into the room, his breath ragged and his face pale. There was blood on his coat. Disheveled and clearly agitated, he stuttered out a message: "There's been... a raid... on one of our safehouses."

Panic spread through the room like wildfire, and the murmurs turned into a cacophony of alarmed voices. The members of the group began to scatter, some hastening to leave while others frantically discussed what this development might mean for their cause.

"Lord Barton," Lily whispered urgently, catching his eye from across the room. He nodded in understanding; it was time for them to make their exit before they were discovered.

As they slipped out of the secret meeting place and into the night, the tension between them was palpable. They had narrowly avoided disaster, but the stakes had never been higher. As they hurried through the darkened streets, Lily couldn't help but wonder if they were truly prepared for the challenges that lay ahead.

The carriage ride back to the Beresford residence was tense, with both Lily and Reginald lost in their thoughts. The raid on one of the Bonapartist safehouses had shaken them both, and they couldn't help but wonder if their actions had somehow played a role.

"Lord Barton," Lily finally spoke, her voice barely above a whisper. "Do you think... that we put the others in danger?"

Reginald hesitated for a moment, his hazel eyes searching hers. "I don't know, Lady Lillian. It is possible. After all, the man impersonating the queen's guard was being followed. If he went to the safehouse, it is likely he led the guard there. It may have nothing to do with our involvement."

Lady Lillian did not seem quieted. "That man. He had blood on his coat."

"If the safe house was raided," Lord Barton said with a measured calm, "the Bonapartists would not have wanted to allow the informant to escape to tell the bow street runners of the location."

"You think they killed him?"

"Likely."

Silence descended upon them.

"I will find out more tomorrow," Lord Barton promised. "In the meantime, promise me you will stick to ladylike pursuits."

She opened her mouth to protest, but Lord Barton interrupted sharply. "It's one day. Surely you can spend one day with my sister and yours doing… whatever it is women do."

She had to laugh at his expression, and the mood lightened.

Lily nodded, her dark brown eyes filled with determination. "Agreed. But afterwards, we have to get closer to Montgomery and Spencer;learn as much as we can."

"Are you sure you want to do that?" Reginald asked, concern etched on his face.

"I do," she said. "I need to know if they are honorable men."

"Very well," Reginald conceded, acutely aware of the fierce spirit that drove her. He did not contradict her. He could tell her volumes about Montgomery and Spencer, but he did not think she would believe him. There were some things she had to discover for herself. "Please be careful. Your safety is my utmost priority."

"Thank you, Lord Barton," she murmured, feeling a strange sense of comfort in his promise. He laid a hand over her gloved hand, and the warmth of it thrilled her as nothing had in the past.

"Now, about tomorrow," Lord Barton said. As they made their way through the now moonlit streets of London, they discussed their next course of action.

As the carriage pulled up to the Beresford residence, Lord Barton helped Lady Lillian out of the conveyance. Their eyes met. Perhaps it was the intensity of their mission, or perhaps it was the unspoken emotions between them which caused a sudden spark to ignite, but somehow, the shadows seemed a bit brighter on this moonlit night.

Lord Barton escorted her into the house where his sister and hers anxiously awaited their return.

# BLUEPRINTS AND WEAPONS OF WAR

*L*ord Barton and Lady Lillian became a common sight at the Bonaparte meetings. There were no more raids which spilled blood-stained men into their midst, and Lily felt that she could almost relax. Lord Barton warned that complacency bred mistakes. She must remain vigilant.

She knew now that Montgomery had paid for the release of several prisoners who seemed to be the most despicable men, and Lord Barton had proved his worth to the Bonapartists by taking Montgomery's coin to free the men, even while he paid for the privilege of being a member of the group. Money changed hands with astonishing regularity, and now that Lily's eyes were open to the transactions, she could not unsee the corruption.

It tarnished Lily's opinion of Montogomery, and she tried several times to interrogate him about his true cause, but Montogomery easily side-stepped her queries with the age-old ease of a man dismissing a woman's concerns.

She had begun to note that Lord Barton rarely treated her so when in private. Instead, he listened to her as if he believed she was an intelligent human being. In the company of the Bonapartists however, he treated her as most men treated women, as a bauble without merit. It was disconcerting to see his easy shift between the two. She had to wonder which was the real Lord Barton. She told herself the real Lord Barton was the one she knew in private, the one presented to his own sister, but the mask was too real. His proficiency in lies unnerved her.

Today, the flickering glow of candlelight cast eerie shadows on the walls of the secret chamber, as members of the Bonapartist group huddled together in hushed conversation. Lily, dressed in a plain gown to maintain her own cover, felt a chill run down her spine as she surveyed the room. She had been to several meetings before, but now, the stakes were higher than ever.

"Remember," Reginald whispered into her ear as they entered the dimly lit chamber, "listening, rather than speaking. Our primary goal is to gather information on their plans to free Bonaparte."

Lily nodded. She did not appreciate Lord Barton's high-handedness, but he was right. Sometimes she spoke her mind too readily. Since her mind was no longer wholly engaged with the same goals as the others, she had to guard her tongue. She was no longer completely certain what her true purpose was. She believed in Bonaparte's ideals, but if Lord Barton was right, and it appeared that he was more right than not, Bonaparte's ideals were not the goal of this group, at least not entirely. Their goals seemed to be rooted in causing chaos and making money. It was despicable, and yet there were some in the group with true belief in the ideals of freedom. Sadly, the more she learned, the more they seemed to be in the minority.

"I understand," she replied, her voice steady despite the fear gnawing at her insides. Never had she been afraid in this group of people, but she had always had the shield of truth. Now, she was lying to them at least by omission. She didn't like how the mendacity made her feel. She moved from Lord Barton's side feeling uncertain.

LILY GRAVITATED toward a small group of women Bonapartists, exchanging pleasantries. She noticed their numbers were smaller this week, likely due to the increased risk since the raid last week. Lily maintained her poise but felt the weight of the danger keenly. She had trusted these women implicitly due to their shared cause, and now, she was unsure of their purpose as well as her own. Certainly, if men could be mendacious, so could women.

The meeting was called to order. Lily focused intently as the strategies were discussed. Reginald asked thoughtful questions, showing his eagerness. When he was asked to describe his military experience, Lily jumped in to save him having to toot his own horn.

"Lord Barton is too modest," she said lightly. "His tactical knowledge has impressed me on many occasions." She embellished Reginald's credentials. His grateful glance heartened her. After all, it was hard for him to sing his own praises. They made a good team, she thought.

Afterward, Reginald caught her eye and tilted his head discretely toward the doorway. Lily extracted herself from a conversation and slipped out to meet him in the darkened alley.

"Well?" she asked without preamble.

"They're moving forward rapidly," Reginald said grimly. "They need funds. I offered some but insisted I would know what my money would purchase, and Montgomery balked. The purchase seemed eminent. I think they are planning the rescue sooner than we anticipated. We need to know where they will take him, in case we are too late to intercept."

Lily hesitated.

"We spoke of this," Reginald said softly.

"Yes."

"Are you with me?"

She nodded, thinking of the evidence of Bonaparte's butchery, the possibility that he or his ilk even financed the reign of terror to make way for his own ascension to emperor. She doubted it was true, but the fact that Bonaparte profited from it could not be avoided. Such bloodshed could not be forgiven even as she saw the freedom he promised.

Reginald grasped her upper arms and turned her towards him. "A decision must be made," he said. "You cannot waver. Speak, or let me take you home."

Lily nodded. She understood that Lord Barton realized her loyalties were divided. She could not continue to be so. It was time for a decision. "I'll press the women about safehouses. Someone must know more." She hesitated. "Be careful."

His expression softened, but footsteps sounded, and

they moved apart. Someone was coming. Lily slipped inside, and Reginald quickly lit a cheroot and took a long draw upon it.

Reginald watched Lily go as he blew smoke into the air. He could not help but admire her courage even as he worried for her safety. This mission was growing more dangerous by the day, and he knew she was conflicted. These people had been her friends, or at least she thought of them as such. He also knew that his own assurance that the Bonapartists would be caught and tried as traitors to the Crown surely influenced her, as well as accounts of Bonapartists' money financing outright murder. It was not a subject for a woman, but it was a subject a spy needed to know, and he could not coddle her as he would was wont to do for a woman and a lady.

Several rough sailors came into the alley to smoke and converse out of the heat of the warehouse. He caught a snippet of their hushed conversation.

"...the weapons are secured in the old smithy on the east side," the skinny one was saying. "I'll show you tomorrow night. You can help me load them on the Errant." The other seemed much more able to carry a load than the first man. Reginald took note of both.

Pretending not to notice the men, Reginald snubbed out his own smoke and reentered the warehouse.

This could be the break he needed. The weapons cache, at last. This vital information could cripple the entire operation. He had not heard of the vessel Errant, but no doubt either Samuel or Jack would know of its whereabouts.

Once inside, Reginald moved towards Spenser and

Montgomery, who were deep in conversation. He eyed them with interest but schooled his features to nonchalance. Casually maneuvering closer, he joined the circle. "Discussing anything of interest, gentlemen?" he inquired lightly.

Spencer shot him a sharp look.

Montgomery replied, "Just finalizing plans, Lord Barton. I understand you'll be joining us on Thursday next?"

"I wouldn't miss it," Reginald affirmed. He met Spencer's gaze. "I'm eager to support the cause however I can." He stuck his fingers in his pocket and jingled his purse.

Spencer studied him a moment longer before giving a curt nod. "Good man. We'll expect you. And your purse." He turned away.

Reginald allowed himself a small smile of satisfaction. Apparently, Montgomery had sought Spencer's opinion and had relented.

He glanced around for Lily but did not see her. Even her momentary absence sent a thrill of fear through him. Likely, she was closeted with some women, but he would not rest until he laid eyes upon her again. For now, he played the patient recruit, biding his time, but his heart leaped in his chest. Soon, they would have enough evidence to dismantle this rebellion before it ever left English shores, but he wanted to get them all, including the ring leaders, and most of all, he wanted to keep his Lily safe.

. . .

As THEY TOOK their seats among the other conspirators, Lily threw a glance towards Lord Barton. He looked relieved. Was he worried about her? She had only been gone for a brief moment when she joined Mrs Dory in the ladies' retiring room. Mrs Dory was not actually married to anyone. She was an old prostitute, discarded by her protector when she got too old to be a pretty addition on his arm. The old woman was a font of information, and Lily could feel the weight of her decision upon her. With each passing moment, the danger only seemed to grow as more and more truths came to light. Separating the loyal Bonapartists from those who only wanted to line their pockets was a monumental feat, but she was committed now. There was no turning back, no matter her misgivings. She must ferret out the truth no matter the cost.

"Friends, fellow supporters of our great Emperor Napoleon Bonaparte," began Montgomery, his voice dripping with fervor as he addressed the gathered crowd. "We stand on the precipice of change, the dawn of a new era where freedom shall reign supreme!"

The room erupted in murmurs of agreement, and Lily felt her heart race with a mixture of excitement and trepidation. She was acutely aware ofLord Barton, who had moved up beside her, his eyes scanning the room for any signs of suspicion or discontent. "Where were you?" he demanded.

"Later," she mouthed, and he let it go.

"However," Montgomery continued, his tone taking on a more somber note, "we must tread carefully. There are those who would see us fail, who would betray our cause to maintain their own positions of power."

Lily glanced at Reginald, feeling a pang of guilt. He caught her eye, giving her a reassuring nod as if sensing her unease.

"Let us not forget that our ultimate goal is the liberation of our beloved Emperor, who has been unjustly imprisoned," said Lord Spencer, his voice cold and calculating. "And let us remember that the price of failure is not only our own lives but also the future of an entire nation. Unfortunately, such endeavors do not come cheap, either in gold or in blood. Our Emperor expects no less than your best."

Lily frowned at his words while she listened intently to the discussions around her, storing away every scrap of information she could gather.

Montgomery called for everyone's attention before announcing a new plan, one that he seemed hesitant to reveal. The hushed murmurs in the room ceased, and even the flickering candlelight seemed to hold its breath in anticipation.

"Listen carefully," Montgomery began, his eyes darting around the room with an intensity that made both Lily and Reginald uneasy. "We have recently come into possession of plans for an extraordinary vessel. A ship unlike any other, capable of traveling beneath the waves themselves."

Murmurs of disbelief rippled through the crowd, but Montgomery held up a hand to silence them. "It is true. This remarkable invention will allow us to approach St. Helena undetected and rescue our Emperor from his island prison."

Reginald's brow furrowed in skepticism, and he exchanged a quick glance with Lily, who mirrored his concern. Although it had been mentioned before, it seemed impossible. The very idea of a ship that could sail under the water seemed ludicrous, and yet Captain Jack had heard rumors of the thing, and the possibility of such an invention falling into the hands of England's enemies was deeply alarming.

"Are you certain this vessel exists?" Reginald asked, trying to keep the incredulity from his voice as he stepped closer to Montgomery. "Such a thing sounds like the stuff of legends, not reality."

Some others murmured agreement.

Montgomery fixed him with a steely gaze, his jaw set in determination. "I assure you; it is very real. It is being built as we speak." As if to add veracity to his words, he pulled from his inner pocket a folded paper and waved the paper about, announcing, "These are the plans of the wonder ship." Reginald assumed them to be a blueprint of sorts, which seemed to have a plan of the very ship upon it. "And with this miraculous ship, we shall free Napoleon and bring about the restoration of the Empire," Montgomery declared. He spoke on with hubris.

Lily moved closer to Reginald. "Cousin," she said under her breath.

"We must learn more about this ship and its capabilities," Reginald whispered. "If it truly exists, we cannot let it fall into enemy hands. I'm going to attempt to steal the plans." His mouth was a thin line, daring her to try to stop him.

"No," she murmured, laying a hand on his arm. She was more certain now than ever. It was one thing to allow Bonaparte to escape to live his life, another to give

England's enemies a miraculous ship such as this. She had trouble believing the thing really existed. She needed to see it for herself. "We don't need to steal it. If I can get a good look at the plans he holds, I can recreate the design."

Reginald gave her a startled look but finally nodded his assent.

Lord Barton seemed worried, his own concern evident in the tight set of his shoulders, but he stepped forward in courage. "You tell us so, Montgomery," he said. "But what is on this hidden paper? Let us see it for ourselves."

Some others murmured their agreement, and Montgomery hesitated.

"WE PUT OUR LIVES FORTH," Reginald jeered. "Our lives and our money, on your word alone, Montgomery. On your word that a ship can sail beneath the waves. It is a fantastic thing, and yet you ask us to take this on faith. Let us see the plans for this miraculous ship. If the thing even exists."

Some in the crowd began to murmur agreement.

Montgomery, edged on by doubt in the crowd, finally spread open the blueprint on the table before them. Reginald shifted to allow Lily to stand in front of him, nearer the paper.

"It doesn't even look like a ship," Lily said with a woefully baffled look on her face. Reginald almost laughed at how befuddled the intelligent woman appeared to be.

"Why is it blue?" she asked.

"It's a blueprint," said Montgomery with derision.

"I can see the print is blue, but it's all just lines." She edged closer, her face clenched in concentration. Others murmured in agreement. "I've never seen such a thing."

"It is a new way to make copies," Montgomery said. "The first of its kind. Just like the ship itself."

"Indeed," said Reginald. "How do we know this ship will even sail?"

"Because," said Montgomery, "I have seen it. It is being built as we speak."

"Built does not mean it is seaworthy," said one of the sailors in the group, as several crowded forward to look at the plans. Reginald shifted, not allowing anyone to dislodge Lily from her spot close to the table. She reached out a finger to touch it, and Reginald realized that where she was pointing was marked as a weapon. Somehow, the thing held a way to fire weapons. It was chilling. Reginald felt his mouth go dry.

As Montgomery divulged the details of their audacious plan to free Napoleon, the air hung heavy with dread, a suffocating blanket that draped over Reginald as he glanced at Lily. She gave a slight nod of her head.

"Once we possess this underwater ship," Montgomery continued, his voice low and conspiratorial, "we can approach the island undetected and liberate the emperor.

Lily and Reginald exchanged a glance, their expressions taut with tension. Reginald knew they needed to somehow relay this information to the British authorities, but doing so without arousing suspicion would be no easy feat. And with each passing moment, the stakes grew higher. Perhaps he could send Lily with the information. No doubt she would refuse to leave for some reason. He wondered how long she could hold the information in her mind before details started to fade. Reginald looked for a discreet opportunity to leave. He glanced at his pocket watch as if he had an appointment, but it was nearly midnight. What would be pressing at so late an hour?

"Cousin," Lily said, giving him the opportunity. "The hour is late, and I am somewhat fatigued."

Reginald immediately took her cue. "I will take you home."

"Indeed, the hour does grow late. Any questions?" Montgomery asked, his eyes scanning the faces of those gathered. No one dared to speak.

"Very well," he said, nodding curtly. "We will reconvene in three days' time to discuss the specifics of our operation."

Once they were out of earshot, they shared their respective intelligence. Reginald said to Lily, "I need to find out where this ship is being kept and inform the authorities before it's too late."

"You?" Lily said.

"Yes. Helms will take you home," he replied, his face set in determination. "I will take a hackney to the docks. Draw out the plans, and I will call upon you in the morning to obtain them. We have to tread carefully, Lily. This group is dangerous, and if they discover our true intentions, they will not hesitate to kill us."

"Then we'll just have to ensure that doesn't happen," she retorted, her dark eyes flashing with resolve. "I'm going with you."

"I am not taking you to the docks!" Lord Barton declared. "And you need to draw the plans before the images fade from your mind."

She considered for a moment. That was true. She was not altogether sure that the ship really existed, but she needed to copy the drawing from her mind's eye.

Sure, Montgomery was waving around the plans for this wonder, but was it built? Did it really work? Would it indeed sail beneath the waves? That seemed unlikely. She had the plans though. Rather than wandering through the docks looking for an underwater ship, they could discern if the vessel was really seaworthy. She suggested this to Lord Barton. "Neither of us need to go to the docks," she said.

"Agreed," he said, surprising her by taking her advice. Then, he grasped her hand briefly in a firm, reassuring grip as he put her into his carriage and climbed up beside her. "Take us home, Helms," he said. "You can recopy the plans," Reginald said, "and we will decide how to proceed from there."

LILY WAS FLUMMOXED by Lord Barton's quick decision, even though he had taken her advice to come to that conclusion. She considered the information she presently held in her mind. A submarine vessel... It was daring and yet mad. Could such a fantastical contraption truly be built? If so, it might actually have a chance of success in spiriting away the imprisoned Napoleon, and what did she truly think of that possibility? It was troubling that an entity not England would have such a wonder.

More troubling was the talk of an armory. Weapons and violence could turn a daring plot into a deadly rebellion with countless lives at stake. Lily shuddered at the thought and let the lines and curves of the plans solidify in her mind.

When they returned to the house, it was quiet. Only a few servants were about, and apparently both his sister and hers had found their beds. Lord Barton escorted her into the library. It was dark due to no fire being lit in the summer heat, and Lily found herself very aware of the unchaperoned privacy of the situation. Although they had been in each other's company for most of the evening and several evenings prior, it seemed somehow more intimate in the library rather than a carriage. The scent of old books around them was comforting to her —home.

Lord Barton got right to business. He found several candles and lit them. A pot of ink and paper lay on the desk, and he invited Lily to sit at the most masculine desk. He moved several papers that seemed to belong to Lord Beresford to allow her to work at the desk. Then, he removed himself, sitting in a wing chair and allowing her some semblance of privacy. She closed her eyes momentarily, centering herself, recreating the plans in her mind, and then began to sketch the drawing.

After some time, she considered whether she had actually copied the ship in its entirety. There was one small section that she was uncertain of, but mostly she captured the whole of the plan. She was satisfied with her work and laid aside the quill.

Having completed the intricate drawings to the best

of her ability, Lily looked up at Lord Barton with a mixture of pride and anxiety. "Well, that's it," she said.

The soft candlelight flickered against her dark curls, casting shadows across her determined face. As her eyes met his, she could see the admiration shining in their hazel depths.

"Remarkable," Reginald breathed, taking in the detailed plans. "I can't believe you remembered all this."

Lily shrugged, a small smile gracing her lips. "It's rather like reading a book," she replied, trying to sound casual despite the pounding of her heart.

Lord Barton came closer to examine her work, and she was suddenly aware of the scent of cloves and tobacco on his person. She turned her face up to him. The moment was suspended as he looked down upon her, his sharp hazel eyes intense.

Their gazes locked, and she saw something in his eyes that made her breath catch—a fierce protectiveness, mixed with deep affection.

"I should take this information to the authorities," he said, but he made no move to do so.

"You seem troubled. What did you learn?" she asked, wondering if he had kept something from her.

After a brief pause, he spoke. "It's about the weapons cache. Apparently, it is to be moved tomorrow night," he replied grimly.

So, he had kept details from her, she thought.

"It's at the old smithy on the east side," he continued. "It's likely where they are storing guns and powder for their uprising. I think I still need to go to the docks tonight. This cache must be found tonight. Tonight, it is being loaded on the Errant. Who knows where it will be tomorrow."

Lily inhaled sharply and stood. "Then it's true. They mean to start a revolution. Here in England?"

"So, it seems," Reginald agreed. "Perhaps it is a diversion to cover the escape of Napoleon. But now I can stop them before it begins. With this information, we can organize a raid on the smithy and remove those weapons from their arsenal."

"You?" she said. "You alone? But how?"

"Not alone," he said. "There are other agents of the Crown, and you have helped immeasurably. Go to bed now. I will be home before dawn." He reached for the blueprint, his fingers brushing against hers in a fleeting touch that sent a shiver down her spine, and suddenly Lily's hand was upon his.

"Don't go," she said.

He looked at her hand, so white against his own ruddy skin, so soft. So warm. A palpable tension hummed between them as they stood together. His gaze roved over her delicate features illuminated by the silvery light of the moon that shone through the library window. He wanted to pull her close, to feel her skin against his, and yet duty held him back.

Reginald drank in the sight of her—her strong jaw-line, her dark eyebrows, and dark curls coming loose from her braid, the fierce intelligence in her eyes that burned like embers. She was like an oasis in the midst of a scorching desert, beckoning him forward, promising solace and comfort within her embrace.

· · ·

"Don't go," she repeated.

"I must," he said.

"I—I have a peculiar feeling," she said, closing her hand over his. The warmth of it was intoxicating, and she turned to face him, transferring her hand from his to his lapels. She pulled him towards her. "This is dangerous," she said.

"It is," he said.

The heat between them was not due to the summer night nor the flicker of the candle flame. "A kiss then, for luck," he said with a laugh, but his voice had a deepness to it, a tremor of passion. Lily did not pull away. Never before had she wanted to be kissed, but she wanted it now. She wanted the assurance of his touch.

"Yes," she answered fiercely, her arms wrapping around him as she pulled him down into a searing kiss.

Her mouth met his in a dance of passion and longing, their lips igniting a single, blazing inferno that threatened to consume them both, as if their very lips were a tinderbox to their souls. Lily felt as though there was nothing else in the world but his lips upon hers, two souls entwined in a passionate embrace that seemed to be without end.

His hands moved to the small of her back while she clung to him with reckless abandon. He pulled her suddenly close until their bodies were crushed against one another. The heat radiating off them could have incinerated the desk behind her along with the precious plans she had wrought, and yet in all that heat, in the shelter of his embrace, Lily felt safe and protected from the tumultuous world outside.

Never before had she wanted shelter. Never had she

wanted to feel protected. She was strong. She was independent. But somehow, in this moment, she felt more than she ever had. She felt his strength and his vulnerability, and in that moment, she was both the weakness and the power of the feminine.

She felt everything that he was feeling—love, desire, passion—all mixed into a single emotion that seemed to echo what she was feeling in every corner of her heart and soul. Suddenly, she realized they weren't so different, male and female, parts of an infinite whole. She wanted this moment to last forever—two lips searing as they became one. She opened her mouth, and following an instinct as old as time, she let him in.

It seemed to break something within in him as his tongue swept inside of her mouth, and her whole body turned to liquid heat. There seemed to be no line of demarcation between them, and the heat reached an unbearable intensity. He paused, breathing, his forehead against hers.

"This is madness," he whispered.

"Yes," she said.

He brushed his lips against her lips, soft as a butterfly's wings. Her whole body was trembling. She had never felt this way—

"If this is madness," she said. "I don't want to be sane." She lifted her chin and let him trail hot kisses down her neck. Some part of her realized that this went way beyond propriety, but she did not care.

He stopped then, his head resting on her bosom, which was rising and falling in passion.

She felt powerful.

She was woman.

Life-giver.

She held everything that was feminine which completed his masculinity.

His breath was ragged, as was her own. She could feel her own heartbeat and his beating as one. His arms held her close, wrapped around her waist. Then, in one gesture, he shifted and lifted her, placing her on the desk so that his face was level with hers. She gave a little squeak of surprise. His deep hazel eyes bored into her soul.

"Marry me," he said, a claim upon her and yet with a vulnerability in him. He hung upon her word. She could say no.

And yet, it was the completion of what they had begun, a commitment that fulfilled their desire, and perhaps love.

Was this love? She faltered, fearing the vulnerability in herself.

"Marry me," he had said. It was not a question. It was a demand—a command—and somehow, it roused her from the heat of the moment. She would not be ruled.

"I don't—" she began, and he cupped her chin and kissed her again, plunging her once again into the flames of desire, and she forgot why she did not want to marry. She forgot everything but the man in her arms as they clung to one another, the world fading away until only the two of them remained, and the searing, unquenchable heat of their encounter.

Presently, he pulled away from her and kissed her forehead with infinite gentleness.

"Sleep well," he said, and without another word, he

straightened his waistcoat, picked up the blueprints, and strode from the room, leaving her adrift in a sea of feelings that had no words.

Much later, she picked herself off of the desk, and on boneless legs found her way back to the room assigned to her. Sleep was a long time in coming.

# AT THE DOCKS

*A*stride his stallion, Lord Reginald Barton raced to the docks, his heart pounding with anticipation. He had in his possession the document that detailed the construction of a submarine—a weapon devised to rescue Napoleon Bonaparte from his exile on St Helen's Island.

He needed to pass off that information to Captain Samuel Beresford or Captain Jack Hartfield. He only hoped that he would be able to find one of the captains in time. He slowed his horse to a trot as he searched the docks for Samuel's ship, the Amelia, but before he could seek to board, he heard shouting and saw Bonapartists moving weapons from a warehouse into a waiting ship—the Errant. He reined in his horse and cursed. How much time did he have left?

As much as he wanted to stop the movement of the weapons, he had to get these plans to Jack, Samuel, or the dockmaster. He could not risk their falling into enemy hands. He scanned the docks, deciding which way to go. Where would the plans be safe? He held the only copy, and the blueprint could not be taken. It was imperative that the authorities learn what the Bonapartists were planning. Samuel's ship, he decided, was the closest. With one last burst of energy, he kicked his horse forward, racing as quickly as he dared on the cobbles. Reginald reached the ship and called to the watch for Samuel to be alerted.

Within moments, the ship was alive with activity. Samuel mobilized his own crew and sent a messenger to Captain Jack for assistance. With the plans for Bonaparte's submarine safely aboard the Amelia, Lord Barton informed the captain of the eminent transfer of weapons from the warehouse to the ship Errant. Leaving a contingent aboard his own ship, Samuel jumped to help his friend and comrade.

Lord Barton, on horseback, took the lead. They intercepted the cache of weapons. Lord Barton raised his pistol and cried out, "Cease and desist."

But the mercenaries were not inclined to obey. One came running towards him, cutlass raised.

Reginald fired point blank. The man went down, but he was only the first. Without time to reload, Reginald leaned down and appropriated the abandoned cutlass.

HIS EYES LOCKED onto the leader of the mercenaries, a towering brute with a thick black beard. Without hesitation, Lord Barton charged forward, sword raised high above his head. His stallion was no war destrier, but the sight of a stallion bearing down upon him hooves flashing, gave the mercenary pause. Belatedly, the man swung his sword, going for the horse's legs, and Reginald barely managed to turn the stallion in time. The horse reared, coming down heavily upon the man, who screamed in rage and pain as the 1500-pound animal's hooves impaled him. Lord Barton was nearly unseated. He swung to the ground, using his horse for balance as the excited animal danced sideways.

Another man came out of nowhere. Lord Barton, now on the ground, raised his sword to meet the attack. With one swift motion, he swung his sword and slashed the mercenary's weapon from his hand. The mercenary was stunned, but the rest of his group was ready to fight back. Another mercenary immediately took his place. Reginald turned, but his horse had bolted.

The two clashed swords, their weapons ringing out amidst the commotion of the docks. Each time their blades met; Lord Barton felt a jolt of adrenaline rush through him. Sweat poured down his face as he fought with all his strength.

But he was outnumbered. Within minutes, the mercenaries had regrouped, and Lord Barton found himself backed up against a stack of crates, his sword arm growing weary. He felt a sharp blow to his side, and he stumbled, his sword clattering to the ground.

As the mercenaries closed in on him, Lord Barton knew that he was done for. But just as he thought all was lost, he heard a loud cannon blast fill the air. The Errant had been hit.

There was a moment of stunned silence, then a cheer went up from the sailors who had joined the fray.

"Captain Jack," said Samuel with a grim smile of satisfaction. It was clear that firing the cannon within the harbor would bring the harbormaster and the guard at a run.

The mercenaries knew this too, and many scattered, fearing capture by the guard.

With the mercenaries momentarily distracted, Lord Barton seized the opportunity to scramble to his feet and retrieve his sword. But just as he was about to rejoin the fight, he felt a strong hand grasp his arm.

It was Samuel Beresford, who grinned at him even as he parried.

The two men charged forward, their swords drawn, and engaged in battle with the remaining Bonapartists. Lord Barton proved to be a formidable fighter, parrying and thrusting with deadly accuracy. Samuel fought valiantly at his side, their swords singing as they clashed against the enemy's weapons.

There was another boom of the cannon, and both men realized that the Errant had returned fire on Captain Jack's ship, but Captain Jack had raised anchor, ready to pursue if the Errant attempted to run.

"Bloody hell," Lord Barton swore, but Samuel knew the harbormaster would be down upon the miscreants in a moment. A battle in the very harbor would not be tolerated.

Leaving the issue of the ships to the harbormaster, Reginald and Samuel fought on until there was no one else to fight. They emerged triumphant, their opponents either lying dead or wounded on the ground. "Well fought, my friend," Samuel said, clapping his friend on the back.

Lord Barton, his adrenaline still pumping, grinned

back at him. "I'm just glad I could be of service, Captain."

As they walked back towards the Amelia, Captain Jack surveyed the destruction. "What were they planning to do with all these weapons anyways?" he asked.

Lord Barton frowned. "I don't know for certain, but my guess is that they were planning to overthrow the government and put Bonaparte back in power."

They exchanged glances, the gravity of the situation sinking in. "Now, we need to report this to the authorities," Reginald said firmly, and I need to find my horse."

"That shouldn't be a problem," Captain Samuel replied, gesturing to the harbormaster, who was bearing down on them with a vengeance.

"I'll let you handle this, then," Reginald said as his wayward stallion came somewhat sheepishly slinking back to the area. Reginald caught his mount and began checking him for injuries as Captain Samuel chuckled.

The captain waved gaily at the harbormaster.

"What is the meaning of this?" the man demanded.

"Do not worry yourself, mate," Samuel called to the man. "We have just stopped a shipment of arms to Bonaparte. I think you will find the rest on board the Errant." He gestured to the ship which was listing badly due to Captain Jack's accurate cannon fire. "Better move quickly," Samuel suggested, or the guns may end up at the bottom of the harbor."

"I believe a number of them are still in the warehouse," Lord Barton provided helpfully as he patted his lathered horse. "And if you have this all under control,

Samuel, I think I will head home. It has been a long night."

"Nearly day," Samuel said looking at the dawn-lightened sky.

And so it was, thought Reginald as he mounted his steed. It would be fully daylight by the time he walked his lathered horse home.

# UNWANTED ENGAGEMENT

*L*ord Barton had arrived home sometime after dawn this morning, and according to his sister, who had the word from his valet, he had gone straight to his bed. Lily couldn't blame him. It had been an eventful past few days. She was glad that he had informed her of his safe homecoming. She assumed that he had delivered the blueprint for the submarine without incident.

While still at the breakfast table, a letter arrived from her mother. Lily opened it with a frown on her face, and at the words, she grew pale.

"What is it?" Grace asked.

"Mother is planning a ball," she said. "My engagement ball."

"Lud," Grace said dryly.

"She wants us home on the morrow. Or perhaps I should say, Grandfather wants us home."

"I did not know you were engaged," Lady Patience put in.

"I am not," Lily said with some vehemence. "But Grandfather is determined I be settled by the end of the month, or when Parliament closes."

"Parliament closed day before yesterday," Patience provided. "Most of the Peers are packing for the country or Bath. By week's end, London will be deserted."

Lily wrapped her hands around her cup and silently sipped her tea. She was not sure what she would do, but she knew she would not marry Lord Rumford. The thought of accepting Lord Barton was not as much of a hardship as she had first thought, although she still doubted that she would be able to pull the wool over his eyes. Would a lifetime with him be giving up her freedom entirely? She was no longer sure. She also was no longer sure that he wanted her. He had proposed in a moment of passion—she felt her cheeks heat with the thought of it—but would he still want to marry her? She was not the sort of woman most men wanted as a bride. She knew this, but she had no intention to change.

There was a meeting of the Bonapartists tonight. She would have to find some way to ask him, she supposed. How embarrassing that would be! Otherwise, she thought, perhaps she could open a school for young ladies in London. There would be satisfaction in doing something useful like that, but after the excitement of the Bonapartist plot, it seemed rather anticlimactic. Would that satisfy her? She was not sure.

"We should go shopping," Grace suggested. "Maybe you can find something that will cheer you."

Lily doubted that something so mundane would improve her mood, but it certainly could not make it any bleaker, and there was some satisfaction in spending her grandfather's money.

LORD BARTON and Lady Lillian had departed the carriage. Helms would stay nearby but covert. Lady Lily Hawthorne stood at the edge of the growing crowd, her dark curls nestled beneath a modest bonnet, her face a vision of resolve. Lord Barton thought she had never looked so lovely. Her deep brown eyes scanned the throng for any sign of Bonapartist spies as she clutched her reticule tightly to her chest. Lord Barton thought it likely that they had moved the meeting after the incident at the harbor. He had tried to convince her that they should not go back, but she was unmoved. She was the most stubborn woman he had ever encountered.

"This is foolish," he said.

"You said that you did not catch Spencer or Montgomery," Lily said. "And if we know where they are, perhaps you can catch them. Besides, I want to know if Mrs Dory is safe, as well as some of the sailors."

"Who is Mrs. Dory?" he asked.

"One of the Bonapartists," she answered. "A drab who has lost her looks. What else does she have? Poor woman."

"A prostitute?" Lord Barton blustered. "Begging your pardon," he said.

Lily laughed. "I do not take offense at your speaking of her person or her profession," she said. "If I remember correctly, you thought the same of me when we first met."

Lord Barton had the grace to blush. Dory, he thought. The name had some familiarity.

"I am concerned for the woman's safety," she said.

"*Your safety* is my utmost concern, milady," said Lord Barton, his hazel eyes filled with worry. He shifted closer to her, their shoulders brushing against each other,

"Lord Barton, I must do this," Lily said softly, her voice firm with conviction. "I could not live with myself if I could do something to prevent these people from suffering and did nothing. It's worth the risk. Freedom and equality are more than mere words to me."

He swallowed hard, unable to hide his emotions. His eyes roamed over her face, taking in the determination etched there and the beauty he found so captivating. "I understand," he said, yet he could not quell the unease that gnawed within him. This was exceedingly dangerous. Certainly bordering on foolish. Anyone could have recognized him at the harbor. It was now the job of others to mop up the rest of this mess. He should steer clear.

"Promise me one thing, Lord Barton," she implored, turning to face him fully. "If anything goes awry, save yourself, and let others know what happened here today."

"Never," he declared fiercely, grasping her gloved hand. "I will protect you, Lady Lillian, no matter the cost. As long as I draw breath, I shall stand by your side and protect you with my life."

His steadfast promise warmed her heart, even as a shiver ran down her spine at his choice of words. She nodded solemnly.

"Does that mean you still want to marry me?" she asked, her tone jocular.

He looked at her in surprise. Did her blithe comment mean she was still considering his proposal?

"Come, then," she whispered, stepping into the throng of unwashed humanity on the street and vanishing like a wraith. She had not waited for his answer.

Reginald followed closely behind, his eyes never leaving Lily's determined form as she navigated the shadowy world. She was an enigma, a woman who defied society's expectations and embraced her independence with unwavering resolve. She was a marvel—a paragon. Of course, he still wanted to marry her, but what brought that topic back to the surface?

As they neared the previous meeting place, Reginald could feel the tension in the air, the weight of secrets and lies hanging heavy like the gathering clouds above. The heat was oppressive. It would only take one misstep, one misplaced word, for everything to come crashing down around them. Now, the Bonapartists would be on edge. Of this, he was sure.

And yet, in that moment, Lord Barton stood tall, filled with a newfound purpose: to ensure that his Lily remained safe from harm, no matter the consequences. She was considering his offer of marriage. He was sure of it. That made his heart sing, even in the midst of danger.

As they approached the warehouse, a figure stepped out of the shadows, blocking their path. Lord Spencer sneered at them, his cold dark eyes filled with menace.

"Well, well," he drawled, "what have we here? You have a nerve showing up here now, Barton."

"Stand aside," Reginald growled, instinctively stepping in front of Lily.

"Ah, but I'm afraid I cannot allow you to continue on this little... errand," Lord Spencer replied with a cruel smile, glancing pointedly at Lily. "Your little play has cost me, Barton."

So, they did know it was him at the docks, he thought. He had hoped that he avoided detection. Since he had not, the gig was up.

"You see, I have invested a great deal in Napoleon's success," Spencer continued. "And I will not let some misguided idealists stand in my way. Ingenious of you to offer your money. That did confuse the issue. Do you have a bottomless purse?"

Reginald's mind raced, searching for a solution. In an instant, he recalled a piece of information he'd gleaned from a previous encounter with Lord Spencer—a weakness that could be exploited. Lady Lillian's previous words came back to him. Mrs. Dory. Now, he put it together. Not Mrs, but Madame. Leaning closer, he whispered harshly, "What pillow talk have you shared with Madame Dory? Something the Crown would like to know?"

Lord Spencer's face paled, his eyes flickering with uncertainty.

"Or perhaps your creditors are more interested in your mounting debts than your loyalty to Bonaparte. Where has all that money gone?" Reginald cooed. "Into Bonaparte's coffers, perhaps? The Crown will have something to say about that."

Panic showed in the man's eyes, proving that the money trail would reveal him a traitor. That was all Lord Barton needed to know.

Seizing the opportunity, Reginald clocked him. The man staggered back, and Lord Barton grabbed Lily's hand. He pulled her past their stunned adversary. "Come, we haven't much time!"

They hurried down the narrow alleyways, hearts pounding with adrenaline and determination. They nearly stepped into another group of ten or twelve Bonapartists. Too many.

Lord Barton pulled Lily quickly into the shadowed doorway of a stone building. Behind them, he heard Lord Spencer howling his outrage. They were trapped. He looked at the street. Which way would Helms have gone? He told the man to have a drink at a pub and then come back for them, but he knew Helms would not be foolish enough to drink in this neighborhood, and yet he wished it would be so. A carriage would get them free of this. They needed only evade capture until Helms brought the carriage back around. He considered the direction of the nearest pub. He turned towards Lady Lillian and realized she was no longer at his side.

Lord Barton watched in horror and disbelief as Lady Lily Hawthorne stepped forward, her dark curls framing her resolute face. The Bonapartist spies sneered at her, their cruel intentions clear even in the dim light of the crescent moon.

"He went that way," she pointed at a far street.

Reginald's heart leapt into his throat, choking him with fear for Lily's safety. For a single moment, he thought to leap out of his hiding place and stand by her side. But reason overcame his impulse, and he knew that doing so would only put them both in danger. He cursed himself for not stopping her before it was too late. Now, showing himself would only prove her a liar and implicate them both. Would they take her at her word?

"He had plans to the underwater ship," she said. "He must be stopped."

The cache of Bonapartists was not too bright apparently and just stared at her uncomprehendingly. "Go!" she demanded. "Catch him!"

"Very well, *Lady Hawthorne*," one of the spies sneered, grabbing her arm roughly. "You shall come with us." They started down the street with some haste in the direction she had pointed.

As they began to lead her away, Reginald's panic rose like bile in his throat. She had obviously not thought that they would insist that she accompany them. She had not known that her ruse as Miss Hawkins was blown. This was quickly turning into a disaster.

And what should he do? In a split second, possibilities flooded his mind. He could not let her sacrifice be in vain. She had saved him yet again, and he could do nothing less than honor and bravery dictated and return the favor. Yet how could he overwhelm ten men? On the other hand, he could not let her be taken. Even with his gun he was no match for ten men, and Spencer would recover and come after them. Bloody hell! He was frozen in indecision. Think, man! he demanded of himself. He forced himself to think as a spy instead of a lover. The need for reason calmed him. He could not chase after her haphazardly. He needed to find Helms and send him for reinforcements, but he could not leave her. Where were they taking her? Indecision dogged him. Which path would be most likely to save her?

He followed the group surreptitiously, never taking his eyes off Lily.

Reginald knew he had to act quickly. His thoughts raced, strategizing how best to save her. If he could escape undetected and find Helms, he could then return and rescue her from certain peril, but every minute she was left behind was an agony. He couldn't leave her. Not for a moment.

As he watched Lily disappear into the darkness, Reginald realized that they were taking her towards the harbor and the ships. Fear blossomed anew. He finally understood the depth of his feelings for her. Her beauty and intelligence had always captivated him, but now he realized that she embodied everything he could ever want in a partner. She was fearless yet compassionate, strong-willed, and loyal to the core.

Reginald slipped away from his hiding place, careful not to alert Spencer, who had come up from behind, rubbing his jaw gingerly.

He would not think of what could go wrong. He could already envision their reunion—the moment when he would sweep Lily into his arms, safe at last. And he would marry her, by God.

Lord Barton raced against the wind, his heart pounding as he urgently made his way towards the harbor, keeping the group of men in his peripheral vision. If he did not find Helms, he would certainly find Samuel or Jack. The night was treacherously dark with only a crescent moon, making it difficult to navigate the narrow, cobbled streets. He wished simultaneously for a moon to see the street and was thankful for the dark that kept him from being discovered. He couldn't afford any mistakes; Lily's life hung in the balance.

"Curse these blasted alleys," he muttered under his breath, narrowly avoiding a collision with an overturned cart. Determination and love fueled him as he navigated the labyrinth-like passages that led to the harbor.

As Reginald rounded another corner, he found himself face to face with a group of seedy-looking men blocking his path. Their leering grins sent a shiver down his spine, but he had no time for fear or distractions. He needed to reach the harbor in order to save Lily from her captors.

"Out of my way," he growled, fixing the ruffians with an icy glare. He pulled his pistol, and to his surprise, they stepped aside without a word, allowing him to pass unchallenged, although in a pinch, he could only have shot one of them. Perhaps they sensed his determination and the unquenchable resolve in his eyes. Perhaps they did not want to question which of their company would take the ball. No one would stand in his way. He had to get back to Lily. Reginald didn't question his good fortune with the thugs; instead, he pressed on, feeling the weight of Lily's fate growing heavier with each step.

Finally, he arrived at the harbormaster's office, where he encountered an unexpected ally, Captain Samuel Beresford, longtime friend and confidante, stood waiting by the door, accompanied by several of his sailors.

"Reginald!" exclaimed Samuel, grasping his friend's

arm in a gesture of solidarity. "I heard about Lady Lily's capture. We're here to help you save her."

"You heard?" Reginald said, surprised.

"Norman," Samuel said, and Reginald noted the skinny sailor that he had seen at various meetings.

"Samuel, Norman. I can't thank you enough," Reginald replied, his voice choked with emotion. "But there's no time to waste. We must act quickly if we're to have any chance of rescuing her."

"I understand your urgency, my friend," Samuel said, his expression serious. "But we mustn't rush into this blindly. If we make a mistake, we'll be unable to save her, or ourselves."

Reginald clenched his fists, frustration, and impatience warring within him. He knew Samuel was right, they needed a plan, but every second they spent devising one was another moment Lily remained in danger. He could not bear to think of what may be happening to her at this very moment. He had failed to keep her safe, but he would find her.

"Very well," he agreed, forcing himself to take a deep breath. "What do you propose?"

"We'll wait for the rest of the crew. Use the cover of darkness to infiltrate the ship and rescue Lady Lily."

"Ship?" Lord Barton said, his voice rising in fear. "What if they set sail?"

"They will sail with the tide," Samuel said with certainty. "They've already missed it, so we have some time. Are we even sure she is on the ship? She could still be in the warehouse area."

"Lud," said Reginald. "I don't know. I lost track of her, but know she is somewhere near."

Samuel laid a hand on his friend's shoulder. "Don't worry, mate. We'll find her." Turning to the sailors, he said. "You, Charlie, go to Captain Jack Hartfield on the Algiers. Tell him I need him to search east and north of the harbor. Jacob, organize half the contingent and search south and west. The rest will be ready to storm the ship itself."

"Aye, Captain," said both men.

"Your sailors are willing to risk their lives for this?" Reginald asked, glancing at the men who stood ready to aid them.

"Indeed, Lord Barton," one of the sailors replied. "We're loyal to Captain Beresford, and if he says we're to help you, then that's what we'll do."

"Thank you," Reginald murmured, touched by their unwavering devotion. "I shall never forget your bravery and loyalty. And tell the others, I can pay you."

"Of course, you can," Samuel said with a nod and a grin. "I told them so."

With their plan in place, Reginald and the sailors set out to face whatever challenges awaited them in order to save the woman who had captured Lord Reginald Barton's heart. He castigated himself that he had not stayed with her, that he had not fought the ten men who took her. He could have shot at least one. Perhaps that would have been enough. He prayed now that they would not be too late.

IN THE SHADOWS of the moonlit docks, Lady Lily Hawthorne stood trembling. As they dragged her forward, she attempted to impede their progress by simply not walking. She fell and was dragged to her feed several times before one of the men simply picked her up for expediency. Her heart pounded in her chest as she listened to the murmurs and footsteps of the Bonapartists surrounding her. She had never felt so vulnerable amongst them, realizing the full extent of her physical limitations against these men. Yet she reminded herself it was not muscles that had gotten her this far; it was her keen intellect. She had to be calm. She had to think. Could she use feminine wiles? She found herself lacking in that department, but she would have to try. She could not over-power these men. She had to use her intellect or her femininity. She was dropped unceremoniously on the ground.

When her latest ploy failed, she came face to face with Lord Spencer. She attempted to bluff her way past him, feigning surprise at his presence.

"Why Lord Spencer! Have you come to join us? What a nice surprise."

"Hardly. I am keeping my eye on you, my dear," he replied smoothly. "Wouldn't want you getting into any trouble. Or should I say, any more trouble?"

She tried another tactic, fluttering her eyelashes and adopting a coquettish tone. "Why, sir, I'm flattered by your attention. I assure you, though, I am quite capable of taking care of myself." She wrenched free of her inattentive captor, but there was no time to run.

Lord Spencer smirked, clearly unimpressed by her feminine wiles. In an instant, he closed the distance between them, gripping her arm tightly and proving just how frail she was compared to his strength. "I warned you, Lady Lily. Don't betray us. It will go badly for you," he said menacingly.

He shoved her back into the arms of another. "Hold on to her," he admonished the man, who squeezed her arm mercilessly.

"Where are you taking me? And why?" she demanded, fear rising in her chest even as she struggled against his grip.

"Maybe I'll keep you for my strumpet," Lord Spencer sneered, dragging her down the street. Unfortunately, in the part of town, gentlemen were in short supply unless they too were looking for a strumpet. No one noticed her struggles, or perhaps, no one cared. They continued shoving her forward until they reached a door that was opened for them, and she was locked in a dimly lit room. The only furniture inside was a bed and an empty pitcher of water.

Keep them talking, she thought, devising a strategy. As long as we're here, there's still hope.

"Tell me, Lord Spencer," she said aloud, forcing confidence into her voice. "How do you expect to free Bonaparte when he's so heavily guarded?"

"Ah, clever girl," sneered Lord Spencer his cruel smile making her skin crawl. "But not clever enough. You see, we have friends in high places who will ensure our success."

That meant there were people involved in the scheme that they had not seen at the meetings. Her heart sank. They would not get all of the perpetrators of the plot. How many had used the poor for this travesty? And the poor would bear the brunt of the arrests, but today, she was worried about her own skin.

"Now, where is Lord Barton?" Spencer asked.

Lily lifted a shoulder in response. "I am not his keeper."

Her glib tongue was rewarded with his fist. The world erupted into stars of pain, and she tasted blood, but she would not yield. "Your plan is doomed to fail," Lily retorted as she spat blood at his feet, her dark eyes flashing with defiance. "You underestimate England's determination to keep Bonaparte imprisoned."

"*Assez!*" barked one of the men, grabbing Lily's arm roughly. He continued in French. "Enough! We've wasted enough time on this foolish woman. Let's board the ship before we're discovered. Once we are to sea, we will throw the wretch overboard."

"Wait!" Lily cried out, understanding the gist of the rapid, guttural French. What happened to being Lord Spencer's strumpet? she thought as she weighed rape against drowning. Her mind was racing for a way to stall their departure. If they boarded a ship, she was lost. "What about ransom?" she said, grasping at straws. "Surely the Earl of Thornwood will pay handsomely for my safe return. My grandfather loves me."

That fact was debatable, but the villains did not know that. Personally, she thought her grandfather would probably be glad to be rid of her. She could feel her lip swelling. What gentleman would want a woman with such cheek that it bore the rewards of a swollen lip? Certainly not Lord Rumford. The thought made her laugh. At least she would not have to marry him. Perhaps she was bordering on hysterical, but her laughter flummoxed the sailors.

The men hesitated, exchanging glances. They knew

the earl's wealth and reputation, but they also knew how fiercely he guarded both. Lord Spencer was against waiting for ransom, but the motion was denied ten to one. The lure of gold and greed won against Lord Spencer's argument, and although the men generally capitulated to him, at this point, they did not. After a tense moment and an argument spoken wholly in French, Lord Spencer reluctantly nodded.

"Very well," he agreed. "We'll send word to your grandfather. But make no mistake, Lady Lily, if he refuses to pay, or if we sense any treachery, you will suffer the consequences. I won't hesitate to toss you overboard myself."

"Understood," she replied, masking her relief with a steely expression. She worried her tooth with her tongue. She tasted blood and realized the tooth was loose. For a mad moment, she thought, her already questionable looks were further marred, and then she realized a loose tooth was the least of her worries. They wanted to take her aboard a ship. If Grandfather didn't pay, they could sell her to the highest bidder. They wouldn't set sail until the ransom note was delivered. Small mercy. Then, they would have to wait until Grandfather's answer arrived. She did not know where they would go, but at least, they would not go far.

As the men began writing their ransom demands, Lily's thoughts turned to Lord Barton. For the first time in her life, she realized she was completely outmatched. She could not reason with these people, and their combined strength was more than ten times her own. She felt like a mouse caught in talons and forced to negotiate with a bird of prey. She could show all the logical arguments for her release, but the bird only saw dinner. "Please," she silently prayed as she worried the loose tooth. "Please let Lord Barton find me in time." The taste of blood in her mouth made her realize how precarious her position was.

REGINALD, Captain Samuel, and the sailors stealthily approached the docks. So far, there was no sign of Lily in the warehouse district. It was probable that the Bonapartists had found another ship to convey what arms they had managed to hide from the harbor patrol, but whether or not Lily was on a ship remained to be seen. And what ship? Reginald felt himself losing hope when the skinny sailor he had seen at one of the meetings ran up to greet them. What was the man's name? Norman. With a quick salute to Samuel, he spoke. "The Scipion," he panted. "I've heard tell the lady is on the Scipion. It was a French ship. It's manned by its old crew. The English crew is tied up on board. One of my mates crews the Scipion," he said, pushing a dark-haired lad forward. The young sailor looked terrified.

"Thank you," Reginald said to the boy, and he seemed to relax being amongst friends and Englishmen.

"Jesse, take half the men starboard," Samuel ordered. "I and the others will go to port. Secure the ship and release the crew. Stealthily."

"Don't worry, Capt'n," Jesse said. "Most of the swells, don' even look at a sailor. Not like you. They won't even notice their crew ain't the same 'till they open their mouth and ain't speakin' French."

Samuel nodded.

Reginald watched, feeling helpless, his hazel eyes scanning the area for any sign of Lily. "I'll find Lady Lillian," he said.

"Norman, catch your breath. Stay with Lord Barton," Samuel ordered.

"Aye, Sir," said the lithe sailor.

Reginald noted that he only had the man's first name, but he would not forget. When this was all over, he would reward the man. For now, the man and the boy both had his sincere thanks.

"May fortune favor us all," Samuel replied, nodding to his loyal crew. The young sailor filed in with the others.

As the sailors dispersed, Reginald crept closer. The smell of saltwater and fish filled his nostrils as he listened intently for any indication of where Lily might be held. His heart skipped a beat when he heard her familiar voice, sharp and defiant even in captivity.

"Over there," he murmured to Norman, adrenaline coursing through him. He could not see her, but her voice was unmistakable.

"Aye," the man said. "She has spirit. Reminds me of my Ella."

"Wife?" Lord Barton asked.

"Daughter. Five girls I got."

Silently, Lord Barton maneuvered through the shadows, each step bringing him closer to the woman he had come to love. He knew that every moment mattered, that their enemies would not hesitate to carry out their threats. But he also knew that he was not alone, that the bravery and skill of his allies would help them prevail.

"Stay strong, Lily," he thought fiercely, inching closer to his objective. "We're coming for you."

Reginald, his heart pounding in his chest, finally spotted Lily at the far end of the dock. She was bound and surrounded by a group of sinister-looking men. Despite her dire circumstances, she stood tall, her dark hair framing her face like a halo, her dark brown eyes filled with defiance.

His concern for her safety momentarily overrode any need for stealth.

"Unhand her, you scoundrels!" he demanded, his voice booming across the docks as he leapt to her defense. The Bonapartists hesitated then reluctantly backed away as Samuel and an abundance of sailors charged forward, engaging them in combat. They quickly realized that they were outnumbered. Apparently, Samuel's sailors had incapacitated much of the French crew while freeing the English, and there were few of the French crew fit to join the fight.

"Are you hurt, my love?" Reginald asked breathlessly as he attempted to untie her bonds, his hazel eyes filled with concern.

Without a word, Norman handed him a knife, hilt first, and he slashed through the bonds that held her.

"Nothing that won't heal," Lily replied, rubbing her wrists where the ropes had chaffed her skin. "Thank you for coming to my rescue, Lord Barton." She held her head high, ever a lady, but her lip trembled.

"You were so brave," he replied, his voice thick with emotion. "I will never again doubt your resolve—"

Something broke within her, and with a small cry, she flung herself into his arms. "I was so scared," she admitted as he wrapped his arms around her. He never wanted to let her go, their lips meeting in a passionate kiss that seemed to suspend time itself. It was a moment of pure bliss.

Some of the sailors chuckled. "Human, after all, the swells," said one.

"Ahem," Samuel interrupted, clearing his throat loudly. "Forgive me, but Regge, this may not be the time." They broke apart, their cheeks flushed with the intensity of their emotions. Lily's hand went to her sore lip.

"You are hurt," Reginald said, noting the bruise on her face. His own face darkened in anger. "Who struck you?"

"Spencer," she admitted, and there was no doubt in her mind that Reginald would not rest until that slight was rectified.

"I want to go home," she said, trying to keep her voice from sounding plaintive.

"Of course, you do," Reginald agreed, his voice firm his hand still on Lily's shoulder. He was not going to let her out of his sight again. "Let's ensure these traitors are brought to justice," he said, looking around for Lord Spencer who was conspicuously absent. Montogomery, however, was found below deck. Samuel threatened to put him in irons. Lord Barton couldn't really care less. Lily was safe, and that was his only concern at the moment.

# RESCUED

*L*ily couldn't help but marvel at the bravery and determination she had witnessed, not just by Lord Barton and his friend Samuel, but all the sailors who came to her aid. They fought so valiantly to save her and thwart the Bonapartists' plans. She felt an immense sense of gratitude for their efforts.

"Lord Barton," she said softly as they stood amidst the chaos, "all of you, thank you."

Lord Barton smiled warmly, his eyes twinkling with affection. "Oh, I am sure you would have managed on your own if I had not been about," he said flippantly.

"I—" She grinned. She realized he was teasing her.

As they left the docks behind, Lily realized it was already the morning of the grand ball her grandfather was hosting, her own engagement ball. The excitement and danger of their adventure now sharply contrasted with the more mundane concerns of her home life. She knew that returning to her family would mean facing her grandfather's wrath and navigating the complexities of societal expectations. But with Lord Barton by her side, she felt ready to face whatever challenges lay ahead. She had to wonder if the ransom note had reached Mayfair. That would surely complicate things.

"Come, take me home," Lily suggested, her hand in Reginald's as they headed up the street.

"Your wish is my command," said Reginald. "As soon as I find my carriage. We may have to hire a hackney, but first, let us walk to a better part of town."

"What makes this part less good?" she demanded.

He raised an eyebrow, but they kept walking leaving the docks behind.

Helms at last found them.

Reginald handed her into the conveyance and told the much-beleaguered man, "Get us out of here, Helms."

"Are you sure, sir?" asked the cheeky driver. "Are there no other dragons to slay this morning?"

"Not today," Reginald said with a laugh. "Take us to Mayfair. The Hawthorne family's estate."

"Yes. There is much to discuss with my family," Lily said.

"Agreed," he replied, his voice filled resolve. "But I think your grandfather will want to have words with me."

"You?" Lily said.

"I have certainly kept you out past curfew. It is a new day."

"You have done nothing of the kind," she objected.

He sighed. "So you say. Let's see what your grandfather thinks."

"Humph."

As Lord Barton and Lady Lily rode through the now

bustling streets of lower London, street merchants called out their wares. The scent of flowers from nearby sellers mingled with the aroma of fresh bread from a nearby bakery, giving life to the air around them. "Are you hungry?" Lord Barton asked.

"Starved," she agreed. "Let's stop."

"I suppose it doesn't matter how late it is now," Lord Barton said. "Or how early. I don't think you will be able to sneak in the servant's entrance no matter how careful you are," he said.

She looked horrified, realizing that she had been absent for more than a night and most of the day. The sun seemed to be climbing higher every moment. Lord Barton was right. There was no chance that the household was still asleep.

With a chagrined sigh, Lily nodded. "You are correct."

They stopped the carriage and bought fresh baked rolls, slathered them with butter and jam, and shared them with Helms, who admitted he had not eaten while they were gone. Instead, he had gone to Bow Street and added to those who were helping to find the villains. Helms had his own tale to tell. At last, they were on their way to Mayfair.

As they approached the Hawthorne estate, Reginald noticed how the dappled sunlight filtered through the trees, illuminating Lily's dark curls, making her seem like an ethereal figure. She licked jam from her fingers. Reginald resisted the urge to pull her hands to his own mouth and suck the sweets from her. The bruise on her face was darkening. Somewhere, she had lost her gloves. She had never looked more precious to him.

"Are you all right?" she asked as she noticed his expression.

"I am. Are you?" he asked tenderly, his hazel eyes filled with concern as he observed her more closely. "You have been through a lot."

"I am quite happy," Lily replied, her voice soft yet determined. "It's just that everything feels so different now."

Reginald reached out to gently squeeze her hand, their fingers entwining, stickiness notwithstanding. "How so?"

"We've been through much together," she said.

"And I believe our love has only grown stronger because of it," he added.

She did not deny it. "Indeed," she said, her dark brown eyes meeting his.

A smile tugged at the corners of Reginald's lips as they approached the wrought-iron gates of the Hawthorne townhouse.

Lord Barton helped her from the carriage. "Are you ready for this?" he asked.

"I am," she said. They walked hand in hand towards the front door where silence loomed. It was early morning, but not so early that it could be considered the previous day. She wondered if her grandfather was awake yet. She need not have wondered. She could hear his bluster as soon as Angley opened the door.

"Lady, we have been so worried," Angley gushed and then recovered himself. "Begging your pardon," he said his ears blushing with his forwardness.

"Never doubted it," said old Patton in a loud voice,

due to the fact that the man was nearly deaf. "The lady is spunky, I tell you."

Lily's sisters, Grace and Betty, rushed over to greet them.

"Where have you been, Lily?" Betty exclaimed, her eyes wide with curiosity. She looked to Lord Barton, and her mouth formed an astonished O.

"Mother was worried sick," added Grace, her expression a mix of relief and confusion.

Mother didn't say a word. She just sniffed. It was obvious she had been crying.

"Never mind that now," interrupted their father, his face a mask of anger as he strode towards them. "Considering the circumstance, Lord Rumford has withdrawn his offer, Lily."

"Thank heavens," Lily muttered.

Her father then turned his attention to Reginald. "And you, Lord Barton, what is the meaning of this?" Her brother, Robert, stood glowering at Father's side like an echo of her grandfather.

"Father—" Lily began but was cut off by her grandfather's booming voice.

"Silence!" the Earl of Thornwood roared, his eyes narrowing in fury. "You have embarrassed our family enough tonight, young lady. And as for you, Lord Barton, I hope you plan to marry my granddaughter, otherwise there will be pistols at dawn."

Lily started to protest, wondering just who would be wielding the pistols, and besides, it was already past dawn, but Lord Barton straightened his spine and met the Earl's piercing gaze without hesitation. "Of course, my lord," he replied confidently. "It would be my honor to make Lady Lillian my wife. If she will have me." His eyes were only for Lily.

"Oh, she will have you," the Earl huffed before storming away, leaving an uncomfortable silence hanging in the air.

Despite the tension surrounding them, Reginald and Lily exchanged a meaningful glance, their love for each other evident in the warmth of their gazes.

"Will you marry me?" Lord Barton asked, and Lily realized that even after all they had been through, he wanted her to say the words. She knew that together they could face whatever challenges lay ahead, spies, traitors and even the wrath of the formidable Earl of Thornwood. She smiled at him, her acceptance on the tip of her tongue when the earl turned back to Lord Barton.

"Do not hesitate to beat her," he said shaking his cane at her. "That has been her father's weakness all of her life. She is entirely too headstrong for a woman."

"Ah—" Began Lily.

"I do not think that will be necessary," Lord Barton said clasping her hand tightly. "I think I shall just love her."

The Earl of Thornwood nodded. Then he tapped his cane on the floor, gaining everyone's attention. "It seems my wayward granddaughter has chosen another suitor," he said. "The engagement of Lady Lillian Hawthorne shall be announced at the ball this evening. She will marry Lord Reginald Barton." He looked at Reginald and raised an eyebrow. "Soon," Grandfather said.

"Yes," Lord Barton agreed. "Soon."

And for once, Lily had no objections. "Soon," she echoed.

"Oh, my baby," her mother sniffed. "My Lily, a bride." And then her mother promptly turned into a watering pot. Lily's father handed her a handkerchief without saying a word.

Lily wondered if Lord Barton was already regretting being made a part of her obnoxious family, but he was smiling ear to ear and looking at her with such love, she felt ready to burst with happiness.

# ENGAGEMENT BALL

The engagement ball was nothing like what Lily had expected it to be, or perhaps it was her own attitude that had changed. She was actually looking forward to it.

Her sister Betty bounced on the bed in her excitement. Even though she wasn't out yet, Mother had agreed that she could come and take a peek at her sister, Lily, as she and Lord Barton opened the ball with a dance.

Grace, who was always the picture of propriety, took one last look at Maggie's handiwork and clasped Lily's hands in her own. "You look lovely," she said to her sister.

"I'm not the pretty one," Lily prevaricated.

"Today you are," Grace said. "You are shining with a resplendent light."

"It's love," Betty pronounced. "Lily is in love."

As the time for the ball drew near, she paced nervously in a secluded corner, sucking on her sore lip and tugging at the lace on her sleeve. She was always more comfortable in simple clothing, but today, she supposed she wanted to be beautiful. She wanted to believe Grace, that today she was beautiful.

A MOVEMENT at the foyer caught her attention. She glanced over at Lord Barton, who paused in the doorway and was using the hallway mirror to arrange his cravat to perfection. Was it possible that he too wanted to be perfect for her? She marveled at the thought. With a determined glint in his hazel eyes, he caught her gaze and winked.

"Lord Barton," Lily said with a hint of exasperation. "Do you think I care one whit about the precise angle of your cravat?"

"Ah, but my dear Lady Hawthorne," Reginald replied, his voice a mix of amusement and mock seriousness, "a gentleman's attire is of the utmost importance, especially on the day he announces his engagement. Will I do?" he asked as the stubborn cravat was finally tied.

She frowned. "Very stuffy," she said. "I think I liked you better wet with sea water."

"Hmm," he hummed, his eyes darkening with the thought. "I think we shall have to wait a bit for such an adventure. It is, after all, the engagement ball, not the wedding."

Lily felt her face heat with a blush, but she was never one to pause at impropriety. "Well, I shall have you know, I have no desire to marry a dull and unadventurous man."

"And I expect you shall be with me in these adventures," he said.

"Equality in all things," Lily echoed solemnly as he raised her hand to his lips for a gentle kiss.

"So be it," he said. "Shall we dance?"

"We shall," she agreed.

The air was thick with perfume and the scent of beeswax candles, while a string quartet struck up a waltz. Grandfather announced Lord Reginald Barton and Lady Lillian Hawthorne, and the couple took center stage in the opulent ballroom where London's elite gathered to discuss politics and revel in their wealth.

But at least one couple were not concerned with matters of finance and luxury. Instead, while they waltzed, they discussed the fate of the sailors who had helped them and the women who worked the streets. Neither brought up the fact that Lord Spencer had skipped away from the law, using his money as a shield, but one day, he would pay, Lily was sure of that fact. One day, evil would be punished and good would be vindicated.

"Together, we are an unstoppable force for good," Reginald said, and Lily could not have agreed more. She had avoided marriage because she didn't want to be dominated by a man, but now, she realized that hand in hand, as equals, they could make changes that neither of them could accomplish alone.

# THE COUNTESS AND THE BARON ~ PRUDENCE

The Nettlefold Chronicles ~ The Baggington Sisters

Cover Art by Mary Lepiane

2018 Mikita Associates Publishing

Published in the United States of America.

www.isabellathorne.com

## PROLOGUE

Miss Prudence Baggington's fine light brown hair had been arranged atop her head with a garland of minuscule white flowers that her maid called baby's breath. She still wore her dressing robe, but the voluminous folds of her wedding gown were draped over the edge of the bed and ready to be worn. She still could not quite believe that this day had arrived. She expected someone to come and snatch the victory away from her.

Outside her window, dawn colored the sky with the most beautiful array of red and orange sunbeams that Prudence had seen in weeks. She had thought to have once heard a saying about a crimson sky in the morning being a cause for alarm, but shook her head and laughed at the silly, childish notion.

Of course there was nothing more beautiful than a rose-hued sunrise. The weather was beautiful and she was about to be wed. At last. She let herself breath in the cool scent of the morning and sighed with relief.

Marriage. Escape was perhaps a better word, but marriage would do. Once married she would be safe. She had dreamed of little else for most of her life, and she had prayed most dearly for these past few years. At last her prayers were answered, though not in the way she expected.

Of course Prudence did not want to stay on as a spinster in her father's home. Perish the thought. Still she had thought her groom would have been the wealthy and oh so handsome Duke of Kilmerstan, but Garrett Rutherford had evaded her every move, and eventually married that little mouse of a woman, Juliana Willoughby.

Prudence huffed. Juliana was on the shelf for years.

How could she have succeeded where Prudence failed? The thought still irritated but Prudence pushed it from her mind. She could not be bothered by that now. It was her wedding day.

She may not be marrying a duke, but an earl would certainly do. She would be a countess. That status had to count for something. A bit of cheer bubbled in to halt her consternation. She would make all the hypocritical biddies who called her "the baggage" eat their words. She smiled at the thought, took up her wedding dress, and twirled around the room. She could not ever remember being so happy. She smiled at herself in the glass.

"Yes, Countess," she said. "Right away, Countess."

She carefully hung the gown again. It was true that her situation was not what she had once hoped, but there was good in it, she thought. One unexpected kiss of passion with a near stranger, an earl no less, had led to the marriage arrangement and the reading of the banns.

She had expected each Sunday to have someone object to her impending marriage, but looking around the church she saw no one speak to oppose it, not even the Earl of Fondleton himself.

At first, Prudence had been nervous about the marriage and about the Earl's absence at each reading of the banns, but the happy day had arrived. Marriage to an earl had not been her plan, but he was titled, and wealthy. He was not old, nor was he terrible to look at. What more could a lady ask? They would grow to know and love each other in time. She was sure of it. Certainly, this was a better option than her current situation.

She shuddered.

The truth was that Prudence would have married just about anyone to get out of her father's house. She, and her mother, had been plotting for months to catch eligible gentlemen in the Nettlefold countryside, but all to no avail. No expense had been spared. They had ordered the most extravagant gowns and perfumes to catch the attentions of the gentlemen. Prudence had been hesitant at first to follow the advice of a London socialite, but her mother paid heavily for the designs, so Prudence capitulated.

She had shrugged her shoulders and gone along with the ploy, even attempting to enact an overly feminine accent that she had been instructed would appeal to the gentlemen's ears. She thought she sounded akin to a banshee, but the gentlemen did take notice. Still, it was a relief to know that she could return to her normal tone, even if some said she had a voice like a man. Perhaps speaking normally would bring an end to the hoarseness and sore throat which plagued her in the mornings.

Prudence had thought all the glitter and glam a farce, but perhaps her mother was right. Perhaps such maneuverings worked. After all, the machinations did end with her engagement. She would be Lady Fondleton.

"Lord and Lady Fondleton," she had whispered to herself in the mirror as the hope for her future lay ahead in an endless road of promise. While their meeting had been abrupt and, of course, improper, there was some romance to it as well. One could not be kissed in a stable without the thought of romance, she supposed.

She brought her fingers to her lips, remembering. The kiss was rather abrupt and rough, but she supposed the Earl had not thought so well of her at the time. He did not know she was a lady. In the dark he seemed to think her someone else, perhaps a kitchen wench or some drab. She would not censure him she decided if he wanted to take a mistress, as long as he was discrete and she was with child first. He would want an heir, of course. She tapped her fingers nervously with the thought. She remembered the first and only time she had met her soon-to-be husband.

Upon literally bumping into one another in the stables of the Inn, Prudence had nearly fallen off balance. She was sure she wind milled her arms in a most unbecoming way, and her hat had fallen askew, but instead of being put off by her unladylike stance, the man caught her. Overcome with passion in that moment, he had swept down upon her, gathered her close to his very masculine form and planted a hard kiss upon her lips.

She had not been prepared. Never before had she felt quite so overwhelmed. She had perhaps just this once earned the nickname of baggage, because she was so thrilled in the moment, that she had not decried his boldness. Instead, she had allowed the kiss. Well, she supposed she did not really have a choice in the matter. She did not even have time to be afraid.

He had her in his arms, one hand laced through her hair and the other clasped to her to him in a very ungentlemanly way. She should have been afraid. He was so audacious and overwhelmingly male, she found herself as meek as a kitten. She could not even utter a squeak. Such was not a disposition that others expected of Prudence – lioness perhaps, or jackal, but not kitten. She was certain that the Earl's passionate kiss had been a sign of their destined future, and then they were well and truly caught.

Once caught in such an embrace and there had been no explaining it. Prudence had swooned in his arms and he had held her. He had kissed her quite thoroughly and she imagined that she looked quite flushed and disheveled with the whole affair when Mrs. Hardcastle came upon them and exclaimed her outrage. She couldn't even blame Mrs. Hardcastle for outing them. After all, the woman knew Prudence was contending for a husband. Mrs. Hardcastle knew her situation, and she saw a solution. Prudence took it. Perhaps she should thank the woman.

Prudence twirled a recalcitrant curl around her finger tucking it into place.

Perhaps the Earl loved her, Prudence thought suddenly. She wondered, could it be love at first sight on his behalf? She could only hope that love might grow between them, but no matter. It would be better than home. She had to believe that.

Still, as the passion of their wedding night approached, Prudence could not help but worry. She remembered the Earl's embrace. It had not been full of love, but full of lust. She shuddered with the thought, but she reminded herself, she would be his wife. She would have stature.

He was simply overcome with passion in the stable. He would not treat his wife so callously. On their wedding night she was sure he would apologize for his previous behavior, and she would forgive him. He would be her husband and offer her his protection. She would suffer his embrace. This she could do.

He would be more caring this time, she thought. He would be gentler and gentlemanly. She had thought of little else but the wedding night for weeks prior to today, though she had never had the opportunity to be alone with her betrothed. In fact, she had not seen the Earl at all. If she were not currently looking at her wedding finery, she would have wondered if this was really the morning of her nuptials.

Father would walk her down the aisle. With any luck this would be the last time the man would touch her. She remembered Father's reaction when the news of her indiscretion reached him. He was, as was to be expected, furious. But after today, his wrath would not be able to touch her. She would be under her husband's protection. She smiled.

Prudence was just pleased to have escaped her father's grasp once and for all. Now, with a wealthy husband, she could lead the sort of life that she, and her many sisters, had always dreamed of. Her sisters. She would allow them all to visit as often as they could. She would shelter them. She would not abandon them like her older sister Temperance had done, running off to a convent rather than marrying. No. She, Prudence, would help them, just as soon as she was married to the Earl.

"Mama," Prudence had called. "I am ready."

Her mother had entered the room with a smile as bright as the rising sun.

"You shall be beautiful," she whispered into her daughter's curls.

Prudence bit her lip. With several sisters well known for their timeless beauty and remarkable features, Prudence was more than aware of her plain face. Plump cheeks and a voluptuous frame softened any definable structure that was applauded in the willow thin bodies of her siblings. Even her eyes were nothing that would cause prose to be written in the throes of passion and love. Brown. Brown. Brown. Nothing more, nothing less. There was nothing special about her, Prudence thought. It was for that reason that she had allowed her mother to doll her up in extravagant costumes that might help her to stand out amongst the crowd of beautiful debutantes.

As Prudence stepped into her wedding gown, which was soon pulled tight by her mother's practiced fingers, she began to worry.

"Mama," she whispered. "Lord Fondleton... he is a good man, is he not?"

"He is an earl," her mother replied as if that were all the answer needed.

Prudence thought on her mother's words for a long while. Titled gentlemen were expected to be above all others in regard to their morality and character. Still... she wondered. He seemed nice enough. He offered plenty of smiles and compliments, but so did her father. In public, he seemed the perfect gentleman. In private, he was a monster.

"Papa is a Viscount," she muttered but, if her mother heard her, the Viscountess Mortel did not respond.

1

Prudence was married for three months. Three months of torturous marriage was more than she could bear. As the mail coach bounced along the rutted roads she only hoped that she could get far enough away before the Earl realized that she had left. If he found her, he would bring her back. If she stayed away, perhaps he could say she was dead. She might as well be dead.

Jasper Numbton, the Earl of Fondleton, was a monster and a rake. Prudence did her best to keep her features illegible of their torment. Not a tear or muffled sob would slip free. Years upon years of practice had taught the Baggington sisters to hide their woes. Prudence had thought marriage her salvation. Now, she carried nothing but a small carpet bag that rode in her lap as if it contained items too precious to be lashed to the top of the carriage.

"Halthaven ahead!" the driver called. The carriage began to slow and Prudence felt her heart begin to thump in her chest anew.

She had taken a risk coming to Halthaven, a monumental risk. It would either be her deliverance or her undoing for if the Earl discovered her escape she might never get the chance again. She was sure he would lock her away. His would be the only face she saw for the remainder of her days.

The other occupants climbed from the coach to stretch their legs but they would not be staying in the remote village. As soon as the horses were watered they would be on their way again, with no recollection of the quiet lady with her face shielded by a bonnet.

Alone in the coach Prudence struggled to pull the wedding band from her plump finger. It had been a source of protection during her journey but she had no need for it any longer. In fact, she wished nothing more than to forget that she had ever been married in the first place. With the ring's removal she felt somewhat lighter, more like herself, Prudence again rather than Lady Fondleton.

She slipped the plain metal ring into a velvet pouch and considered pushing it into the carpet bag, but decided it was best to leave it closed just now. It was best the contents of said bag remain secret. Instead, Prudence put the velvet pouch into her pocket and pushed the golden ring to the very bottom.

She wished she could forget about it entirely. She wished she could have left it behind, but of course, she could not. The ring was the only jewelry she carried. She had left the more costly ornaments at the manor. She did not wish to be accused of theft, even though as the countess the jewels were rightfully hers. She knew the Earl did not love her, but if she took anything of value, Prudence knew he would hunt her down. She hoped that leaving empty handed would keep the Earl from seeking her too vigorously.

Then, with as much pride as she could muster, she tucked her small bag close and descended the mail coach. She thanked the footman for handing her down. She had no coin for a tip except the one that was promised to the nuns, but she was grateful for his kindness. He smiled absently and looked away. For once, she was happy to know that her plain features would help her to be easily forgotten.

She had never been to Halthaven before, nor had she ever intended to visit. It was a shock to see the rush of activity in the isolated town. The arrival of the mail coach had spurred the excitement of the locals. Doors opened and slammed shut as patrons rushed to collect their letters or packages. An old woman with a cane and one milky blue eye watched Prudence with interest. Prudence turned her face away and held her bag close to her chest with two hands as she slipped down the street away from the crowd.

A sign swung and creaked in the wind, announcing a tavern named the Broken Bridle. Prudence was not sure of the level of clientele that would be housed within, nor did she care. The patrons could not be more repugnant than her own husband. She pushed her way into the dark and dank hall and made her way to the barkeep.

The burly man in a once white apron, polished the glasses that sat in a row on the counter. His face was mostly covered with a surplus of facial hair. Both his hair and his beard looked like they could have used a trim weeks ago. He grinned at her, and she felt somewhat at ease by his ready smile.

"What can I help ya fer?" he grunted while replacing a glass and choosing another to shine. His eyes were on the glass.

Again, Prudence noted that she was not worth the lingering stares that would follow her sisters every time they showed their faces outside of the manor. Once again, she thanked God for her plain features.

She cleared her throat.

"If you would be so kind," she muttered hoarsely, cleared her throat again, and began anew. "If you would be so kind as to direct me toward Halthurst Abbey, I would be most grateful."

The man raised his gaze to look her over. Prudence stood under his appraisal from her bonnet to her toes with a nervous patience. Then, he gave one curt nod and turned his attention back to the glasses.

"Gon' be a nun, are ya?" he asked.

As a married woman Prudence would never be allowed to take such vows against those she had already stated, not while her husband lived, but there was no way for this man to know that. Rather, she would give whatever excuse might kept her identity concealed until she arrived at her destination.

"Yes, sir," she whispered. "I wish with all my heart that I would be worthy to dwell with the holy sisters." She lowered her head and did her best to give a modest and pious nod. Perhaps he often directed ladies toward the Abbey. Prudence wondered if her own sister had stood here all those years ago and made the same request.

"You'll not get there any time soon," he revealed. "All this rain we've seen has got the throughway flooded. Bridge is washed out and no way across 'cept on foot."

"Oh," Prudence felt deflated. She turned to glance out of the window and saw that the sun was already well in the sky. "If I were to walk could I arrive by nightfall?" she asked.

The barkeep held one finger to the tip of his nose while he thought.

"Perhaps ya should wait 'til mornin,'" he offered.

"I'd rather not wait another moment, if it can be helped," she revealed. "If you think it can be done, please point me in the proper direction, and I shall go."

"I ought ter say no," he shrugged, "but ya look like a sturdy enough gal for it. Ya got a strong pair of boots on them feet of yours?"

Prudence shifted her feet beneath her gown. She was wearing her best walking boots in preparation for the journey but they were still made more for fashion than crossing the countryside. Another product of her London advice, she mused sadly.

"Of course," she lied. Prudence did not care if she had to climb barefoot up a mountainside if it meant getting to the Abbey before darkness fell upon her. She was road weary and ready to be free of her burdens, if that were at all possible.

The man narrowed his eyes. For a moment she worried that he might call her bluff, but it seemed that he decided to allow her to make her own bed, if she so wished it.

"Well," he nodded, "my daughters are brawny girls so I learned not ta expect less from a woman. It's not a trek for the weak but I see you'll not be swayed." He explained that she should follow the main road to the end of the village. Then, she should take the fork in the road to the left. Once she came to the bridge she'd have to find a more shallow place to ford, but the road led straight to the Abbey if she just stayed upon it.

"Don' go to the right or you'll end up in the Baron's Wood," he warned. "It's mighty easy to get turned around in the woods. We might not find ya 'till Michaelmas since we've no way 'o knowin' if you didna get to the Abbey, what with the road out and all."

She thanked the barkeep and offered him her last coin. The rugged man, who could scare the leather off a cow, let his shoulders droop as he looked upon her extended hand.

"Keep it, miss," he gave a soft grin. "If nothin' else, give it to the sisters up where you're goin'. They've done a world a good for this village. That's to be sure." Prudence realized that there was more heart in him than met the eye. She folded her hand back around the last coin to her name, tears welling in her eyes at such a simple kindness.

With a croaked word of thanks she left the tavern and made her way toward the edge of the village.

For a moment, she almost felt a hope that her faith might be renewed in humanity. Then, she recalled why she had found herself in the tavern in the first place, and she cursed the world of men, mostly her father and her husband. Then she bit her tongue and asked forgiveness. She should not go to the holy sisters with a curse in her mouth.

"If only you would take them both, Lord," She prayed. "I do not wish harm upon them, for that would be ungodly. I only wish they were in Your Presence rather than mine. I am too weak to suffer them."

## 2

Night did fall before Prudence reached her destination. She had trudged along with a determination that she had not known she possessed, yet the time wasted finding a shallow place to cross the river had cost her precious hours.

She had removed her boots and stockings, tossed her skirts over her shoulder, and still not managed to climb up the opposing bank without leaving herself drenched from waist to toe. The added weight of her dresses slowed her to the point where she even considered walking for a mile or two in only her undergarments until her skirts dried. Her sensibilities would not allow it, so she placed her boots back upon her feet and dragged the sodden folds through the mud behind her.

When the light of the day began to fade she was thankful that the twinkle of candles in the windows of the Abbey had come into view in the distance. That, and the ring of a bell that chimed every quarter of an hour kept her to the path, even when she was no longer certain that she was upon it.

Her stomach growled with the memory of her last meal, a bit of bread and cheese that had been stolen from the kitchens before her escape from her husband's home. The final morsel had been consumed shortly after she had begun to plod her way through the sodden trail away from the village. She prayed that the nuns might allow her a bite of something, anything, upon her arrival. The thought that she might have to wait until a communal morning meal made her groan in agony. Already, her head was beginning to ache and her stomach twisted and cried out.

Prudence was near delirium when she arrived at the steps of the Abbey. She had been muttering nonsense into her bag for nigh on an hour, recalling the journey they had completed and how much better off life would be away from the Earl.

"May I help you?" a soft voice startled Prudence from her reverie. She looked up into the soft, brown eyes of a frail looking nun who might have been the oldest person Prudence had ever laid eyes upon.

"Oh!" she gasped. "Umm… well…"

Now that she was here, she knew not what to say. She snapped her bag shut with a little squeak. She thought for a long while about the best way to begin. Rather than pry, the nun simply stood and waited with silent understanding.

All of a sudden, Prudence fell to her knees in supplication. "I pray you," she said.

"Pray to God," the nun said with a stern expression.

Prudence, still kneeling, clutched at the nun's grey habit. "Please, I've nowhere else to go," she cried. "I do not know what to do."

The nun's face softened as she bent down. "What is the matter my child?"

The old woman crouched at her side and pulled Prudence against her with surprising strength. Her fingers stroked Prudence's matted tresses and her cooed soft words of love and support. Prudence wished that she could stop the world in this moment and live in it forever.

She wiped the tears from her eyes and looked up into the face of her savior. The woman had clear blue eyes, and laugh lines about her lips, but the rest of her face was covered by her wimple.

"I don't know where to begin," Prudence whimpered.

"What led you here?" the old nun asked.

"My sister," Prudence said. "I hope she is here."

"Your sister?"

"Temperance!" Prudence exclaimed. The prospect of her sister being so near made Prudence want to rush into the Abbey and call out for her sibling. "My sister," she explained. "I need to see my sister."

The old woman narrowed her eyes, taking in all that Prudence was and, perhaps, measuring her against her sister. Prudence hoped not for there was no comparison. Temperance was the most beautiful of the Baggington sisters. In fact, before she had abandoned Nettlefold for the Abbey five years prior, Temperance had been the gem of the town.

"I see," was all that the nun said. She must have made some significant determination for she stood, set Prudence upon her feet, and ushered her inside. After a moment, she spoke again. "I will speak with the Mother Abbess."

Prudence wondered what the Mother Abbess would do. Would she allow her to stay?

"May I take your things while you wait?" the nun said as she settled Prudence before a simple fire in a gaping hearth.

"No!" Prudence exclaimed and clutched the bag to her breast. Then, she recalled her manners and softened her tone. "Thank you," she amended. "I should like to keep it, if you don't mind."

"As you wish," the nun nodded and left the room on silent footsteps.

Prudence used the moment to evaluate her surroundings. She had been led into a bare room with little more than a writing desk and a pair of padded chairs. The walls were adorned with several paintings of the religious persuasion, but overall the room was bare.

Despite the empty expanse, it was not cold. In fact, she felt at once at home. If it would not have been rude, she might have curled up in the opposite chair and drifted off to sleep. Instead, due to the ruined nature of her gown, she chose a spindly wooden piece that was worn to the point of comfort from ages of use.

The door creaked open and another elderly, though not quite so old as the first, nun swept into the room with a grace that would befit The Queen.

"What is your name, child?" she asked as she settled herself at the writing desk.

"Prudence," she said after some hesitation.

"I am Sister Beatrice," the nun explained, "Mother Abbess of Halthurst Abbey. Your claim to be Temperance's sister would make you a Baggington, yet you have not identified yourself as such. What is your *proper* name?"

Prudence could see that, while the Mother Abbess seemed obliging enough at the moment, she would not put the question to her again.

"I am Lady Fondleton," she said with a heavy heart. "Wife to the Earl of Fondleton, Prudence Numbton, formerly Baggington."

"Thank you, Lady Fondleton," Sister Beatrice replied. She folded her hands upon her lap and looked upon Prudence with a firm expression. "The convent is no place for a married woman. Are you widowed?"

"N-no," Prudence stammered. It would not do to

admit to a member of the holy order that she had very much prayed for just such a thing. "I am here to…"

"To see your sister," the Mother Abbess nodded. "Yes, I am aware."

"May I?"

"Temperance has some very important decisions to make." Sister Beatrice seemed disinclined to allow it and Prudence felt her hope sink into a puddle at her feet.

"I know that her decision to join your convent has meant that she should forsake her previous life," Prudence could think of no way to convince the nun other than to beg, "but I have come here for sanctuary. Even as a nun she is my sister, though you might not see it that way…"

"A nun?" Sister Beatrice raised one eyebrow. "When has your family last heard from Temperance?"

Prudence hung her head. "Not these past five years, since she left, though I cannot blame her." The admission broke her heart.

"Temperance has not yet joined our ranks," the Mother Abbess revealed.

"She hasn't?" Prudence was dumbfounded. Her sister had left home all those years ago with the vow that she would never marry, and never return. She would be a nun, she had sworn so. Though dozens of letters had been sent by all of the Baggingtons, Temperance had never responded. Prudence heart sank. "Is… is she still here?"

"Oh yes," Sister Beatrice replied with a smile and a laugh at her visitor's clear relief. "She is a novice. Though it has taken her longer than most to take her vows, she has finally decided to make the ultimate commitment this coming spring. We are happy to have her as she has shown great promise these years in our care."

"Yes…" Prudence knew not what else to do other than agree.

"I suppose, as a novice, she might still receive a visit," Sister Beatrice gave a solemn nod. "Though, I hope that you do not intend to sway her from her determination to devote her life to The Lord."

"Not at all," Prudence promised. "I swear to you that I come here in my own need. I have no intention of uprooting Temperance or her devotions."

"We do not swear, Lady Fondleton," the Mother Abbess replied, "but I thank you for the truth of your words."

Sister Beatrice slipped from the room and left Prudence once again to her silence. She did not know what to make of her reception. She had yet to be certain that she would be allowed to stay and every moment without that promise increased her fear.

"Prudence!" a delicate voice echoed in the hall. The patter of slippered feet could be heard rushing through the hall.

"Calm, my child," Sister Beatrice's cool voice came from behind.

"Yes, Mother," Prudence heard her sister reply along with the slowing of her footsteps.

Temperance Baggington, the eldest and most beautiful of all the daughters, stepped into the room with a perfectly contained posture and expression. Her beautiful hair was contained under her wimple. Prudence could not help but wonder if the nuns had cut it all off.

Temperance's face was smooth and white, her lips pursed momentarily and then she broke into a smile, but that was the only indication that she was glad to see her sister. She kept herself still and sedate.

"Lady Fondleton," she said with a nod.

"Please do not call me that," Prudence said with a huff of laughter.

"Is it true that you have been wed?" Temperance approached her sibling and grasped her hands within her own. Her eyes sparkled with the excitement of seeing her sister, but she maintained her composure for the pair of watchful eyes that entered the room a moment later. "I ought to offer you my congratulations."

Prudence knew not where to begin. She shook her head. "No. Do not congratulate me. There are no felicitations to be had," she informed her sister. Prudence threw a glance towards the nuns. How could she speak here? "My marriage was not what I had hoped," she explained.

"Most unions are not," Sister Beatrice replied.

"It is more than that." Prudence widened her brown eyes and implored her sister to understand the truth without words. She could not dare to make her confession in front of such a pure soul as the Mother Abbess. In fact, she dared not say a word to anyone if it could be helped.

"I beg you," she cried. "Do not send me back."

"Lady Fondleton," Sister Beatrice said with a sigh, "one cannot run from their responsibilities. A convent is not a place to hide from life."

Prudence dared not say that, in her opinion, it was exactly the place that one went with the desire to hide from life. That, of course, would get her nowhere.

Instead, she remained silent and squeezed her sister's hands, begging her to remember with her heart the language that they once shared.

"Remember Father," Prudence said.

Temperance's eyes widened and she tightened her grip on her sister's hands.

"If you might only give me a chance," Prudence begged. "I promise that I will not be a burden."

"The convent is no place for a married woman," the Mother Abbess repeated. "We have no power to keep you here against your husband's will."

"He does not know where to find me," Prudence persisted.

Temperance loosed her hands from her sister and turned to the nun "Reverend Mother," Temperance said in a soft murmur that she must have learned in her time at the Abbey, "I beg you to reconsider. Prudence has never been one for dramatics. I assure you, if she is seeking safe haven it is within reason. At least, surely she must spend the night."

"Still," Sister Beatrice continued, "far be it from me to keep a gentleman, an earl no less, from his wife. The Abbey is not meant to withstand such things. I am sure the Earl's wrath would rain upon us. It is not within our power to hide you from him here."

"Please, Reverend Mother," Prudence said.

The Mother Abbess then turned to Prudence. "Is he a hateful man?" she asked.

"Hateful," Prudence thought on it for a long while. "I am not so certain that hateful is the word. Monster, is more like. A wolf in sheep's clothing. A wolf is akin to a dog." She spat bitterly.

Sister Beatrice nodded.

Prudence felt as if she could not express enough the danger that her husband presented. This nun could have no idea of his plotting or manipulations. Even worse, the sick nature of his mind.

"Jasper is different," Prudence said with grave sincerity. "He is unlike any other man, gentleman or no, that I have ever met. There is something... wrong about him."

"How long have you been married, child?" Sister Beatrice asked.

Prudence admitted to the few months which she had been formally wed. Still, it felt like an eternity.

"My child, I have had dozens of ladies come to my doors in shock at the changes of life after marriage," the nun explained. "Few are prepared for the truth of it. Ladies fill their heads with fairy tales and that is not what marriage is. Love is one thing, but reality is quite another."

"I assure you that I am not blinded by idealism," Prudence persisted.

"Still," the Mother Abbess continued, "we have no right to keep you here when you belong to another."

Her words brought about a finality that both Prudence and her sister knew better than to attempt to argue against. The Reverend Mother allowed that their guest might remain for the night only. In the morning, she would be returned to the village with express instruction to be delivered back to her husband.

**3**

Prudence could not fault the nun. She had a convent filled with women to look after and, while Prudence had hoped to hide amongst them, there was little that they could do to circumvent the will of an earl, or any gentleman of note for that matter. Still, she could not help but be crushed at the knowledge that her entire plan lay in pieces, a failure.

She thanked the nun for the offer of a bed and bath for the evening, declining the later for sake of her own sanity.

"If you are to stay with us you will bathe, my lady," the Reverend Mother instructed. "Cleanliness is next to godliness."

"I am fine, I am sure," Prudence protested still clutching the bag close. "I would not want to inconvenience you."

The Mother Abbess gave her a look, and Prudence was sure she thought Prudence did not want to bathe in such meager accommodations. That was not the case.

The old nun folded her arms over her ample breast. "Lady Fondleton, you may be more civilized than our usual ways, but you are worn by the road and I should expect a higher level of cleanliness during your stay within our walls. After your wash you shall also be fed, if you wish."

Prudence was not ashamed by the lecture. She was not one who was used to such a slovenly state. Yet, neither did she wish to bathe in the presence of these women of faith, for she had been offered the aid of their hands despite her assurance that she could manage on her own. The temptation of a meal was the only thing that allowed her mind to sway.

Temperance linked her arm through her sister's and steered her down the hall and toward the bathhouse.

"Really," Prudence muttered, "I am leaving in the morning, I shall not need a wash."

Temperance rolled her eyes as she had used to when they were children. The gloss of her midnight tresses glinted in the candlelight.

"Prudence, you ought to bathe," she whispered. "You are waist deep in mud and leaving a trail with each step. We shall clean for a month after your visit."

Prudence glanced behind her where there was, in fact, a trail of crumbling dirt in her wake. With a sigh of resignation she agreed to the task. At least the nuns would be civil about it, she thought. At the very least they knew how to keep their own council, unlike most ladies' maids.

Her gown was stripped and hastened off to be cleaned as best as was possible. If there was any chance of saving the dress, it would be attempted, though Prudence thought it might be best to just cut it to rags at this point.

Temperance and one other postulant were given the task of bathing their guest, a lowly job Prudence realized for the others were surely fast asleep in their beds at this hour.

Prudence was surprised when her sister remained silent.

*"Really Prudence, what were you thinking?"* were

the words that she had expected to hear from her sister's mouth. Instead, Temperance set about her task with singular focus. Five years cloistered and she had seemed to forget how to speak.

"Temperance," Prudence put her hand upon her sister's arm as she reached out to untie her undergarments. The other postulant, a freckle faced girl with brassy hair and eyes that were set wide in her face, never gave her name as she hauled buckets of boiled water into the basin.

Temperance looked into her sister's eyes, resigned to their fates. There was nothing more that could be done now that the Abbess had made her decision.

Prudence released a deep sigh and turned her back to allow her sister better ease in the task. She felt fingers at the laces upon her back.

Then, a gasp.

Cool air hit Prudence's back as the sheath slipped from her shoulders and down along the winding curves of her body. What had once been peaks and valleys of pale, milky skin was now mottled with purples and greens. The sickly pallor of bruises newly acquired beside those in the later stages of healing brought both postulants to her side.

Soft fingers traced the ridges of her back, puckered welts from where she had been beaten with a strap. Ligature marks from restraints marked her limbs, a telltale sign of the Earl's preferences.

A soft plea to The Lord was whispered as trembling fingers traced the tender flesh that was scarred and scabbed in several places. There was the distinct shape of a human bite mark. Hidden beneath the fabric of her gown, Prudence's body was a graveyard of violent memory. Nary an inch was left unmarred save that which might be exposed to public view. Jasper Numbton was practiced enough to keep his violent perversions masked to outside world. Rather, his wife had been left to suffer in silence as she learned to hide the marks and bear through the pain of his assaults.

Not a word needed to be said to send the other postulant racing from the room in terror.

"It's alright," Temperance murmured as she wrapped her arms around her sister's naked frame. "He cannot hurt you any longer, little sister. I promise you that."

Prudence did her best not to shrink away from Temperance's protective embrace. The kindness of human touch had been forgotten for such a long time that it was all that she could do not to flinch as the gentle hands guided her into the warm waters.

"There is nothing that can be done," Prudence sobbed as tears began to stream into the bath. "if the sisters won't let me stay, where will I go?"

"There must be a way," her sister said with a vigor that seemed to spring forth from some forgotten reservoir.

"I am wed," Prudence whispered in her meek voice a mantra she had been taught to repeat in recent months. "I *belong* to him."

"You belong to God," Temperance spat.

"No," Prudence said. "God has forsaken me."

"Blasphemy," Temperance said. "A gentleman of this ilk has no right to a wife."

"You say that," Prudence protested, though the word of support was like a balm to her wounds, "but you forget what the world is like outside of these walls. Men are unkind. Have you forgotten?"

Temperance's eyes grew dark, almost black with anger that seethed just beneath the surface.

"I have never forgotten," she asserted. "Nor will I." Her voice was low, dangerous, and certainly nothing that might come to be expected from one who was soon to take her vows of poverty, chastity, faith, and charity. For a moment, Prudence glimpsed the spark that she had once known her sister to possess. That is, before it was covered with the demure focus of one who was to wash every speck of dirt from her sister's exhausted limbs.

They continued in silence, the practice of sisterly conversation having been forgotten in their isolations.

When the door opened once more, Prudence expected the figure that entered to be that of the mute postulant. Instead, it was none other than the Mother Abbess herself.

"Stand, my child," she instructed with a soft wave of her hand as if she might compel Prudence from the waters.

Instinct forced her to shrink down into the warmth so that the suds that floated along the surface of the bath masked the flaws of her flesh.

"I must see for myself," the Reverend Mother allowed an expression of pain to cross her features, revealing that she hoped that what she had been told was not true, or perhaps an exaggeration.

Prudence glanced at her sister, still kneeling beside the basin. Temperance nodded in silence.

With her breath held tight in her chest and her eyes

cast downward, Prudence rose from the water to reveal the freshly cleaned surface of her skin.

It was worse than the Mother Abbess had anticipated, there could be no mistake about that. Now that the mud had been washed away, several more bite marks had become apparent. Areas that had merely looked unclean, were now unmistakably an extension of the pattern of bruises that trailed across her body.

The Mother Abbess's hand flew to her mouth, and when she took it from her lips she said in a soft voice. "The church demands a wife submit to her husband, but this…" She shook her head. "I do not believe The Lord requires a wife to submit to torture." She waved Prudence back to the cooling water. "You will stay here as long as necessary until I might find a safe place to hide you away," she promised.

Prudence felt as if she could cry anew, but there were no tears left in her. Instead, she sank down in shocked silence at the turn of events in her favor.

"It is well that the road is out for it shall prevent visitors, and questions," the nun continued. "That shall purchase us a few days' time to form a plan."

Prudence was peppered with questions about her husband and the likelihood that he might pursue her. Without a doubt, Prudence confirmed their worst fears.

"He is a proud man and likes nothing more than a challenge," she admitted. "In fact, I am not entirely certain that he would not take great personal pleasure in… the hunt."

She shivered at the realization that she was now little more than prey in his game. Lord Fondleton would come after her with his full effort. No expense would be spared. She had hoped that leaving the jewels would satisfy him, but she knew that was not so. He would not rest until he had won. She wondered if there was anywhere that might be safe. Perhaps even the colonies would not be too far for his extensive reach.

"There is one more thing…" Prudence grimaced as she stepped from the water and pulled a long length of cloth around herself for both coverage and absorption.

"Are you with child?" the Mother Abbess asked with wide, fearful eyes.

"Not that I am aware of," Prudence shook her head. She could see the relief in the eyes of the other two women. A child would present another layer of complications. She might be able to run from him, but he would not allow his heir to be taken. Just to be safe, she sent a plea to the heavens that her womb remained untouched. Her husband had seemed to be more intent on other pleasures than the act which might get her with child. "Just one more thing…" she said again.

"Then, out with it," the nun pressed. "We haven't all night."

Prudence pressed her lips together in a nervous gesture that prevented her from groaning at her plight. She had only barely been accepted into the Abbey, and only for the state of her health. There was no guarantee that they would be forgiving of any further surprises.

She padded over to her carpet bag, which sat in the corner. The sound of her damp feet upon the cool stone floor was all that could be heard. She would have to get used to the silent nature of these women. The bag had been left open, but she pulled the mouth wider to peer inside. A small yip greeted her.

"You're awake!" she whispered, her face transforming into a wide grin.

"You said there was no child!" Sister Beatrice exclaimed. "What have you done?" It was clear that she thought Prudence had stolen a child and carried it in her bag. The truth was not so far from her assumption.

She reached into the recesses of the nearly empty container. She had packed no other clothing save the dress she wore. Those that she possessed would have drawn too much attention. Besides, she thought, she hated them all.

Instead, she had brought only her most prized possessions. She still felt a twinge of regret at the loss of the comb but knew that her mother would forgive her in the haste of her escape.

Her hands cradled the tiny life within and she drew it from the darkness and held it against her breast. There, it curled against the cloth that covered her body, opened its mouth into a wide yawn, and settled against her.

"Why it is a puppy!" Temperance exclaimed and rushed to her sister's side to peer at the small creature.

"Whatever made you bring that creature with you?" Sister Beatrice asked, though it was clear from her tone that she had a heart that was fond of animals. Prudence held the small brown pup, as plain as herself, out to the nun who took it with a small gasp and a sigh.

"She was the runt," Prudence explained. "Jasper was going to have her drowned. I heard him speak of it. I couldn't leave her, I just couldn't bear the thought. We both escaped. Together."

Sister Beatrice looked indignant at the prospect of the loss of life.

"I shouldn't allow it," she murmured while her fingers stroked the feather soft fur of the animal's ears. "Really, it's a luxury… an extra mouth to feed."

"She's too small to cause any issues," Temperance reasoned. "Really, I doubt she can do more than hobble at this point. A rag of milk will fill her belly. That is not too much to spare. I'll even forego my own glass if you'd like, Mother."

Sister Beatrice was humming to the waking pup as she rocked back and forth. A tiny, pink tongue flicked out and tasted her hand. Her heart melted before Prudence's eyes.

"I shall have to find a place that can take you both," Sister Beatrice concluded. "It shall be your duty to keep her care. I'll not have a spectacle in my abbey."

"Of course," Prudence could not keep the grin from her face. It appeared that they had both been saved this very night. She and Posey, as she had come to call the pup during her trek along the winding road to the Abbey. She had let the animal down from her bag as she sat for a moment to rest her blistered feet.

The small brown puppy had done its best to waddle through the field of flowers that bordered the lane, attacking each small flower with a vengeance that was contrary to her minuscule size. Prudence had laughed at the battle between the pup and its namesake. Posey, she had decided would be her name.

Sister Beatrice made her farewells so that she might compose a letter to be delivered by the groundskeeper that very evening. The cover of darkness would prevent any suspicions while also allowing her to act with utmost urgency. Prudence wondered to whom she might be writing and how they might come to her aide.

Temperance assisted her in dressing. The rough woolen gowns that the postulants wore were nothing more than a sheath compared to her usual gowns. Still, she did not complain. She would disguise herself as a shrub if that is what it took to evade Lord Fondleton.

The offer of sustenance for herself and the pup was accepted with gratitude. Temperance procured a small hunk of bread and butter along with a bowl of some sort of mash that Posey gobbled up without hesitation. Prudence was proud to witness her growth and knew that it was only a matter of time before the dog was as healthy as any.

Prudence was weary and relieved for the offer of a small room with a sleeping mat in the corner and a pile of warm blankets to crawl beneath. She wanted to ask her sister to stay with her, to rest at her side as they had when they needed to guard against the terrors of the night as children, but Temperance had murmured her farewell and slipped away into the dormitory where she would be expected to sleep amongst her peers.

It still hurt Prudence to think that her sister was to be so removed from their family. Yet, she could not blame her. Temperance had received the brunt of the burden that the Baggington sisters had to endure as a result of her pure and extraordinary beauty.

Prudence had always thought it amusing that the gossips of Nettlefold proper referred to herself, and her family, as *the baggage*. It was true that they carried a surplus of secrets indeed, she had often thought. Only, the mental rather than physical sort. Little did the gossips know just how many secrets their family concealed in the isolation of the cold manor walls.

Prudence fell to sleep that evening without a nightmare. It was the first time in months that her mind had drifted into the relief of blackness. She cared not if she slept until lunchtime. She cared not if she did not even wake at all.

*CLICK to Continue Reading*

# ALSO BY ISABELLA THORNE

### *THE LADIES OF THE NORTH*

The Duke's Winter Promise ~ A Christmas Regency Romance

The Viscount's Wayward Son

The Marquess' Rose

### *RESCUED BY RUIN*

### *THE SEDGEWICK LADIES*

LADY ARABELLA AND THE BARON

HEALING MISS MILLWORTH

LADY MARIANNE AND THE CAPTAIN

### *SPINSTERS OF THE NORTH*

THE HIDDEN DUCHESS

THE MAYFAIR MAID

SEARCHING FOR MY LOVE

### *THE LADIES OF BATH*

The Duke's Daughter ~ Lady Amelia Atherton

The Baron in Bath ~ Miss Julia Bellevue

The Deceptive Earl ~ Lady Charity Abernathy

Winning Lady Jane ~ A Christmas Regency Romance

The Ladies of Bath Collection

Printed in Great Britain
by Amazon

35829802R00185